Fox & the Peach

Fox & the Peach

Nick Thaler

Santa Monica, California

FOX & THE PEACH

Text Copyright © 2010 Nick Thaler

Cover Art by Stephen Sampson © 2011 Madness Books

All Rights Reserved. No part of this book may be used or reproduced in any manner whatsoever without the written permission of the Publisher. This book is a work of fiction. Any references to historical events, real people, or real locales are used fictitiously. Other names, characters, places, and incidents are the product of the author's imagination, and any resemblance to actual events or locales or persons, living or dead, is entirely coincidental.

ISBN: 978-1-936573-00-4

Library of Congress Cataloging-in-Publication-Data is available on file.

Published by Madness Books
171 Pier Avenue, #328
Santa Monica, California 90405 USA
www.madnessbooks.com

Madness Books, in association with Global ReLeaf, will plant two trees for each tree used in the manufacturing of this book. Global ReLeaf is an international campaign by American Forests, the nation's oldest nonprofit conservation organization and a world leader in planting trees for environmental restoration.

Without limiting the rights under copyright reserved above, no part of this publication may be reproduced, stored in or introduced into a retrieval system, or transmitted, in any form or by any means (electronic, mechanical, photocopying, recording or otherwise), without the prior written permission of both the copyright owner and the above publisher of this book.

For my mom and my dad

Acknowledgements

First and foremost, I'd like to thank Jim Strader for his passion and belief in his book. I also want to thank Adrienne Levin for all her support these last few years and Jeff Marriote for his helpful edits. I'd also like to thank my academic advisors including Dan, Lewis, Michelle, Marta, and Ellie as well as my CSUN and UNLV cohorts. Thanks also to Ani, Adam, Dave (though he still won't read the book), Stacy, Matt, Yashar, Justin, and Jeff. I'd like to acknowledge my family including Mitzi, Milt, Keiko, Dwight, Ben, and Kanoe for all their support. My mom, for her love, care, guidance (and patience!) in raising me. Finally my dad, who was my first fan and editor – this book wouldn't exist without him. Thank you all.

Fox & the Peach

Prologue: Slaughter in Sato Village

To the casual eye they would have been invisible, three figures slipping through the brush and trees without so much as a rustle. With the grace of herons, they ghosted down the slope toward the tiny camp and paused at a ledge overlooking a sheer white cliff. A stream trickled through the valley below, where little mud huts lay peacefully along its banks in neat rows. The moon was full, brightly illuminating the still night, but it did not matter to the three figures standing together in their black masks and padded clothes – they were shinobi, and they had come to this village to kill.

One of them flashed a hand signal to the others: *"Filthy animals,"* it said. Though his face was hidden beneath his hood, the other two could read his contempt. The Yan Tribe was the only ninja clan that developed its own hand code for silent conversation. *"We should have done this long ago."* His name was Kawaru, the youngest of the group. This was his third mission, but he had first tasted blood years ago and had found it much to his liking.

The other two glanced at each other. Only the young upstart's prodigious abilities stayed Rinji's hand at that moment. The older shinobi quickly banished his anger and raised two fingers. Tsukimi, the woman of the group, gave a brief nod as her body shimmered and faded away. The others heard her soft tabi boots pad to the east. Rinji gestured to Kawaru and pointed to the river. *"Strike from there,"* he signaled.

Kawaru grinned wide beneath his thin cloth mask. He closed his eyes and summoned the chi needed to form his invisibility shield. As always, there was a brief tingling on his skin, as if he was stepping into drizzle, and then the slightly unsettling sensation of floating. Once he was unseen, he impulsively signaled to Rinji, *"Of course, My Lord."* If Rinji had seen that sign, he might have struck down Kawaru immediately – the idea of master and vassal among the Yan was a filthy notion that only lesser humans possessed. To the Yan, all within the tribe were equal except for the Dai-Yan, their Shadow Lord.

Rinji didn't see what Kawaru had signaled, but his heightened senses picked up the rustle of the younger ninja's fingers. As he switched his own invisibility on and dashed down the sheer ledge, he briefly reflected on Buddha's lesson on patience. Kawaru's time would come.

*

A small brown rabbit hesitated as it reached the edge of the rice paddy, its nose twitching urgently in the cool air. The night was still and the sky was clear of predators, but something seemed amiss. The creature barely had time for a muffled squeak before a boot darted out of the rows of rice stalks and slammed down hard onto its head. Kawaru laughed silently as his heel crunched and pressed down harder. A warm wetness seeped up his cotton leggings and sent a chill down his spine. He flicked the remains into the bush, uncaring that villagers might smell the blood with their own heightened senses. The residents here may have appeared fearsome to some, but to Kawaru they were as insignificant as that rabbit, small lives that were his for the taking. He slipped into the rice paddies banking off the river and passed through them without letting a single stalk sway. Crouching in the shallow paddy water, Kawaru unsheathed his kodachi and waited. Two minutes passed before he heard the trill of a great egret. The signal. He rose and gracefully flowed into the village

Inside the first hut was a lone old man, likely a hermit, resting comfortably in a hammock with a pipe slowly smoking by his side. A brief jab to the throat finished him instantly. Kawaru flicked the blood off and observed the corpse – it remained still. Ah, a real human then, hiding out among these tanuki. Kawaru had heard that some eccentrics actually liked living among the othermen, but he was nonetheless disappointed; he had hoped to witness a transformation right away. Still, there were so many yet to kill.

The second hut proved to be far more interesting. A young couple – perhaps the farmers of that rice paddy – slumbered, blissfully unaware. Both died soundlessly. Kawaru watched the bloodied corpses sag and sink like wet cotton dolls, compressing upon themselves to revert back to their natural animal form. The dead tanuki was bestial in its natural form, a hybrid of dog and raccoon. Their pointy teeth were bared in silent snarls as they met death, and their brown fur was blackened by blood. Kawaru gleefully laughed out loud – this was far more entertaining than killing mere humans.

Suddenly a cry went up and the camp came alive. Kawaru cursed under his breath and wondered which of his companions had been careless. It did not matter, the tanuki would all die tonight. The ninja closed his eyes as his practiced hands flew into motion. He summoned a body double that split from his body and immediately dove out of the hut and into the battle. Through his double's eyes, he saw tanuki, in various states of transformation, running around in panic and disarray. He couldn't see the other ninja. Kawaru quickly restored his invisibility and followed his double outside, lurking carefully behind its shadow.

A large bearlike tanuki reared up and struck at the double with a mighty blade that jutted directly from its shoulder blade, as if it were an actual arm. The double dissolved into a black fog and then Kawaru was upon the creature, stabbing deftly upwards underneath its chin. The sword bit through flesh and the creature let out a roar before abruptly lumping over, still standing in front of Kawaru. Its blade-arm faded into a small claw and the body shrank to its normal proportions as the tanuki died.

Kawaru heard a faint wail and rolled under the incoming throwing knife. It sizzled past his ear and buried itself in his enemy's corpse, still dangling from his sword. Kawaru turned and studied the little child before him. This tanuki had turned herself into a beautiful girl, nine or so, perhaps trying to instill sympathy in the attackers. Kawaru only laughed and plucked out the knife with his free hand, casually flinging it back at the thrower even before she could ready a second one. The girl caught it in the eye and her head flopped back. The shinobi didn't bother to watch the transformation this time – it had suddenly become a boring affair.

He slid his sword free and sent out another body double. Once again, he waited until a tanuki attacked the illusion, and then countered with a vicious blow. Some of the tanuki were starting to group together now, combining their transformation powers to create great visions, images of ghosts and demons designed to baffle their attackers and send them fleeing. A giant red-fanged devil leered down from the sky and shot a burning fireball toward Kawaru. He merely sheathed his sword and closed his eyes. All ninja were trained to meditate in the heat of battle as a method of dispelling trickery, and few were as adept at teaching it as the Yan. When his eyes were open again, the swirling mists and half formed demons that had begun to emerge were gone, replaced by a dozen or so small, furry animals huddling together in a circle. He suppressed a derisive laugh as he snatched a small clay bomb from his belt and tossed it into the center of the group. Only one tanuki noticed the round object roll toward them and as he knelt down to pick it up, a large explosion sent his body flying. The smoke cleared, revealing the burnt and bloody corpses of the others. Kawaru whipped out his sword and twirled it triumphantly in his hand before slamming it back into its sheath.

*

Tsukimi was on the east side of the village, surrounded by her kills. Kawaru nodded once to her and signaled. *"How many are left?"*

"*None, here. Rinji is taking care of the last few, north,*" she responded. Kawaru gleefully noticed that the kunichi had only slain half a dozen. Besides the grenade and the initial kills, Kawaru had killed three more of the animals, bringing his total to seventeen. It seemed proof enough that few Yan could match his abilities, and none as young as him.

"*So you killed six. We were informed that thirty lived in this wasteland. That means Rinji should have handled seven.*"

Tsukimi ignored the implied boast and turned away. She found no joy in slaughtering helpless creatures, no matter what the Dai-Yan had ordained. Justice, she reminded herself, was the code of the Yan, and these animals were the vassals of that monstrous Oda Nobunaga, warlord and scourge of Japan. Although Makoto felt otherwise, she wholeheartedly agreed that these devious creatures had to be eliminated. Only one daimyo had hired the Yan to eliminate this potentially troublesome village, but all men, great and small, whispered fearfully of Nobunaga's bloody war and the countless lives it cost.

And yet, she could not help but feel some disgust at herself. She didn't spend eight years training just for this sort of butchery and didn't enjoy it as some others apparently did. She eyed Kawaru carefully. The young shinobi was restless, scanning the horizon for more tanuki. He abruptly stopped and stared at someone in the distance. It was Rinji, swaying slightly, as if injured. He appeared to have lost his sword and wielded a crudely fashioned iron hammer. "Stay there," he called hoarsely. "There are more of them around us. We must regroup."

Kawaru couldn't help but laugh at the blatant trickery as he flung a throwing knife at the man. It flew thirty paces and buried itself neatly in Rinji's chest. The ninja stumbled to his knees.

"Traitor!" he screamed. "Kill him now!" In an instant Tsukimi's blade was out of her sheath. She regarded the distant figure cautiously.

"Are you certain?" she signaled.

"Kill him! What are you waiting for? He has betrayed us!" Rinji clawed at the knife in his chest and let out loud wheezing gasps. Tsukimi hesitated and the two shinobi warily eyed each other. Kawaru frowned. Could he have made a mistake? Would they both have to pay for his carelessness? He struggled to control his fury and instead focus on the problem at hand. He would have to strike first, before Tsukimi could make up her mind. He slipped out the poisoned needle tucked in his upper right sleeve.

Suddenly, Rinji's head flew off in a bright spray of blood. Both shinobi stared aghast as the corpse shriveled and twisted, brown fur sprouting out to reveal yet another tanuki. The real Rinji appeared behind the corpse.

"That was foolish, Tsukimi," he signaled. *"I would never speak out loud when there is danger about. Kawaru was right to strike first."* Kawaru felt an impulsive grin rise. *"But!"* Rinji added. *"Kawaru, always aim for the head of shapeshifters. You thought you struck the chest, but you only hit its shoulder. Such is their devious nature."*

Tsukimi bowed low. *"Forgive me Rinji. I was careless."*

"Both of you were careless today," Rinji responded. Before either could respond, he darted forward and rammed his sword's hilt deep into Kawaru's stomach. As Kawaru doubled forward, Rinji drew the youth into a tight headlock. *"Who do you think alerted the tanuki, you fool?"* Rinji signaled with his free hand, each motion accentuated in slow, deliberate jerks before the youth's eyes. *"Your penchant for finding our work amusing is well noticed, rest assured."* He released Kawaru with a kick and the shinobi fell over retching. Tsukimi nodded to Rinji in silent approval but the other shinobi merely shook his head. *"We are done here. Return."*

The other two ninja bounded away as Kawaru lay on his side, each breath a painful gasp. Several minutes passed before he could stand. When he could, he walked over to the corpse of the be-headed tanuki and looked down with his pale gray eyes, regarding the creature carefully. Then he took his sword and methodically hacked the body to pieces.

Part 1
Blooming Fruit

1. Little Fox

The peaches would be sweeter than usual this year. Momo set down the basket of silk and stretched her arms in the cool breeze of the late spring that had finally decided to arrive. The buds on the peach tree hadn't yet formed, but her keen nose picked up the scent of sugar and nectar and she knew that the fruit would be exceptionally delicious when they were ready. The small, round-faced girl licked her lips and turned her gaze to the winding path.

Every evening she ventured into town for her father's business. As the adopted daughter of Haruhiro Takamoto, the esteemed silk weaver of Yubikawa village, it was her job to deliver each day's goods to the merchants who pawned their wares on the main street. She hated their stares, their crude jokes, and their pinches, for she believed herself ugly and alien, their attention a joke among themselves. *Foundling,* they whispered behind their stalls and in the town square where she shopped for her father and brother. *Witch,* others would say, for it was well known in the village that she was nearly sixteen and still unwed. Although her body was slight and boyish, it was developed and last year a few suitors had come calling. Takamoto had made it obvious then that he wouldn't mind her wedding and becoming another man's burden, but none of the village boys ever visited twice. It only took a few months of this before the rumors spread among the locals.

Momo broke into a run and jostled the basket down the path with an uncanny strength. She was less than five feet tall, and was often mistaken for a child from a distance, but as she came closer the cold expressions of the villagers revealed that they had recognized her. She smiled at a village boy who happened to be in her path and kept the smile on as he glanced at her and darted into the bushes. Momo didn't bother looking back as she entered the outskirts of town.

Yubikawa had become prosperous in the last decade, one of the land's central hubs, with travelers regularly stopping by on their way to do business at Buzen castle. It was widely known that the current daimyo himself had once journeyed through the village. Momo could still see the spot in front of the inn where he had planted a chrysanthemum in thanks for the hospitality. A line of rocks cordoned that area and no man had trodden there since, even though the flower had withered and died within days.

People hurried about their business in the cool dusk air. Narrow dirt streets crisscrossed around carefully constructed wooden houses arranged in neat rows. Slanting evening light sparkled off of the rice paddies, casting a dark reddish glow down across the long stretch of fields. Momo stepped onto the main road and smiled pleasantly at those who happened to look at her. If she had ever felt anything from their stares, it had long since turned into aloof indifference. She knew who she was, and what her worth was to these people. Not everyone regarded her so coolly, though she wished that the old merchant Gen would. He was waving eagerly and motioning her over. She put on her friendliest smile and stepped over to him.

"Good afternoon, Gen-san. How is your health today?"

"Fine! Fine! Oh, it's good to see you. What about your health? I had heard you had taken a chill, Momo-chan?" The old man grinned and gave Momo an excellent view of his yellowing teeth. Her sharp nose picked up the decay within them. She pretended to blush.

"Thank you Gen-san, but I am much better now. Taku was very kind to run the errands while I was ill." Taku was her brother, her adopted father's true son. She loved him dearly.

Gen mimed sympathy and caressed her arm. Momo fixed her eyes on his and stared hard. A good daughter was expected to be meek, but that was a quality Momo simply didn't have. For a second the old man saw something flash within her eyes before a doe-eyed serenity clouded it over, and he hastily withdrew his arm. *Impudent child,* he thought. *I know what you are.* "Ah yes, Taku-san, yes…he was able to carry out your duties? Quite impressive of him!" He chuckled uneasily and then peered at the silks. They were neatly folded and ready to be dyed and processed. "Marvelous, marvelous. Takamoto-sama truly has exceeded himself. I will take the whole basket!" Momo nodded, expecting this. The recent eastern wars had made her father's business flourish of late.

After her business with Gen had concluded, Momo went to the marketplace. As always, she paused at the meat stall, the tantalizing smell of fresh blood and flesh drawing her over. Meat was too expensive to buy often, even for one as well off as Haruhiro Takamoto, but smelling it was one of the small pleasures that she derived from her day. As usual, the butcher rudely waved her on without bothering to say anything. Takamoto was well respected in the village but his two offspring were not. Momo wasn't sure which one of them harmed the other's reputation more, but the outcome was the same nonetheless.

"Momo! Hey, over here!" A young barefoot girl ran toward her. Her skin was peasant dark, far more deeply tanned than Momo's, and her hair was wild and unkempt. Still, she might have been pretty if not for the harelip that had split her mouth. Momo turned away as if she hadn't noticed her, but Usagi grabbed her shirt. "Hey silly! I heard you were sick." Usagi grinned through her deformity and her eyes shone. "It's so good to see you back!"

"Thanks Usagi," muttered Momo. She hadn't in fact been sick, but for a whole week after her last "incident" she had sequestered herself in her room. She had spent that time crying, too unhappy to even eat. Taku had taken over the chores and her father had berated her endlessly, but after a few days her depression lifted like a veil, and the familiar and calm emptiness had returned. Of course, none of the villagers knew about this, but keeping secrets in the Takamoto household was a well practiced art.

"I wanted to go flower picking with you. My mother said we could create lovely arrangements if we bring back some chrysanthemums and cherry blossoms. I was hoping you would be well enough to go today!" The words came out in a breathless tumble and a small string of spittle dripped from her mouth. Momo had to look away again. It shamed her how the split in the girl's lip repulsed her, but there was nothing to be done about it. Momo often felt alone and desired the companionship of others, but not from one who was more deformed than her.

"Forgive me, Usagi. I can't. I still feel ill."

"But—"

"Please give your mother my regards," Momo sighed. She trudged back up the hill to her house. Although her basket was now empty, it felt heavier than it did on her way down. *Perhaps I have not killed everything inside my heart after all,* she reflected, surprised at her own disappointment in herself. That stab of self-pity was actually somewhat satisfying.

*

"Disturbing news," muttered Haruhiro Takamoto. Kenji Nakano, samurai and constable of Yubikawa, nodded once. As both policeman and messenger for Lord Motonari, Nakano was the village's link to the outside world.

"Very disturbing," Nakano agreed. He had just turned thirty and was still lean and eager with the righteousness of youth.

Takamoto bowed low to his friend. "Thank you very much, Nakano-sama. I'll keep you informed of anything I hear."

Nakano bowed back and stood. "Thank you. I appreciate your willingness to help me. I know how difficult it is." He left the house and brushed by Momo with barely a glance. The girl averted her eyes as she walked in.

"There you are!" snapped Takamoto. "You lazy brat! It's time to prepare dinner."

"I'm sorry, father," mumbled Momo. She kept her eyes on the floor. It lately seemed that she saw more of the ground than of her father.

"Go prepare our food," instructed the weaver. In the other room, the looms of his apprentices went silent. The three boys always listened in on Takamoto's tirades against Momo. He seemed to sense their gleeful anticipation and calmed himself down. "No, wait. There's no point in putting this off, Momo."

Momo set down the basket and dared to look up at her father. Takamoto's body had aged incredibly in these past ten years. He had grown heavy and his face was sallow like old parchment. Momo smelled agitation in his sweat and sake on his breath. *So you have been drinking again*, she thought. She followed him outside.

"To the river," he said. His house, the only building on top of the hill, marked the end of the village. Beyond it lay a thick forest. They walked past the silkworm grove, a flat grassy area that had been cleared and filled with cages, and further on to the bank of the Finger River. The sound of burbling water calmed Momo's nerves somewhat. She sighed and wondered if Usagi had gone ahead and picked those flowers.

"Nakano-sama visited," her father was saying. He spoke with his hands behind his back as he stared down at the murky water. "He's brought some bad news." He looked at her suddenly. As always, she instinctively cringed before this stern and powerful man who had never shown her anything but disapproval. He wasn't a violent man and he had never hit her, but neither had he ever shared a smile or a kind word. For Taku it was different, but then he was the weaver's actual son. Momo tried to appear meek before him, as a daughter of the Takamoto family was expected to.

"Nakano-sama has given me news of Oda Nobunaga. Have you heard of him?" She nodded. Rumors brought by travelers informed the village of a warlord who had occupied the Imperial castle in Kyoto, home of the Emperor. Those same rumors also whispered that Nobunaga had enlisted the aid of allies that were not human, but instead strange and terrifying beasts that could confuse and trick men with their foul magic. Yubikawa villagers largely ignored the news or spoke of it in light, casual tones, for their village was well to the west of Kyoto, and Lord Motonari was an experienced and capable warlord in his own right.

"It's been confirmed that he is using othermen in his armies. Tales of kappa and oni in his ranks have spread amongst the villagers," Takamoto continued. "Lord Motonari and other western daimyo have agreed that they need to band together before Nobunaga conquers all of their lands, including this one. And in this plan, Momo, they want a full account of any othermen in their provinces." He began to tick off his fingers.

"Specifically, tengu, neko, tanuki, kappa, oni. Kitsune." After he said the last he peered intently at Momo, waiting expectantly.

Momo felt her stomach lurch. Nearly sixteen years had passed since Taku had brought home an injured fox. The boy had been ecstatic, miming joy in strange chirps, the most emotion he had ever shown in his young life. The fox's leg was broken and mauled by predators, and Takamoto had allowed the boy to keep it as a pet. However, it wasn't long before he realized that the fox, who he thought would soon heal and escape on its own, had instead found a permanent residence inside his house.

"I have kept your secret for fifteen years," the weaver continued. "Encountering an otherman is an honor for any man and nobody ever came to claim you. But keeping one in my house was always risky. I can see now that keeping this secret has had consequences."

"Father—" Momo began. He rode over her words.

"Nakano-sama has informed me that all who aid othermen and henge are to be arrested on sight. I've taken care of you for nearly sixteen years. It's time you did the right thing and left us." Before she could respond he abruptly spun around and stomped off. As he left, Momo thought she saw him glance back for a second, but then he was gone.

*

"I see you choose to be blind." Takamoto stepped into the

kitchen where Momo was washing the rice for dinner. The apprentice boy who had been assisting ducked out of the way of her father's path. "I didn't expect you to return to my house."

"Takamoto-sama—" began Momo.

The blow caught her against her cheek.

"Don't speak out!" he roared, his face deep red. "Two weeks ago, you spontaneously transformed, becoming a wild beast. How could I have explained that if any of the villagers were around? If Nakano was around? If we had not been alone, who knows what might have happened!" That episode began while Momo fetched water for her father's bath. Her head had been throbbing all day from a dull headache and it had suddenly exploded in a blinding pain. The bucket of water splashed noisily to the ground as Momo fell on all fours, breathing heavily. She heard a strange dull laughter from somewhere and when she stared at her reflection, the whites in her eyes had yellowed. She had shifted right then, transforming into her fox form, and fled the house in a panic. Taku found her hours later, shivering by the river. She had no memory of why she was there.

Takamoto raged on. "And after that incident you sit in your room for days, a crying, pitiful girl who is completely useless to me. No, not useless! Dangerous! Leave this place before you attract any more attention!"

Momo's cheek burned where she had been slapped, and beads of sweat popped onto her forehead. She rubbed her cheek and struggled for her wits. Her sudden banishment had been much too much for her to handle. After Takamoto had left her at the riverbank she had walked back to the house, hoping that it was all a mad whim that would blow over. She now struggled to say something.

"No! You will *not* endanger my household." Takamoto fumed on, raging over her. "You will leave at once! You will—" He was cut off as a large clumsy figure stumbled into the kitchen. Taku's thick frame pressed against Momo's tiny one and he moaned mournfully. He shielded Momo from his father.

"Taku," whispered Momo. The boy, no, now a man, was the one who had brought her home and played with her and loved her even as her wits had rapidly exceeded his own. He was the only person she had ever opened her heart to, even though he could do nothing but smile and bob his head back at her. He was the other source of shame in the Takamoto household, the one who shared a burden at once similar and yet so different. Taku turned around and hugged her furiously, tears pouring down his vacant face.

Takamoto shook his head, the redness dissipating from his face like evaporating water. "Son, what are you doing? Please Taku-chan, come here. Please." Taku shook his head and cried out, refusing to let Momo go. The girl felt a sudden and powerful urge to get out, to escape this overwhelming stench of human misery. The smell of Taku was generally pleasant, smooth and clean as milk, but today he had a sour reek. She twisted her body, slipped under his hug, and darted out the door. Taku yelled piteously and fell to his knees.

The old artisan looked down at his son, now a giant of a man. He remembered when he first saw Taku, the same time he had been informed of his beloved wife's death. Taku had never learned to speak, but he had learned to laugh on his fourth birthday, the day he had brought Momo into the house. Takamoto turned to his apprentice. "Go," he said. "Go get her." The boy bowed and ran outside.

Taku sat with his head buried in his hands, sobbing in large, staccato gasps, shoulders shuddering violently with each spasm. Takamoto walked over to his son, placed his hand on his head, and quietly stroked his hair.

11. The Green Man

For the next three days Takamoto ignored Momo as much as was possible. He took his meals with his three apprentices at earlier times than usual to avoid dining with her, and left the silk and the list of groceries by the door before she woke up. It suited her fine—ever since their fight she had no desire to see him either.

Not for the first time, Momo considered what she could do with her life. She had often dreamt of finding her own kind, other kitsune, in a village far away from humans. With little to do during the day, she often spent hours reading. Her father owned a decent book collection and peddlers occasionally brought in new ones. She mostly read about the henge, the othermen whose talents involved shape shifting and illusions. She read of the tanuki, raccoonlike beings who had the unique ability to project their illusions out on others, and the neko, reclusive cat henge who lived on small islands off the western coast.

There were several books on the other intelligent species as well: kappa, the river folk, and tengu, the mountain men, as well as the mysterious and ancient race of oni who never died from age. However, there was precious little information about her own kind. One old book from Hokkaido briefly mentioned the kitsune as a race of tricksters who drew on the power of the full moon, but the alien drawings of two-legged foxes casting sinister glares at unwary travelers seemed ludicrous to the little girl. The books had no answers for her, but neither did this village.

"Women don't need to read," Takamoto said to her on the fourth day, as she sat in her room perusing an old and well-read scroll about kitsune who dwelt in the northern lands. She looked up in surprise at his sudden intrusion. Her father's broken veins had lately given him the look of a ripe pomegranate.

"I am no woman," she retorted fiercely. Takamoto narrowed his eyes at her tone but finally nodded.

"My ancestors would be shamed at how I let you treat me. If not for my respect for othermen, I would have cast you out years ago. Instead I took you in and spent my money educating and feeding you." The two of them stared at each other, one angry, the other defiant. To Momo's surprise, her father broke first. He sighed heavily and his lined face took on a weary turn. "Momo, I'm sorry. In truth, I'd always felt the gods had honored my household by bringing such an exquisite creature to my doorstep. Kitsune are considered good luck, and it is true that business has prospered lately."

Shocked at the sudden change of attitude, Momo bowed low as a wash of gratitude overcame her. "You honor me, father," she said in a small, tremulous voice. He had never spoken so much kindness to her in all the years she lived there.

"You may stay," he said hoarsely. He cleared his throat. "But you must work, too. I will show you how to boil the silk cocoons. There is much need for weavers in Moji and in other large cities. You will learn the trade and then live your life as a human." His smile faded. "But Momo, no more transformations, ever again. I forbid it."

Live as a human? Her burning resentment was quickly extinguished by the shame of her ingratitude. "Father, you are too kind to me," she murmured. "I am not worthy of your generosity."

"Perhaps not," Takamoto replied. "But you have been good to my son. Your brother." Takamoto smiled then, a brief smile that made Momo's heart ache. The two shared an awkward bow, and then Takamoto left. When she was alone again Momo waited, fearful that her father would change his mind and return. After a while she opened the door and peeked out. The looms hummed quietly and the apprentices kept their heads low; Takamoto struck anyone who spoke while working. Slipping past the workroom, Momo ducked outdoors.

 The day was overcast, a sharp contrast to the mild weather that the gods had blessed the village with over the past few days. Momo turned her nose to the wind and caught the sweet smell of honey coming from the forest. She licked her lips. Taking a moment to glance around, she ducked into the brush and knelt down. Mud smudged her simple white dress, but it hardly mattered. Closing her eyes, Momo muttered a quick prayer and allowed the gods to envelop her body.

 First her hands sprouted fur, a light red color that quickly darkened into burnished brown. Then her face shifted, stretching like molten metal before firming into its new form. Ears sprouted like lilies along her hair and her back arched painfully as her hands turned into paws. The teeth were her favorite part—those simple square human teeth sank in, yielding to the sharp and pointy ones that sprouted forward. Those teeth meant meat, and the hot taste of blood. They meant rabbit and fish and all the other delicacies of the forest that simple humans missed. She permitted herself a small smile.

 Her father and her worries all melted away like snow at first light. Now it was only about the hunt, the myriad smells wafting across her face like brief shafts of sunlight. She caught the honey one, and holding onto it as dearly as a fisherman onto his line, darted from the brush. As a fox she was inconspicuous, of interest only to the occasionally hunter and predator roaming the forest. But none were fast enough to catch Momo, who had had years perfecting her agility and grace. The honey beckoned strongly and she embraced its overwhelming aura like a drug, letting it consume her entire being. She suddenly realized with renewed clarity that she hated being a human. She hated their rules and codes and her obligations and now her father wanted her to remain one forever. A yip flew from her mouth that almost sounded like a laugh.

The scent carried her down the river and up a grassy knoll. She skidded to a stop when she heard the sound of singing. Momo quickly shifted back to her human form. Naked only for an instant, a glowing light surrounded her body, fading into a clean white dress. Other than a few smudges on her hands, no trace of the forest showed.

The hive hung precariously off a low branch. Usagi sat beneath it, uncaring of the bees humming lazily above her head. She sang softly, almost imperceptibly, as she stared at it.

"Little bee, little bee, where are you going? Ah, Momo-san!" Usagi sat up, delight springing onto her dark face. "I didn't expect anyone to find this place!"

"Usagi," Momo said. She approached the girl, avoiding her

face. "What do you mean?"

"This place! This is the isle of the Green Man. It's my little secret." Usagi giggled as a bit of spittle dripped down her face. "I guess it's ours now."

Momo glanced up at the hive. It was thick and heavy with honey, easy for the taking. As a fox she could spring up and bite a chunk of the comb before any of the bees could react. "What secret is that, Usagi?"

"Look around you," Usagi said. "See how green this knoll is? The forest stops before the edge, giving way to the soft grass and its flowers." The ground was enshrouded in thick stalks of grass, but Momo hardly found it remarkable.

"It's not really an island, Usagi. We are still in the forest."

Usagi pouted. "True, true. But the Green Man is real, did you know that? He was the one who brought me here in the first place! He is large and kind and has wood for eyes. He can give me all kinds of beautiful things."

"Can he give you honey?" Momo thought about just reaching up with her hands. Stings didn't bother her any more than scrapes or bumps or any of the other trifles that humans dealt with. All of those disappeared when she shifted, yielding before smooth, unblemished skin. Of course, the bees would then turn on Usagi.

"Oh no, that's not what he does, Momo-chan!" Usagi

scolded. "Don't you know this honey is for those bees? The Green Man disapproves of humans stealing from their poorer cousins."

"Bears eat honey," Momo said, somewhat sulkily. "So does Father, during festivals." Mentioning her father reminded her of their agreement. *Live as a human.* She grimaced. Usagi cocked her head, mistaking the expression. "Oh, of course we can eat honey," she said happily. "Only we should farm it, as we farm for rice and potatoes. Did you know there are beekeepers in Kyoto?"

"I didn't!" That piqued Momo's curiosity. She always enjoyed tales of the capital city.

"They do!" Usagi said proudly. "I read it in a book. Men and women raise bees like your father raises silkworms, only they are harvested for their honey. So you see, we don't need to steal from these poor bees, who are only trying to survive. If we eat their honey, they will starve!" Momo didn't know how to respond to that. "You know," Usagi continued, "I think I would like to be a beekeeper someday."

Momo backed up, embarrassed by the girl's disclosure and constant push for friendship. She hardly ever spoke two words to Usagi and yet Usagi always spoke so freely to her. "I hope you do, then," she said. She turned to go. "This is truly a nice place."

"You are leaving? Don't you want to hear more about the

Green Man?"

"What is there to hear?" Her father would be expecting her soon.

"Well, he is the guardian of the poor folk. Creatures of the forest, and farmers and young children. He protects the weak from the evil and he never judges you, no matter what your station in life is. Peasant, bee, cat, flower, he watches over all of us. And he loves halfway places."

"Halfway places?"

"Yes!" Usagi said. She grabbed for Momo's arm but Momo carefully stepped aside. "He dwells in secret and only comes out in places that are in between. Solstices, beaches, sunsets, and islands of grass! That is why this is his home."

"Why would he come to our village?" Momo asked, somewhat irritated. She was too old to listen to this nonsense, and Usagi certainly was too old to be spouting it!

"He comes to all villages! He is everywhere, Momo-chan. You just have to look for him."

Momo nodded politely and sketched a brief bow, as humans were apt to do when in a hurry. "I must go," she said. "Father is expecting me to carry the day's work to the village."

Usagi smiled, hardly perturbed. "Come back sometime. If you wait until dusk, you might just see him. If you do, he might share some honey with you."

I was going to do that anyway, Momo thought. She took the long way home, annoyed that Usagi would be expecting her to walk on two legs, just like a good little human would.

*

Takamoto was in the back talking business in hushed tones, so Momo was undisturbed as she returned to the house and hoisted the silks onto her back. The villagers were as cool as ever toward her, though Taku amused her by tromping alongside for awhile, mimicking the expressions of some of the particularly dour folk. They split at the sweet foods stalls as Taku fumbled for a coin and Momo unloaded a third of her silks to a midwife who was an accomplished seamstress.

The middle of the town had a small inn where locals gathered to eat and swap stories. Momo generally avoided that center of humanity, where the men leered and the women stared, everyone inebriated with sake. Therefore, she froze when a voice called her name from one of the windows. "Momo-san!"

Turning, she saw Kenji Nakano sitting alone at a table. He seemed a decent sort of man, as distant as the others yet without the same contempt. Of course, he was highbred, sent from the noble courts to serve as both policeman and liaison to the outer world. "Would you care to join me for a minute?"

"The silks, Nakano-san," Momo began, but he cut her off. "No one will take them, Momo-san. Please, leave them by the window." She hoisted the basket onto the sill and went around through the front entrance. Coarse laughter drifted on the air, laughter that wavered as she stepped into the dimly lit straw-littered inn. The innkeeper was a stout woman whose name Momo never bothered remembering. She offered Momo a scowl before wiping down the clay counter. The scattering of men, local and foreign, glanced over at her. A trio of soldiers muttered something approvingly but stopped when she sat at Nakano's table.

"What is it, Nakano-san?"

"Please, call me Kenji," he said. She was taken aback at his cordial attitude. "Would you like some tea?"

"No, thank you. I will be late and my father will worry if I linger."

Kenji nodded and sipped from a small porcelain cup. His eyes looked tired, and whiskers jutted out from his skin. "Momo-san, are you happy here?"

Momo blinked, hardly expecting such a direct question. "What do you mean?"

"What I say. Are you happy here?" He set the cup down and peered intently at her. Momo averted her eyes.

"Happy? Of course I am, Kenji-san, thank you for asking. Father treats me so well and Taku is dear to me." She tried to sound cheerful, as well-trained girls were supposed to. She smiled, feeling her cheeks scrunch up. Kenji smiled back, somewhat sadly, she thought.

"I see. I am glad to hear it." Kenji glanced over and Momo followed his gaze. The three soldiers had gotten up to pay their bill but two others were sitting down. Many strangers passed through Yubikawa these days. The merchants, Momo's father included, were thrilled by their patronage, but there was also unease in the air. Momo smelled that unease springing from Kenji's sweat.

"Are you worried about me, Kenji-san?"

Kenji's eyes flickered back to her. "These are hard times, Momo-san. Very hard. There is talk…coming in from the east. I don't mean to scare you, little one, but war may come soon to these lands."

"What do you mean?"

Kenji sighed. "I should not speak of such things to a girl, but…" Momo picked up another scent from him… apprehension? No, it was still fear. But now it was fear directed at *her*. "But you are a special case, aren't you?" Kenji's eyes pored into hers and his hands were flat on the table. "I think you should hear the truth."

"Kenji…Nakano-san…I'm afraid I don't know. Please, tell me." Momo tried to hide the fear from her voice and failed. *He knows. He knows he knows he knows. And he is* frightened.

Kenji shook his head. "I just want you to realize…should you ever need help, Momo-san, you can come by my house. Please, don't hesitate to stop by, anytime. We can talk. But only if you are willing to talk."

Momo opened her mouth to speak but he cut her off. "My apologies, Momo-san. It is rude for me to speak so bluntly. Please, I will escort you out." Twenty pairs of eyes followed the two of them as they stepped outside. He bowed formally to her. "It is probably no concern. These are troublesome times and yet…" at this he laughed, "and yet, what times are not?" Momo bowed back as a group of horses thundered by, a great black banner hanging from the front one. Kenji Nakano watched the horses and their riders storm east, the dipping sun reflecting off their burnished steel, and then offered Momo a small shrug. With that, he turned and strode away, leaving Momo behind as she wiped the dust from her eyes.

*

She hunted. The colors were keen, the air rich with smells. She dove through the brush, playfully chomping at crickets that leapt inches from her teeth. They would be hers if she really wanted them, but she was well fed. Rice porridge and fish stew, a bountiful meal that her father had laid out before her. They did not speak of their new arrangement, but Momo had found a new outfit waiting beside her bedroll. An apprentice's outfit, brown and sturdy, designed to last for years. Such an outfit would fit her well, but it would be left behind whenever she transformed. The apprentice boys seemed to suspect something, because they watched her more closely than ever. The air of the house was filled with change. Even Taku sensed it, pacing and looking as agitated as a dog before an earthquake.

But none of that now. She hunted for the sheer sport, the thrill and the chase. The day grew long as shadows crept across the ground and the skies buzzed with cicadas. She trampled across the brush, defying other creatures to challenge her, but none came. A rabbit darted before her and she bared her teeth and engaged. It would be a short chase.

The kill in her mouth, Momo strutted beside the river. A familiar scent tickled her nose. Honey. Though her belly was satiated, her sweet tooth was not, so she trotted toward that tantalizing scent. Tonight she would feast.

Usagi was lying beneath the tree, as she had the day before. She idly stared up at the hive, humming the same song the bees hummed back down to her. Momo dropped the rabbit and licked her chops, tasting blood. This time she did not change. Instead she waited and watched the human girl as she lay there, a peaceful smile stretched across her deformed features. Momo sighed and lay her head down on her paws. Usagi's languor was infectious.

When her eyes popped open again, it was twilight. The sky

hung heavy and dark and the sun winked its light over the edges of the trees. Usagi was standing and singing to herself at the edge of the green isle. Momo's animal ears could hear the words perfectly.

"Green Man please save us from trouble. Green Man please save us from harm. Green Man, thank you for your blessings. Green Man, thank you from my heart." Usagi's voice was sweet, so much sweeter than her face. Momo watched her face the big tree and bow. Then the young peasant girl left.

Momo eyed the bees as they climbed, one by one, into the hive for the night. She then looked guiltily at the dead rabbit before her feet. She wouldn't be eating it anytime soon. Why did a well-fed girl like her need to kill? Arching her back, Momo dipped her head toward the hive and the grass island that contained it, and then sped off for home.

III. The Clashing of Interests

An immense waterfall hid the entrance to the Yan tribe's hideout. A gorge spanning twenty feet across and several hundred feet down stretched out in front of it, deterring any intruders from discovering its location. The leap over the chasm and through the roaring white water into the hidden cave beyond was one of the final tests for all Yan shinobi. Failure at that point in their training was rare but the cost was final. Beyond the waterfall, like an elaborate ant colony, was a network of passages that tunneled through the mountain and yawned out to a small clearing nestled in the middle of the vast forest. Humble gray cloth tents dotted the idyllic grassy land, providing an illusion of peace hiding the deadly wasps within. Only the Dai-Yan had an actual building; a cedar hut placed in the center of camp. A small Shinto shrine lay behind it.

Makoto sat in that shrine underneath the red torii gate that towered before the bronze and iron dais. The red gate was one of the simplest symbols of their land – two red beams connected at the top by a third curved one. The stark simplicity of the symbol appealed to all the Yan, who valued purity along with justice and strength, their other virtues. To many, Makoto seemed an ideal of such virtues: young, powerful, serene, with a deep intelligence behind his dark eyes. He sharpened his katana in quick, deft strokes against an oiled stone and avoided looking at Tsukimi as she quietly mended a shredded robe. They had not spoken in some time.

Tsukimi sneaked a peek over at her lover, two years her junior. They had first met six years ago when Makoto had voluntarily sought after the tribe. Most who attempted such a mad pilgrimage lost their lives early on but Makoto had persevered, striving hard even as those with more potential surpassed him. His unrelenting belief in the Yan code earned him a place among them and he now carried a distinct grace and calm that Tsukimi dearly loved. His huge, innocent eyes looked sad as he inspected his blade. Today was his first mission under Lord Motonari and he had sunk into a dark mood after hearing the news.

"Bad luck," muttered Makoto, breaking the silence. "This goes against our doctrine. It'll end ill."

Tsukimi paused in her knitting. "Makoto," she said gently. "We must obey the Dai-Yan, and he's agreed to offer our services to Lord Motonari. We're carrying out what we're trained to do."

"No!" Makoto's eyes flashed bright. "We're slaying the gods' very own creatures, and for what? For money." He spat it out like a poison. Tsukimi sighed – they had been having this argument ever since she'd returned from her last mission. Makoto had been boiling the rice when she slipped into their tent and when he gazed coldly at her bloodstained outfit, it confirmed everything that he really believed.

"I agree that this is slaughter, but those tanuki worked for the warlord Nobunaga. Any who live in Motonari's lands could be spies for Lord Nobunaga, and it's a daimyo's right to be concerned for his fief." Privately she also felt some approval of Motonari's wishes, though that was for personal reasons. Her own home village was near Kyoto and she felt a loyalty to them that was not quite displaced by her Yan allegiance. The thought of these strange trickster othermen dwelling near her family instilled a deep unease.

Makoto smiled as his frustration faded. "I understand why you think so, Sachiko-chan," he said, using her real name. "But for me…" He didn't finish the thought. Instead, he sheathed his katana with a resolved *clack* and stood up. "It's time." As always, they didn't kiss, but he gently squeezed her hand as he passed. Tsukimi felt a hot flood of electricity as they touched. After he left, she knelt by the shrine and prayed silently to whatever gods might be listening.

*

The interior of the Dai-Yan's hut was spare, consistent with how rest of the tribe lived. An elevated platform at the end of the room had a single chair for their lord. A ceremonial red robe and a massive black hat covered the frame of the burly man who sat before the three ninja. Although he was fifty he could still defeat any of them easily with his highly developed techniques – tradition upheld that only the most powerful among their tribe could be Dai-Yan. Kawaru tried to hide his hunger for such power as he knelt beside his two companions.

To his left was Makoto, a man only a few years older than himself. Kawaru knew little of the man other than that he was Tsukimi's lover. Otherwise, Makoto did not stand out in any way that even remotely interested him. The other one though, was far more intriguing. The powerful, muscular woman to his right was Tanin, one of the old shinobi from the Dai-Yan's youth. Still their master's closest aide, she was only sent out on the most important missions. This would be Kawaru's first time fighting with her.

Tanin always wore a smiling white cat's mask over her face. Long black hair spilled from that mask like a black fan cloth, completely obscuring any traces of flesh. Rumors hinted that she had been horribly burned years ago, and that the flames destroyed her tongue, explaining why she never spoke out loud. She suddenly shifted slightly and turned her mask toward Kawaru as if sensing his thoughts. He kept his gaze to the floor, feeling those squinting cat eyes crawling over him. *I'll figure you out,* he silently promised. Tanin spooked him in an unnatural way and he hated the sensation. The Dai-Yan's voice interrupted his thoughts.

"Tanin will lead. Two days from here, by the Finger River, is the village of Yubikawa. Reliable sources have informed us that a kitsune hides out there disguised as a merchant's daughter. It is my wish that you three eliminate her."

Makoto bowed low, indicating he wished to ask a question. After he was acknowledged he asked, "Beg pardon Lord, but why send three? Three easily dealt with a whole village of tanuki. Shouldn't one be more then enough for a single kitsune?"

The Dai-Yan folded his arms and nodded. "Yes, that is possible. However, Lord Motonari has warned me that there may be others roaming around those parts." His eyes briefly turned to Tanin. "Spies have informed us that there have been tengu sightings not far from the Yubikawa border." Tanin's body seemed to be quivering with strange energy as her master addressed her. "The tanuki village was easy because we had the advantage of surprise. Now the othermen may be more prepared. We cannot take any risks."

They went through the traditional rituals performed before each mission. First they each threw salt before the ground to ward off any spirits of ill luck, and then burned the carcass of an animal to placate the god of Death in case he had cast his eye on them. The Dai-Yan then stood and clapped twice, which was the official signal to depart. The three bowed low one last time and then quietly ran out, single file past the camp into the caves that led to the waterfall. Each easily sailed across the gorge and dove into the woods. They vanished into the trees as swiftly as stars obscured by clouds.

They kept pace together, dodging tree branches and pitfalls as effortlessly as any forest animal. None of them spoke. Makoto tried asking a question once but Tanin ignored it and Kawaru only smirked. By evening they had covered almost fifteen miles and it was only when the stars were fully out that Tanin signaled them to stop. They set tripwires and traps around the small clearing they settled in, and Tanin shot down two squirrels with a single flick of her wrist. Makoto built a smokeless fire and roasted the meat while the others finished securing the area. As their meal cooked, Makoto stared deep into the fire, orange flickering across his veiled face. His eyes were filled with dancing, desperate flames.

*

Her hands felt clumsy on the fragile creature's body. "Easy now," the apprentice said, a young lad who instructed Momo in mechanical tones. "Too hard and you crush it."

Such a delicate thing! Momo marveled at the silkworm, a miraculous construct of nature. To her, it looked like a little fuzzy speck but to humans it was an invaluable asset. Her father's very livelihood depended on the silkworms' survival and wellbeing. And now she held that livelihood in her hand. "You're gonna raise the larvae," the boy said. "You'll feed 'em until they mature and spin their cocoons. Then you get to boil the cocoons that'll unravel the silk."

"What happens to the worm?"

The boy smirked. "That worm's cooked after we get the silk. That's why they never turn into anything."

"That's cruel," Momo sighed.

The boy snorted. "Silly girl. You're gonna need a thicker skin if you really want to work with us." He walked out contemptuously.

Momo watched the little worm crawl across her hand. She carefully dropped it into its cage, whispering a prayer for the creature. How sad, she thought to herself, to be snuffed of life before even having a chance to fly!

The three Yan warriors stood in a grove of peach trees on the south end of Yubikawa. They were waiting for evening to fall and had veiled themselves after Tanin's first kill. Makoto watched his shadow grow steadily longer and reach out towards the village. Despite years of training designed to calm his nerves, the ninja shivered.

"Wind kisses my brow; a silent farewell to youth; autumn cuts too fast," he whispered to himself. He wished that Tsukimi was with them. She would have had an appropriate, comforting answer to his haiku. They often spent their idle hours speaking only in poetry.

"Be silent," Tanin signaled with a flick of her fingers. Her mask gleamed in the sunset light. Neither Kawaru nor Makoto had seen her eat, or use the bathroom, or clean herself, but she always seemed alert and poised like a hunting cat ready to spring. She was imposing too, almost as tall as Kawaru, who was a good head taller than Makoto. She put away her weapon of choice, a pointed three edged sai, and flicked her fingers rapidly. *"We move in two groups, at the Hour of the Ox. The silk weaver's house rests on the hill up from here. I will handle any resistance inside. You two go around the back."* Tanin's cat eyes were polished marble, her face an eternal smile. Makoto risked a glance at the small girl she had neatly dispatched when they had

secured the area.

She had met death so quickly her face had not yet formed an expression of surprise. Three neat holes were in her neck where the sai had penetrated and dried blood stained her brown neck like dead flowers. A single peach blossom was clutched in her right hand. Kawaru had sneered upon inspecting the body.

"A deformed one," he had said. *"Look at how her lip is split. Truly this is a village of weaklings. They probably keep all kinds of freaks here."* Makoto had resisted the urge to respond. Since starting this mission he had realized how much he despised Kawaru, who had proven to be nothing more than an arrogant, bloodthirsty killer. There seemed to be all too many Yan who had those traits these days. The ancient Yan ideals of justice and purity seemed like distant stars to the disheartened shinobi.

Tanin adroitly scaled one of the trees and perched on a branch. Kawaru grinned at Makoto. "There won't be enough to go around," he whispered. Makoto felt his temper twinge and he finally glared back at the younger ninja, unable to contain himself. Kawaru's gray eyes widened briefly at the challenge, then narrowed. His grin remained fixed, white, hard, and toothy. They locked gazes until Makoto looked away, disgusted with it all. The breeze picked up, and a chill air swept through the grove. Dusk had arrived.

*

Gen packed up his supplies. Villagers hurried by, heading home for their evening meal or out to the inn for a drink. The merchant folded the last of the silk patterns neatly into his basket and closed it. When the giant shadow fell across him he didn't bother looking up.

"She will be at her home," he said after a moment. Three gold coins clunked down by the dirt and the shadow retreated. Gen grinned and picked up the money. He scraped the coins with a small knife until the images engraved on them faded away into obscurity. That one's seal would not be welcome in this part of the country.

*

The apprentices finished for the night, leaving Momo to clean the cages. She took to the job reluctantly. Ever since she had been a small child, Momo had found solace in the grove. But now that she was one of *them,* one of the harvesters who nurtured and raised the silkworms for the sole purpose of taking their silk, she felt a pang of regret. What they were doing was unnatural. Everything that humans did seemed unnatural, from their artificial poses and gestures to their manipulation of the land, as if they were gods who walked the earth.

Images of her secret forays into the forest came to her

mind. There she knew she belonged. She was built to roam and hunt, to walk unconstrained by the laws and lands of man. But there too, there was something lacking. She was not a creature built of only instinct, without a need for any mental stimulation. The foxes dwelling in the forest avoided her, and they could not provide the form of companionship she yearned for. She needed conversation, and laughter, and emotions that the lower beasts did not possess. The humans seemed too rigid for her, the animals too wild. Where was the balance? Could she ever find it, or was she doomed to forever to carry on alone, teetering precariously from one end to the other? She wasn't sure.

One of the apprentice boys hurried past, casting her a sharp glance. Takamoto had acquired the three boys all within the space of last year, when it seemed clear to him that he had no real heir to his business. The skinny village lads were the reason Momo's reputation among Yubikawa villagers had fallen so dramatically of late. She knew of their concealed whispers, and their rude attitudes in her presence only emphasized her isolation. She shook her head, already knowing she could not put up with this farce for long. Momo could never be one of them.

Taku's familiar babbling voice snapped her out from her brooding. Looking around, she realized it was nearly dark and the apprentices had gone inside. Sometimes at this hour she and

Taku would sneak back outside and look for fireflies, but the season was not yet dry enough for the beetles to emerge. As if honing the point, a soft drizzle suddenly filled the air as a thick mist enroached. Taku took her hand and beckoned her toward the house. A cheerful grin was fixed on his face and his hands bore fresh nicks. He must have been carving wooden blocks again, a hobby of his that Momo never understood. She smiled at her brother and let him lift her to her feet. They walked together down the path back towards the house.

As they rounded the last bend, her nose prickled suddenly with the metallic scent of blood. Taku, oblivious, continued to walk ahead, humming tunelessly. Momo grabbed his arm and pulled him back.

"No! Taku, wait." He may not have understood her words but he clearly saw the expression of fear on her face. His eyes widened to two full moons. "Stay here." She crept forward, following the scent. Crickets buzzed and she relaxed slightly – if nothing had disturbed them, it was probably a false alarm.

Then she saw the body of one of the apprentice boys sprawled in a ditch. The wind wafted the smell of his blood to her, then the scent of an unfamiliar man. There was no other sign of the intruder. The wind shifted again and then the stranger's scent was behind her. She started to turn, and a gloved hand clasped her mouth. Someone hooked his arm around her neck and dragged her back toward the path. The cold touch of steel grazed her throat. Momo twisted her body but the arm maintained its position, as strong as pure iron.

Taku barged forward, bellowing furiously. Her unseen assailant hesitated and Momo quickly shape-shifted, her body contorting and shrinking down to a fox. The man yelled in surprise and dropped her as she scurried away on four legs. She turned around in time to see a black-clad figure duck under Taku's wild punch and kick him in the stomach. Taku grunted in pain, but followed with an elbow intent on smashing the man's head. With amazing swiftness, the man slid away and struck at Taku's nose with an upraised palm. The big man gurgled and crumpled to the ground.

"You should've killed him." Kawaru turned off his invisibility and approached the unconscious man.

"Leave him, it doesn't matter," Makoto responded. *"Where did the kitsune go?"*

Momo, who could not make out the rapid hand movements, was torn between running and helping Taku. While she hesitated she realized that the two black clad figures were looking at her. Before she could move, an intense, piercing pain split her back. She felt warm blood run through her fur as her legs turned to water. Her breathing hoarse, Momo fell on her side, shivering uncontrollably in the icy rain.

Kawaru drew another throwing knife, perfectly balanced it

in his hand, and flipped it over. He aimed this one at her head.

It never reached its target.

A metallic fan suddenly flew out and blew the knife off its course. A tremendous red figure walked forward and plunged a gigantic axe haft first into the dirt. The shaft, over six feet tall, seemed far too heavy for a human to hold. Makoto looked up and stared at a monstrous figure nearly two heads taller than he was. In the dim twilight he could make out red skin and malevolent eyes peering out over an extraordinarily long, narrow nose. Two huge black wings protruded out from the creature's back.

"Tengu," Makoto whispered as the two shinobi flew into action. Kawaru whipped out his sword and chopped viciously down at the shaft with the intent of breaking the axe head off. Makoto went invisible and leaped toward their new enemy with his sword aimed for the creature's thick trunk of a neck. The tengu's eyes somehow followed his invisible form and his other arm effortlessly swung into Makoto's chest. The blow, combined with his momentum, broke two of his ribs and he fell to the ground, gasping.

"How did he do that?" breathed Kawaru as he hacked again at the axe's haft. His blade snapped in two on the third blow and the tengu's weapon remained intact. Kawaru cursed and flung two throwing knives at the mountain goblin. One glanced off the tengu's arm brace, which he had whipped back protectively across his chest. The other buried itself in the meaty flesh of its shoulder. A crippling blow against any human, the wound only seemed to enrage the tengu. It growled low and swung its axe one-handed up and over its head, and down at Kawaru.

The blade smote through Kawaru's double, which shimmered and disappeared. Kawaru's true form lurked a few paces back, and he readied three more knives. The tengu snorted at the illusion and turned his attention to the other ninja. Makoto had propped himself up with his sword, muscles quivering in agony, just in time to see the hulking figure bear down on him. The tengu struck quicker than anything Kawaru had ever seen, cleaving the other ninja neatly in half. Makoto's blood gushed out in a fountain and soaked the dirt path. Kawaru's nerves gave way and the young shinobi scrambled away from the battle.

With beady eyes the tengu watched Kawaru flee before wrenching the knife from his shoulder. He flicked the weapon aside, then walked to the unconscious form of Momo. The drizzle slowed to a stop as he lifted the small fox with his free arm and hoisted her onto his shoulder. He bunched his legs and jumped once, then used his wings to further propel him into the air. With mighty thumping flaps, the tengu sailed up and over the house, and vanished into the iron curtain of clouds.

IV. Consequences

The floor ran thick with blood. Tanin finished her gruesome job with a final slice and dropped the apprentice boy to the floor. He had died slowly, his eyes bulging in terror as she extracted information from him. The Shinto religion believed that every object has a god behind it, and the spy had sworn to each one of them that he had no idea where the tengu had come from. He pleaded for his life, blubbering like a gasping fish that sparing him was reward enough for his work, but Tanin hadn't been satisfied. That's when she chopped off the first finger.

The masked woman didn't turn around when Kawaru walked into the silk weaver's home. It was still in good order, looms ready to be spun, an evening meal spread out and not yet cold. The weaver and another apprentice were out back, their throats slit, their bodies left for scavengers.

"Makoto's dead," Kawaru began. His eyes flicked to the dead boy and then back to Tanin. Black hair tumbled in a huge wave down her back, blending in perfectly with her shrouded costume. In the dim night the effect made her white mask shine unusually strong.

"*Someone else is involved.*" Tanin's fingers flickered rapidly, and the slight tremble in them revealed her rage. Her cat mask smiled on as she turned to face Kawaru. "*The tengu knew when to attack.*" She kneeled and wiped her blade on the dead boy's tunic. "*This spy was useless. He knew nothing.*"

"*So now what?*" Kawaru asked impatiently.

"*We return. Matters have grown complicated, and we may need a third.*" She spat the words from her fingers in bitter acceptance.

The younger ninja sneered. "So we run, just like that? Does our honor mean so little to you?" The woman turned her mask back on Kawaru and he shivered. It was like staring at a giant moving doll.

"*You speak with great arrogance, boy. See where that takes you.*" She walked toward him and he instinctively sidestepped out of her way. He watched her stride out into the night. The darkness swallowed her until only a white cat head floated away like some vengeful spirit. He cursed under his breath, pulled his mask over his head, and ran after her.

*

The next few hours were a hazy blur of wind and darkness. Momo remained in her animal form, nestled over a massive shoulder that her light-sensitive eyes perceived to be red. The hardened muscle jostled her back with every step that the creature took, but the pain had dulled significantly since the thing took her. She had tried to struggle at first, but that only aggravated the wound. After a while she dozed.

When dawn arrived, she found herself lying on a mossy bank beside a gentle stream. They were in the middle of the forest, with pine and cedar trees looming in from all angles. Still half asleep, she watched a butterfly bob and flicker by and she wondered if it had all been a horrible nightmare. But as she tried to sit up a sharp lance of pain ran down her back and she whimpered slightly. The sound roused a large figure that rose from its bed.

"Ho, so the little one is awake, is she?" The voice was low and inhuman, but surprisingly friendly.

Momo curled her tail underneath her and cringed. As she did, the scabs on her back broke open again. "Don't do that!" the creature protested. "They say a kitsune can heal whenever it transforms. Time you learned a bit about yourself." Momo looked up at the speaker.

The tengu stood a head higher than the tallest man she had ever seen, with expansive black, leathery wings nestled on a powerfully muscled back. It might have been a statue of polished red ivory, with every cord of muscle clearly standing out and glimmering in the morning light. A wound on its left shoulder was clotting, the blood blending in almost perfectly with the skin. Its only clothing was a pair of ragged brown trousers that showed signs of much travel. A proud, long nose jutted out like an extended finger beneath black eyes and bushy eyebrows. Its hair was elegantly tied into a warrior's bun and its face was clean-shaven. Gripped in its left hand was a dark iron war axe. The mountain goblin noticed her appraisal and grinned.

"It's rude to stare, little fox," it laughed. "But while we have a moment to talk, allow us to introduce ourselves. I'm Banken, and this is my partner Aiken." Suddenly another tengu materialized beside a pine tree. The second one was smaller then the first and wore a red bloodstained bandage across its chest, but other than that, the two were practically indistinguishable.

"Little kitsune," Aiken said. "You no doubt have many questions, and we can't answer them all right now. But be assured you're safe with us. We're heading east, away from this land. Friends are waiting for us."

"Wait!" Momo suddenly found her voice. "Please, tell me. What about Taku? What of my family?"

"They're alive," Banken replied stoically. Aiken's eyes widened slightly but she remained quiet. "A shinobi in a cat mask attacked your house but Aiken drove her off. She took a blow across her chest for your friends, little one, so be thankful." After a moment's pause he added, "Two were slain, a boy and a girl with a deformed lip."

Usagi. Momo's heart sank low. She cared little about the apprentices, but her eyes watered for the small girl who had so tried to be her companion. *May the Green Man protect you in your journey.* Now she'd never have a chance to make amends.

"We should go," Banken suggested. "We need to keep moving in case we're being followed." The other tengu nodded and with amazing dexterity, collapsed its axe. The shaft was segmented into three parts, each slightly narrower than the last, so in its final form the weapon was the size of a small hatchet. Banken did the same with his axe and dropped the weapon into a pouch hanging from his belt. "Come, we can speak while we walk. I trust you're strong enough?" Momo concentrated and slowly shifted into her human form. As Banken had predicted, her wounds completely closed, and although a burdening weariness swept through her she found that she could walk. Then she looked down and realized that she was completely naked. Horrified, she started to revert back.

The two tengu laughed uproariously. "You think we care about such things?" cried Banken. Aiken's tone was less mocking.

"Little fox, do you really not know the limits of your

powers? Shift again, and wait. Healing is exhausting and you're tired. But your dress will come to you." Momo nodded, feeling her face burn with shame. The tengu watched as her smooth white dress slowly shifted into existence over her naked body. Then it rippled and disappeared.

"You can do it," Aiken encouraged. "Kei says that forcing it only makes it harder. Try to relax." Momo concentrated again and her skin rippled. After a moment, a familiar dress flowed over her skin and hung loosely on her frame. She looked down as the tengu nodded approvingly.

"Good enough," grinned Banken, his teeth neatly filed and pointy. "And if kitsune are like any of the other henge, you can walk barefoot through the forest. Come on."

The tengu began moving at a rapid pace. Momo's mind raced with questions, but these strange goblins intimidated her too much to ask them. The forest sparkled with the early spring dew and there was a faint smell of moss in the air. A tantalizing scent tickled Momo's nostrils like a curious insect and she turned to see that they passed a small grove of peach trees. A wave of emotion abruptly washed through her body and the kitsune sank down to her knees. She cradled herself and began to weep.

Banken looked at Aiken with impatience. "She was raised by humans, you know. She's got the values of a human woman, unfortunately. I hear they're weak."

Aiken hissed then, an irritated sound that Banken knew to avoid pressing. "She just lost her friends and her family, Banken! That'd be hard on anyone, even you. Don't think women are weak, human or otherwise." As Banken retreated with a muttered apology, the smaller tengu knelt beside Momo and spoke in a motherly voice that sounded odd in its low tone.

"I know it's hard. I am sorry this has happened, but often the worst moments come all too quickly. I know you grieve, but the assassins who are after you will be on our trail soon. Once we leave Lord Motonari's fief we'll be safer. In a few days we will meet allies who will take us to sanctuary. If you can stay strong until then, you'll have time to mourn your loved ones."

"And where is sanctuary?" asked Momo between sniffles.

The tengu smiled gently but Momo shivered as she heard the answer. "The city of Kyoto, located in the fief of Lord Oda Nobunaga."

The tengu gave her some rice balls. After she ate them and drank some water she felt a little better. Banken had gone on ahead to scout the trail, but Aiken remained to talk. "Lord Nobunaga has extended his friendship to all forms of life. Motonari, the wretch who owns the land where you lived, has hired a clan of assassins to dispatch those who are not human. Those like us."

"Why?" Momo asked. That seemed nonsensical to her. She had never thought anyone would actually want to hurt her.

Aiken sighed. "It began when one of Lord Nobunaga's lords brought over a clan of oni from China. Normally the oni stay uninvolved with human affairs, as do all othermen. However, these particular ones aided the lord in a decisive battle that overthrew one of Nobunaga's rivals. That was the snowball that has cascaded into an avalanche, dragging the rest of us othermen into this war."

Momo felt dizzy. "War?"

Aiken nodded. "It's been going on for months now. Lord Nobunaga seeks to unite this country using othermen and several of his rival daimyo have foolishly conspired to kill all othermen in retaliation. Foolish, because that leaves us little choice: join Nobunaga or die." The tengu's eyes flashed like glowing embers. "But I promise you this, Momo-san. As long as we are with you, you will be safe."

Aiken fell silent and though Momo had more questions, she found she didn't know where to start. The terrain of the forest grew more and more strange to her as her nose picked up the scents of new flowers and unfamiliar animals. As evening fell she thought she caught the scent of an old badger that had roamed around her home, but she wasn't certain. The forest continued on, an uncaring blanket of trees that stretched as far as Momo could tell. Takamoto had once told her that the forest that bordered their home would take days to fully cross and she now realized he had not exaggerated. She felt a pang in her heart. Despite their differences, her father had finally shown her kindness and she prayed that he was all right.

Eventually Banken returned and informed them of a clearing up ahead. They made camp there, the tengu deftly setting the fire and roasting several rabbits. The kitsune found she had an appetite, despite all that had transpired that day. She wondered how Taku was doing, and wished that he was here. Banken and Aiken distracted her with tales of the east, of fiefs that had fallen under Nobunaga's rule. Momo had heard of Kyoto, the human capital city, but she could not believe that it was as vast as they claimed. She felt subdued and exhausted and didn't speak much, although when she asked why the two tengu shared the same pallet, Banken broke off into such chortling laughter that he started choking. Aiken shot the other tengu an irritable look before smiling indulgently at Momo. "We're mates, Momo-san. I am Banken's lifelong partner. He and I are promised to each other until we leave this earth." Momo found that notion comforting.

That night she had a fitful dream of her father's last outburst. Her father was screaming with rage, and as Momo quailed in the corner, beads of blood began to drip from his pores. Takamoto stumbled blindly toward her as his face turned into a mass of raw red, and Momo screamed in terror. This time Taku did not come to rescue her, and she woke up crying pitifully in the middle of the night. Aiken was there in an instant and held her like a child until she drifted off again into a peaceful, dreamless slumber.

They rose at dawn and proceeded once more across the unchanging forest. Momo asked the tengu if they knew of any more kitsune.

"We don't," Aiken admitted. "We have worked with tanuki, kappa, and even a neko, which is practically unheard of. However, you are the first kitsune I have ever encountered. I think that is why Lord Sharada—" Banken nudged his mate briefly and she fell silent. The male tengu reached into his pouch and withdrew a small figure of an old man smiling benevolently.

"This is Inari, little one. He is your god, the god of kitsune. You may have it as a keepsake, at least until we find another of your kind. Although they have not answered Nobunaga's call yet, I know there are other kitsune out there." Momo accepted the small jade token and ran her fingers over the deeply carved indentations. Taku had always loved to carve.

"Where are these other kitsune?" she asked quietly.

Banken replied quickly in an evasive tone. "They are hiding somewhere east of Kyoto. That is all that we know at the moment." Momo frowned as she pocketed the Inari figurine.

There was something amiss, but she could not pinpoint what it was.

Throughout the course of the next two days, Momo found herself gravitating toward Aiken, and they spent most of their time talking. Momo found it amusing how little Aiken knew of womanly manners. She could not speak the feminine dialect, nor perform any of the chores or duties, but Aiken just laughed when Momo pointed that out.

"Those are human responsibilities, little fox," she said. "Humans focus too much on society, and their duty to it. The tengu, as well as the kitsune, do not care for such pointless matters." The female tengu seemed intent on keeping Momo's attention occupied, and the kitsune found herself with little time to mourn her lost family. The weather remained fair and the forest was beautiful, and by the third day she was positively light on her feet.

On the fourth day, they encountered the soldiers.

It was just past noon and the three of them had set up camp for their meal. Aiken was showing Momo the proper way to start a fire while Banken hunted their food. When the male tengu returned, he had taken out and extended his mighty axe. He had a serious, almost wolfish quality to his expression.

"Aiken," he said. "There are humans. I've been spotted."

Aiken looked up from the fire and dropped the kindling. "How many?"

"Six soldiers, from the look of it."

"Where are they headed?"

"West." Banken said it with a grave finality, as if that piece of information was particularly important. "Let's go."

"Momo, wait here." Aiken stood up and extended her axe. The two of them dove into the trees, leaving Momo alone in the small camp. She did not have to wait long. Before five minutes had passed, they were back.

"Where did you go?" asked Momo. The tengu ignored her.

"We should go north, away from the main road. It's too dangerous here," Banken said. His skin glistened with exertion.

"No," responded Aiken. "Bands of thieves are to the north. This is the best course. It's a regrettable thing, but it's unlikely it'll occur again."

"Where did you go?" Momo repeated.

Banken looked down at her with pupils constricted like a snake's. His teeth seemed especially long and sharp as he grinned at her. "No worries, little fox. But let's break camp. We'll eat our meal later."

As they walked, Momo noticed that both tengu were avoiding her - even Aiken seemed unwilling to catch her eye. The forest seemed as tranquil as ever, with the constant chattering of cicadas and chirping of birds, and Momo wondered what was so wrong. Then a fresh gust of wind burst through the trees, and her keen nose picked up the sharp scent of human blood.

*

Tanin stood in front of the Dai-Yan. As an old companion and his closest confidante, she did not need to kneel when ceremony did not require it. The ninja lord gently stroked his beard.

"So. It looks like there were spies for Nobunaga in that village as well. How did our networks fail to catch this?"

"Our spy has been retired," Tanin signaled to him. *"More useful ones will be sent in to replace him."*

"Do so," responded the Dai-Yan. "This is troublesome. Indeed, the presence of tengu is very disturbing. It has complicated matters."

"We have a vendetta," Tanin reminded him. Her fingers flicked the final word with extra intensity. When a member of the Yan was killed, it was a matter of honor that the murderer was disposed of, whether the shinobi were paid for it or not.

"Even you cannot handle two tengu," the Dai-Yan replied. "Rinji and one other will accompany you. Makoto was weak, and Kawaru young. They were caught off guard."

Tanin nodded. *"With your permission, I request Kawaru again. It is time his potential shone."*

"I was thinking Tsukimi," said the old man. "Or perhaps Shinji. One who possesses the old blood." The old blood granted powers extending beyond the trainable arts of shadow doubles and invisibility. Only a handful of the Yan still carried the ancient bloodline and the tribe coveted those who did jealously. An entire network of Yan ninja were dedicated to hunting out new talent.

"Let's not waste our prodigies. This is no trouble for me. I would have slain the tengu bitch if she had not caught me off guard. As it was I easily drove her off and killed those humans she tried to protect. Kawaru has felt the sting of defeat as well. He will not shy from the hunt. Most importantly, he needs to learn a lesson."

The Dai-Yan smiled at his old companion. "Be wary, Tanin. These creatures mix with tanuki, who have great illusionary powers. You above all should know that the illusion of power is often power sufficient."

The cat face was expressionless, as it always was. *"They will all die,"* she assured him.

*

The moon was a sullen sphere of cold light to Tsukimi's eyes. *Moon viewing,* she thought bitterly to herself. *That's what my name means. And Makoto loved moon viewing with me.* She thought back to when Kawaru had told her, with that infuriating smirk, how her lover had been brutally slain by that monster. His gray eyes mocked her even as he expressed sincere regret that she could not accompany them on their resumed hunt. It took every ounce of her will to not strike down the impudent boy.

She looked back into the tent she and Makoto had shared. His side was cold, as it had been for the last week. *As it will be forever*, she reminded herself. The Yan were taught from an early age to let go of earthly possessions. To the eyes of the others, what she and Makoto shared was nothing more than the exchange of physical pleasures. But their greatest secret, the one that would have earned the wrath of the Dai-Yan, was that there was so much more than that.

There was love.

Tsukimi focused on her inner energy and tapped the hidden source of power within, the old blood that sang of generations of magic derived from the ages when the gods walked among men. Green fire surged out of her clenched fist and encircled it, the flames shimmering hungrily as she glowed like a firefly. Her irises burned with green dots as she grabbed her belongings. She had a vendetta of her own to fulfill.

V. The Traveling Troupe of Penken Satsumoto

"There it is!" Banken whooped in sudden delight. He swiveled his head to face the others and grinned wide in triumph.

Momo avoided his gaze. Two days had passed since the incident with the soldiers. She was afraid to ask the tengu what they had done to those humans, more so because she already had guessed the answer. The accusing, metallic smell of human blood and the tengus' guilty eyes had silently confirmed her suspicions. Since then, the kitsune resolved to escape and make her way back home. She was growing more worried about her father and Taku each day, but it was hard to leave under the tengus' careful watch.

Aiken glanced at her and then caught up to her mate. "We must have crossed the border some time last night. Penken wouldn't dare make camp so close to Motonari's fief." Banken nodded in agreement.

"Come, little fox. You'll be safe soon."

Momo caught up with them and saw a few colorful tents set out in a nearby clearing. The sudden break of the trees surprised her. Had they finally left the forest? A fresh gust of wind blew in her face and her nose picked up the scent of cooking meat and humans.

"Who are they?"

Banken rubbed his stomach. "Friends. This is the end of the woods, little fox. From here on we'll travel on the main road. Our kind doesn't need to hide in these lands."

I'm not like you, she thought angrily, and she blurted out, "I want to go home."

Aiken's black eyes narrowed. "Don't say such foolish things. We've risked much to get you this far. You can't go home now."

Momo drew back from the imposing figures as fear fluttered through her stomach. Aiken's suddenly cold attitude unnerved her more than anything. "But," she managed, "I'm worried about my father and brother. Are they all right?"

"They're fine!" snapped Aiken. "Perhaps we'll send word to them later."

Banken shook his head. "I'm sorry, little fox. There's no going home now." He turned his back to her and walked toward the camp.

Once, years ago, a circus troupe had passed through Yubikawa. Taku nearly frothed at the mouth as the jugglers and magicians streamed through the village. Momo, who was six at the time, could still recall being lifted up onto the large boy's shoulders as he ran toward the parade. Her developing animal senses were overwhelmed by the smells of smoke and men and the sounds of music and foreign languages. She had buried her face in her large brother's meaty shoulder and he had calmed her by humming a tuneless lullaby. The two spent the better part of the day by the seafood stalls, sucking down roasted eels and sea urchin and spending too much of their father's money. Momo quelled a nostalgic twinge as she followed the tengu into the camp.

This troupe was somewhat different from the other one. The one from Momo's memory had a blind man singing a lewd song while comically attempting to take swigs from a bottle in between verses. This one had two sentries with spears who each bowed low as the tengu approached.

"Banken-sama," one said, "Master Penken has been expecting you. Ah, is she…?" The sentry looked at Momo with a strange eagerness.

Banken waved him aside and stepped into the clearing. "Penken!" he roared ferociously. "Where are you, you old lazy dog?" A few men who were filling a latrine looked up but did not seem particularly surprised at having a giant red goblin in their midst.

A fat, unshaven, middle-aged man hurried out of the largest tent. "Banken! I thought I caught the stench of feces this morning. Quit stinking up this place!"

Banken motioned to the diggers. "It's your poor management of the camp that causes the stink, fat man. Maybe if you ate less, you would shit less." Momo started at the exchange but Aiken didn't seem to care about what they were saying.

Penken only laughed uproariously. "Stupid goblin." Although he was a good two heads shorter than the massive tengu and considerably softer looking, he clasped hands firmly with Banken. "Welcome back."

The tengu grinned. "Good to be back. We have brought a guest with us." Aiken motioned Momo forward and she reluctantly approached the fat man.

Up close, he was an odd sight. His head was almost too big for his body, giving him a slightly comical appearance. Dirty stubble protruded out underneath a pug nose and his hair was greasy, black, and short. Thick gold and silver rings adorned his fingers as if he was some wealthy merchant, and his breath stank of stale alcohol. With the exception of the jewelry, the fat man reminded Momo of the beggars and peddlers who occasionally wandered through Yubikawa. Despite his slovenly appearance, he managed a formal bow.

"Ah, I apologize for my friend's barbarous attitude. I'm Penken Satsumoto. Welcome to my camp! Please, please, you must be tired after such a journey. I'd love to hear your tale, but only after a bath and a hot meal."

Momo was swiftly escorted away by two young girls around her age. They took her to one of the two wagons in the camp, which turned out to be the women's quarters. There was some awkwardness when one of them tried to remove her illusionary dress but then the other laughed.

"Kimiko-chan," she chided. "Can't you tell?" The girl was taller than Momo but still had a child's look about her face. Her skin was healthy and unlined and her black eyes seemed to shine green when caught directly in the light.

The other girl blushed. "I'm sorry," she told Momo. "I had no idea—"

Momo cringed, feeling the girl's awkwardness. "What do you mean?" she asked. The first girl tittered.

"Don't worry, friend. There is nothing to fear here." The girl's pupils slipped into a deep emerald as her body shifted and her ears turned upwards as fur sprouted on her face. Momo was suddenly facing a human shaped cat. It wiggled its ears at her. "I'm Kei," it said. "Here, you don't have to hide what you are."

"I'm Kimiko," the other girl said. She seemed to just be a normal human. She looked at Momo shyly. "Are you a neko too?"

Momo had read about the cats that could shift into humans but the books were sparse on the subject, nearly as sparse as on her own kind. She stared with her mouth wide open. Kei giggled again and shifted her body back into her human form. "Who are you sister? Tell us!"

"Momo," she managed.

"Like a peach! How adorable! Well, Momo-san, welcome to our family! Penken-san is taking us all east to the capital city of Kyoto. Othermen from all over the land are going there, to be under the safety of Lord Nobunaga's rule. So tell us, what's your story?"

Momo related the last few days' events as they bathed her. Kei and Kimiko comforted her when she got to the part of Taku getting knocked out, and both sighed with relief when they heard that her family had survived.

"You're lucky," said Kei. "I was in my cat form when the soldiers came to my master's home in Okayama. They tied up my master and his wife and threatened to burn everything down if they did not turn me over. I was hiding under the porch the whole time. I watched one crazy samurai fly into a fit of rage and cut them both down." Kei's eyes filled with tears.

Momo nodded quietly as her thoughts turned again to her family. For some reason, narrating what had transpired made the events all too real. She resolved that as the troupe broke camp, she would slip away.

"I know what you're thinking," Kei suddenly said. Momo looked at her in surprise. The young girl's face was serious. "You want to go back, don't you? But that's only going to endanger them. If ninja were hired then they'll find you and kill anyone in their way to get to you. Stay with us, Momo. There are those who can protect us here."

"Who? Who can protect me? This is a circus troupe."

Kimiko and Kei exchanged smiles. "This is Penken's circus troupe," the neko said. "There is nobody like us in the entire world."

*

A small fire burned low in the dug out pit centered in Penken's yellow tent. Banken and Aiken sat cross-legged, their heads brushing the top of the canvas. Hot tea brewed in a pot, but Penken had a flask of sake in his hand. He took a swig and offered some to Banken. The tengu shook his head and stared reflectively into the fire.

"She fears us," he suddenly said. "A regrettable incident occurred two days ago. She is still naive, and knows nothing of the ways of this world."

Penken shook his head. "Too bad, too bad. But she'll learn quickly with us. You say she was raised by humans?"

Aiken nodded. "She's an unusual one, caught between her

human upbringing and her kitsune nature. I think her family must have abandoned her to the humans, why we don't know yet. Right now she lives like a child does, day to day. Right now all she wants to do is go home."

"Impossible anyway," Penken said. "You said the ninja killed her human guardians?"

The female tengu ran her hand over the wound on her chest. It had closed over but still burned to the touch. "There was a woman," she replied. "Her blade moved too fast for me to follow. It was like her shadow was the weird weapon, she an illusion. I could not protect them, and we lied to Momo about that." She hung her head. Banken put an arm around his mate.

"It was necessary," Banken said gruffly. "She's fragile as it is. If she had known that Takamoto died who knows what she'd do?"

Penken shrugged and took another swig of his bottle. "If the Yan are involved then we're in great danger. We'll pack up camp tomorrow and head east immediately." He belched and tossed the empty bottle aside.

Banken shook his head disapprovingly. "You need to stop that. You can't lead if you drink so much."

The fat man shrugged and patted his belly. "Leave me my comforts." His form shifted into a two-legged tanuki. "You say the Yan wiped out an entire village of my people?" He shaped his arm into a crudely shaped axe and slashed it through the air. "I say let them come." He shook his head and lay down. "It's time to sleep, ugly goblins. Gorofuku will watch over us."

As Penken began to snore, the tengu stepped outside. Under peeping stars, they squatted outside the tanuki's tent and passed the night silently, watching the camp for any signs of trouble.

*

The next morning, Momo stepped out of the wagon she had shared with the two other girls to find that the camp was nearly packed up. She looked at the valley ahead, where a road snaked ahead across the plains, eventually crossing over a thin line of sparkling water. Turning around, she stared longingly at the vast thicket of trees that would lead her back to Yubikawa. Homesickness nearly brought her to her knees, but then a gnarled black staff bounced against her shins.

"Sorry about that," an old man snickered. He had jaundiced skin and his ropy white hair was filthy and matted down. Something in his eyes reminded Momo of Gen, the lecherous merchant in Yubikawa. She quickly stammered an apology and darted back toward her wagon where Penken's men were hitching horses. She felt the old man's gaze on her and was thankful for the kimono she had donned that morning. She paused on her way up the wagon steps as Banken approached. When she turned towards him she realized that the strange human had disappeared.

"Walk with me, little fox! The sun'll do your pale skin good," Banken boomed. "It'll take about four weeks," the tengu told her as the troupe threaded down the valley. They moved at a pace that seemed excruciatingly slow. "We have left the Mori lands, and are now in another lord's fief, but until we reach Kyoto, we are still in some danger." He grinned suddenly. "But don't worry too much, little fox. We have real fighters with us now."

The troupe consisted of approximately thirty people. Most were men, hardened warriors, bronzed by the sun, and wielding battered but sharp spears and swords. Momo could only compare them to Kenji-san, and he seemed as soft as butter next to these strange men. Of women, she only saw a plump cook, a few serving women as lean and hard as the men, and her two companions. Kei and Kimiko rode in their decorated wagon and did not emerge at all, even after the troupe had started moving. With the exception of the tengu, everyone appeared human, but one particularly large man stood out from the others.

If the tengu capped a tall man by a full head then this man beat them by another half. He was imposing too, with muscle nearly as thick as on the horses that pulled the wagons. His face was grotesque: broken teeth hung half out of rubbery lips, and his flesh was sickly and pale. A dumb, vicious look was in his dull eyes and his hair was unwashed and tangled down to the small of his back. Banken saw her staring and nudged her.

"That's Gorofuku," he whispered. "He's the guardian of the camp. With him here, we're quite safe."

"He can't be human!" Momo whispered back in awe.

"You've caught on. Actually, several among us are not. Penken himself is a tanuki, who as you know have the ability to create illusions. Gorofuku there is an oni, and Penken has placed an image of a human over him. It is safer this way, even if we are not in Mori's lands anymore."

"Oh." Momo felt disturbed by how unnatural it all was. "But what about you two?"

Banken snorted. "I'm not letting anyone change me into an ugly human. Tengu are known to travel with troupes. We're signs of good luck and are famous for our singing and dancing."

Momo reflected on what she knew of the oni. Most of the tales about them had originated in China, their homeland. They were described as fierce creatures with two horns jutting from their forehead and a monstrous face that would scare even the most stalwart samurai. Their skin was horned and as thick as leather, deflecting all but the sharpest of blades, and they were said to be as intelligent as humans if not more so. Their legendary ferocity earned them high positions in any warlord's army. To Momo, the ugly human before them seemed nothing like the great ogres she had read about.

The troupe crossed the river and reached the main road by the late morning. Travel became much quicker on the smoothly paved road. Momo soon saw signs of civilization, farms and rice paddies in the distance and peasants going about their business. A couple of times children ran alongside the troupe, calling for tricks and gaping at the tengu, who merely laughed at the attention. One man finally pulled out five colored balls and juggled them deftly, to the whooping delight of the children. Another took out a samisen and plucked out a tune. The sun crested the sky and Momo found herself shucking the kimono that Kei had given her the night before. She quickly shifted the white dress onto herself and stepped into the wagon to return the gift.

The two girls were seated comfortably on their beds. Kimiko was mixing paints while Kei dallied through a book of poetry. They looked up and smiled as Momo entered.

"Too hot out there?" Kei took the kimono. "You don't want to stay out too long, Momo-chan. You might get a peasant's tan!"

Kimiko playfully slapped Kei. "Don't tease her!" She smiled shyly at Momo. "You know you can change the color of your skin, right Momo-san? Oh, you are so lucky! You can be beautiful or ugly whenever you want."

Kei dropped her book and stretched languidly on her cushions. "You're already beautiful, Kimiko-chan. You don't need shape-shifting powers!" She spoke in bored tones, as if they had had this conversation several times.

"So," Momo said, "what are we supposed to do? Nobody has given me any work."

Kei laughed, a bright and trilling sound. "No no, Momo-chan. There are no jobs for us three here. When we make camp in town, we will show them our wares." She winked cheekily at Momo in a way that made the kitsune feel uncomfortable.

"What do you mean, 'wares'?" she asked.

"Well." Kei shifted slightly and her clothes faded from a modest cotton robe into an elegant silk one that hinted at the curves of her body. "Circus troupes are expected to entertain, aren't they? We maintain that image. While with us, you'll entertain the men who seek the heavenly pleasures. Like us. That's what our work is!" She trilled out a little laugh.

*

The massive oni itched. Gorofuku scratched at the flea-bitten clothes Penken had given him – much to his regret, the tanuki wasn't powerful enough to constantly maintain the illusion of clothes along with the human form. It was just another minor irritation in a slew of them that he was forced to put up with on this mission. Bored, he eyed the women's tent with some interest.

"Nice, isn't she?" Gi-chan caught up to Gorofuku. The old man leaned on his gnarled stick, feigning weakness as he always did. "I wonder if she's still a virgin." He grinned, revealing a mouth full of rotting, brown teeth.

Gorofuku shrugged, ripping a new tear in the shirt. "Perhaps we'll find out later," he rumbled. He fixed his eyes on the road. "It's stupid how we traveled for weeks just for a fox girl. I'd like some reward for it."

Gi-chan's black eyes sparkled. The old man's white hair fluttered in the wind like tentacles. "Indeed. We can be customers too, Goro. Next time we stop, I say we pay the fox a little visit."

*

They made camp that evening in a flat field beside a wealthy farmer's home. The man had allowed them to stay for a few coins and then went inside, uninterested in their business. Tents sprang up, wagons were unhitched and arranged in a circle, horses were led to water, and a large cooking fire was started in the center of it all. One man set down his spear and began to sing a song about tengu and their mischievous tricks. Men passed around flasks of sake and clapped to the tune and, far from being offended, Banken began a strange and intricate dance to the man's words. He balanced himself expertly on sandals that had large blocks jutting from the bottom, and in the glow of the setting sun he looked like the incarnate body of some ancient god. By the women's wagon, Momo sat with a bowl of rice and vegetable stew. Aiken was beside her, her long shadow completely shrouding the little girl.

Momo felt a small bit of peace sitting with these strangers, listening to their foreign music. She also felt intensely homesick. "Aiken," she said, "who were those men who attacked us?"

Aiken looked straight ahead, not answering right away. She pitied the young girl, who earlier that day had adamantly refused to work as a pleasure woman. Penken had reassured her that nobody would force anything on her, but Aiken knew that eventually some man would insist. That was the ways of the humans, and othermen had to learn how to adapt to these ways if they wanted to survive.

"Aiken?" Momo tried again.

"Yan." she finally answered. "The Shadow Tribe. Of the schools of shinobi out there, the Yan is the top. They are currently centered in Motonari's fief and work for him."

"Everyone is drinking and having fun! We don't seem like we're ready for an attack."

Aiken nodded, pleased by the young girl's insight. *She's learning to be cautious,* the tengu reflected. "Don't worry. It's all part of the farce. Penken's men know better then to drink themselves to a stupor." *Except for Penken himself,* she added silently.

"Will the Yan come for me again?"

Aiken looked at her. Momo's face was still remarkably round, like a child half her age. The innocence of those cheeks contrasted sharply with her eyes, which stared with that fierce intensity that had always struck the tengu as unusual. *These fox folk are truly a mystery, even to Penken,* she mused. *How valuable is one, exactly?* "I think so," she finally answered. "But we'll be ready for them." She thought back to the cat-masked woman, the one who had given her the scar she would bear for the rest of her days. Aiken had ambushed the Yan from above with her spear aimed for a quick kill but the ninja somehow fended off the surprise attack and drove her off with casual ease. "We must be ready," she said softly.

*

"The messenger brought some interesting news. There are rumors of refugee tanuki hiding out in the village of Uchiwa, north in the Yamano province. We need you two to get there before any more trouble starts." Penken puffed on his pipe. "It is regrettable that you are needed again so soon, but will you do it?"

Banken sighed. "And Momo?"

Penken looked away. "No harm will come to her, of course. But she'll have to work as the other two do. It's the human way, and that's our way now."

"Are you so enamored by humans, Penken?" Banken growled low. "This is war, I know, but can we not avoid turning completely to their ways?"

Penken tapped ashes onto the ground. "She'll work," he repeated. "As we all do. It was a mistake to lie to her about her father. Someone must tell her he's dead so that she severs all ties to her old life. With us, she'll find a new home."

The tengu felt sick as he walked over to the pallet shared with Aiken. He sat down with a grunt and stretched his wings mightily.

"I know," Aiken said. "I heard you two."

Banken playfully pulled at his lover's nose. "I'm sorry. I know how you feel about the little fox."

"Like you don't?" she harshly returned. "It pains me to leave her like this. For awhile, I almost felt like—"

The other tengu squeezed her hand. "It's inevitable," he finally said. "We must leave tonight. It'll be better this way."

*

It was near midnight. Momo tiptoed past the slumbering forms of her two companions. Quiet as a hunter, she slipped from the wagon and headed towards the tengus' open pallet. The camp was completely silent, the sentries posted somewhere beyond and everyone else fast asleep. She felt an eerie chill shiver down her spine. Momo had been unable to sleep, with thoughts of Taku and her father continuously playing through her mind. Finally she had rolled out of bed. Aiken would send word to her family that she was safe.

She crossed over to their pallet and her heart lurched up towards her mouth. The bed was neatly made and the gear the tengu had brought was gone. *Perhaps they only moved,* a voice offered but inside she knew with a sinking feeling that they had vanished.

"They're long gone, little one," a reedy voice cackled behind her. She spun around and recognized the old man from that morning. He was only slightly taller than she was, and bent over a wooden staff. His skin was completely folded with wrinkles but his two cheeks popped out like little cherries when he grinned. "It's just you and us now." He flashed his rotting teeth at her. "What's your name?"

Momo stepped back, over the pallet, never taking her eyes off the old man. Her nose picked up the foul stench of unwashed flesh.

"How rude! When strangers meet, it is good for them to exchange names so they can be friends. Call me Gi-chan, little one. Would you like to be friends?"

"No!" Momo hissed. "Leave me alone."

The old man tottered forward on his cane, favoring his left leg heavily. His long white hair trailed behind him as he approached. "Oh, you don't like Gi-chan now, but soon you will find I can be quite nice. Your friend the cat girl has known me for some time. You will find it quite enjoyable too, you'll see." He crooned the words and for a second Momo felt hypnotized by his eyes. Rooted to the spot, she could only watch as he reached out an arm.

"Are those real clothes?" he murmured. "Let me see."

The kitsune sprang into action. With a fierce shriek she shifted her mouth and her teeth contorted into sharp needles. Her mouth distended to fit the row of fangs that suddenly appeared, and with a vicious snarl she snapped forward and sank her teeth into the old man's shoulder. They bit deep and the old man screamed. Rage and disgust escalated and the sweaty taste of the old man made her want to retch. She shoved the man away as her teeth returned to their human shape and she gagged, trying to spit out blood.

The farce over, the old man dropped his cane and stood there clutching his shoulder, breathing in staccato gasps. "You bitch," he moaned. "Oh, you'll pay for that." A second figure appeared behind the old man. "Gorofuku," Gi-chan said, "teach this fox bitch a lesson in proper behavior."

The oni was a fearsome sight in the waning moonlight. His illusion had been dropped, revealing a towering beast from a child's nightmare. Horns protruded from the devil face, and in sharp contrast to the tengus' long, almost comical noses, his was a short and ugly snout. Yellowed tusks gaped over lips that were turned down in an angry snarl. In one hand he carried a nasty iron hammer that he was tapping gently into his open palm. His skin was the color of dried curry.

"Stupid fox," he rumbled. He reached his free arm out to grab her. Momo tensed, feeling the hairs on her back rise up in anticipation.

"Gorofuku!" Penken's furious voice roared out. "Stop this at once!" The three froze at the sound of the tanuki's voice. He stumbled out of his tent, naked and in a two-legged animal form. "I will not tolerate this."

"Look what she did to me!" howled Gi-chan, shaking blood drops in the tanuki's direction. Penken scoffed.

"Most likely you deserved it. I told you two before not to harass the girls. If you want women, wait until the next town."

"You hear that, little one?" Gi-chan sneered at Momo. "You are Penken's woman now. Remember that well and start acting like one." He stumbled away, grunting at the pain of his shoulder. Gorofuku waited a moment longer.

"Yugotaro will know your name, tanuki," the oni rumbled dangerously.

"Is that a threat?" Penken challenged. "Get out of here!" Gorofuku scoffed and matched Penken's eyes for another second before turning away contemptuously.

The tanuki went to Momo. "Go to bed," he instructed. "We'll talk tomorrow." He walked away, stumbling slightly as he climbed back into his tent. Momo stood silent and still and then slowly sank her knees onto the tengus' bed.

*

With a snake's patience; I wait beneath milky stars; Too soon to strike true.

Tsukimi composed the haiku in her head and then let it slip from her memory, a gift to her beloved Makoto's spirit. She had only slept a few hours each night as she relentlessly pursued the trail of the other three Yan. Despite covering their tracks, Tsukimi could still pick up subtle signs – the slight impression of a boot here, the strange alignment of a twig there – and stayed true to the trail. She ate her cold ball of rice silently and reclined underneath a thick canopy of trees.

Images of Makoto danced through her mind. She had been eighteen when he had donned the garments of a full Yan ninja and joined them in the hidden grotto. Unlike him, she had spent nearly her whole life in the Yan, sought after when she was a child for the unique powers that she carried in her blood. Makoto had not been exceptional in any particular way, though he was capable, but what stood out in her mind was his good heart. *You had no place among these killers,* she thought to herself. *What karma could have turned our lives onto this course?*

Despite her talents, it was doubtful that she would be forgiven for her desertion. It did not matter. After she had avenged Makoto's death she would put her fate in the hands of the gods. Perhaps she might even be granted the chance to join her love in the afterlife. That would be reward enough for this final task before her.

VI. Two Cats

Rinji perched on the highest branch of the cedar tree and peered west, back toward where they had started. Although nearly forty, his vision remained as sharp as an eagle's and he easily made out the thin strip of blue known as the Finger River. That river was the lifeblood of the Mori lands, darting and snaking through countless villages, farms, and cities until it crashed into the maw of the great waterfall that marked the Yan's hideout. He then turned around and surveyed the small border checkpoint where two tiny guards stood stalwart and ignorant of how close they had come to death. As time was short, the Yan would spare these men and circumnavigate the checkpoint as they tracked the tengu.

He felt the tree rustle gently as Tanin suddenly dropped down beside him. For not the first time, he marveled at the masked woman's amazing grace and dexterity. Rinji was a veteran of the Yan, having served for twenty years, but even he was unable to hear her approach. Even after four days in the forest, the tall woman's lithe outfit didn't show any signs of wear and she still appeared alert and well rested. Rinji bowed his head respectfully at the kunichi.

"We will leave in four hours," she said. *"Their trail is still weak and we dally here too long."*

Rinji nodded, somewhat uneasily. Although the Yan always served the Dai-Yan unquestionably, this was the first time their master was working exclusively with one particular lord, in this case the aging Motonari. While it was clearly intolerable to let Makoto's death go unavenged, Rinji reflected that it was their constant allegiance with Lord Motonari that led to his death in the first place. He feared bringing up his worries to Tanin, of course – the old companion of the Dai-Yan was fanatical in her service to him – but his misgivings would not end. Politics were the concerns of lower humans, not enlightened beings. Rinji also had a more practical viewpoint on the situation; part of the Yan's survival relied on their neutral attitudes toward daimyo affairs. In siding so clearly with Motonari, they were at great risk of earning the wrath of other lords, including Oda Nobunaga himself. And unlike Motonari, Nobunaga was still young and very hungry.

As the othermen have been forced to a side, so have we, he reflected grimly to himself. But to Tanin, he simply signaled, *"as you say. Is Kawaru back?"*

The other shinobi nodded and then with deceptive ease, leapt down from the branch. Rinji craned his neck and watched her land deftly on her feet with the reflexes – and the looks – of a cat.

He took his time, testing each branch carefully before landing on the grassy knoll where they had set up camp. Kawaru had a fixed smirk on his face as he sharpened a knife with swift, deliberate strokes.

Until this mission, Rinji had always been assigned as Kawaru's leader. Now, under Tanin, both were equals and he found the younger shinobi intolerably insolent. He watched with disapproval as Kawaru balanced his blade expertly on his forearm and then tossed it in the air and seamlessly into his sleeve. Tricks and antics were for circus performers, but Kawaru strutted about as if he had an invisible audience. The younger shinobi then stood and signaled something to Tanin, cleverly hiding his hands from Rinji's view. Little things like these were too minor to openly confront, but the tension was building between the two shinobi.

"There is nothing unusual to report," Kawaru said to Tanin, fully knowing that he was infuriating the older man. He felt incredibly bored and made little jibes like that as passing amusements until the real fun could begin. It infuriated him that a single being, otherman or not, could drive away not one but *two* Yan. Granted, Makoto was hardly a worthy fighter, but the

gray-eyed shinobi felt great personal shame in running from the battle. He still remembered the fear that had flooded through him as he watched Makoto die, and how his legs forcibly turned and ran from the battle. *Not this time,* he vowed to himself. *This time I fight.*

Tanin flicked the signal indicating it was time to retire, and Kawaru gratefully lay down. In his mind, he played out the scenario of the recent battles over and over again. As sleep overtook him, a smile that almost resembled one of peace draped over his young face.

The other two shinobi looked down at him.

"I am getting tired of this," Rinji said. *"He is far too arrogant to follow our ways. He is a mad dog, nothing more."*

Tanin nodded, but then answered. *"I had misgivings of taking this boy when we found him, but he is unequaled in skill and potential. We will guide him, mold him to be a true warrior. He must gain the humility to work with others. Otherwise, he will not return to camp, whether we succeed or not."*

The other shinobi smiled beneath his veil. His eyes turned back to Kawaru and he watched the boy's chest rise and fall. Perhaps, if the upstart failed to learn the lessons of the Yan, there would still be some satisfaction after all.

*

"So they're gone," Kei said as she leafed through her book. "The tengu are Penken's hunters. It's not unusual for them to leave all of a sudden."

Hunters. Momo considered what that word meant. "They didn't even bother to say goodbye," she replied in a small voice. It was odd that she felt so hurt by their abandonment. One day ago, she would have liked nothing more than to get away from the strange, alien goblins who seemed to laugh and kill with indiscriminate ease. Now she found she dearly missed them, despite how little time she knew about them.

"It's war." Though said in a flippant tone, Kei's casual words echoed Aiken's. "Penken needs them elsewhere. I am sure they will return soon, Momo-chan." The neko placed an arm on her. "So, you talked to Penken today?"

"Yes." Momo sighed. There was too much happening at once and she suddenly felt like crawling away and hiding somewhere dark and cool. Their conversation had not gone well. Penken had apologized for the tengus' absence and assured her that his men would not harass her in the future, but he couldn't directly answer her when she asked if she was expected to entertain other men. Instead, the fat man turned away as a troubled expression crossed his face and taking a swig from his bottle, he curtly dismissed her.

Momo had wanted to cry, then. She couldn't even fathom what "entertain" really meant. She knew what humans and all living creatures did with each other when they reached maturity, but her experience with men was limited. The men who had approached her father's house were old and ugly and cast leering looks her way as they bargained with her father. Three of them had managed to negotiate a deal but when they tried speaking to Momo, they were quick to realize she was no ordinary human. One look, a slight yellowing of her eyes, and the men hastened back, tumbling over themselves as they hastily sketched bows to a baffled Takamoto. Those encounters had deeply upset her and she still shuddered at the memories.

Seeming to understand, Kei crawled over to Momo's bed and wrapped her arms around her. Momo felt that the young girl's enthusiasm and compassion eerily resembled Usagi's and she bent her head and mouthed a silent prayer to the dead girl's soul. Misinterpreting it, Kei only hugged her tighter.

"It's okay, sister! I won't let anything bad happen to us. Kimiko-chan and I will look out for you. Sex can be unpleasant the first few times, but soon you will find it as routine as anything else you do. Pretty human women often live this way and trust me, our kind can do it without even feeling anything."

"But we are not human, Kei-san," Momo answered. "Why

must we do what they do and live like they do?"

Kei let go of Momo and patted the shorter girl's head like a pet's. She giggled, suddenly in a goofy mood. "You would rather live as an animal all day? Run around in the forest, chasing mice and sleeping in bushes?"

"Yes!" Momo's harsh answer caught the younger girl off guard. "Why not?"

Kei pursed her lips. She had spent all her fourteen years in the residence of wealthy merchants. She had been discovered rummaging the alleys as a kitten with only vague memories of a mother who had been caught by trappers. Her masters had pampered and fed her, and let her walk around freely as human and cat. She often was sent to other homes to spy on competitors and gather information, but she had never lived in the wilds as she had heard neko were said to do. It all seemed quite intimidating.

"I don't know," she said slowly. "There would be Kimiko to think of."

Momo nodded. "Of course, you are right." She felt a real kinship to the two girls in the short time they had known each other. They did not judge her, as the villagers of Yubikawa did, and the fact that Kei was not human lowered several barriers that Momo had erected while young. She crawled to the edge of the wagon and peeked out.

Evening had arrived, casting a cool orange glow over the

landscape. The rice paddies and farms had grown sparse as they entered an uninhabited mountain range. Kei had said that in a few days, they would cross over and arrive in Okayama, the city where she was raised. There, she had solemnly warned Momo, she would be expected to entertain any customers who might seek her out. "It'll just be dancing, singing, pouring drinks and the like," Kei said. "You really don't have to sleep with any of them. Unless you like them, of course. Or if they pay Penken enough. Which they rarely do," she hastily added. "Anyway, you're just an apprentice so you can hang back and let Kimiko and I do everything. You won't be expected to actually perform or anything, not yet."

That's not the life I choose, the kitsune thought angrily. The casual and resigned attitudes of the other girls saddened her. *Tomorrow, or the day after, I will leave them and go into the mountains. I cannot endanger Taku but I cannot stay here. I will be alone.* She felt tears brim in the corner of her eyes, and she hastily wiped them away as she closed the curtain and faced Kei.

"Shall we get dinner then?" she asked her friend.

*

The cat-faced shinobi hissed in delight as the three of them came across the main road. The trail of the tengu had merged in a grove where the signs of horses, wagons, and several more men indicated a large party. The increase in numbers did not particularly worry any of the Yan; they were more than prepared to take on several opponents at once. However, it would have been difficult to tell if the fox and tengu had joined such a large party. Then as they reached the road, Tanin picked up on the unmistakable large footprints in the soft dirt road. She traced her finger along the large outline and turned to the others.

"We stay true to the path," she signaled. *"They travel within a large group, due east."*

"Good," Kawaru said. "More for me to kill."

The other two shinobi ignored him and switched on their invisibility. They ran down the road, leaving no imprints of their own behind. Kawaru cursed under his breath and made haste to follow them.

"We'll reach them sometime tomorrow," Rinji whispered to Tanin. Though he could not see her expression, he knew that the shrouded woman's body was quivering with eager anticipation.

*

Momo's second night with the troupe proved to be less eventful. She spent most of it with the two girls, chatting and exchanging stories with each other. Momo felt embarrassed about how little she had to say about her own life, but Kei and Kimiko seemed intrigued by Taku and his childish antics. For her part, Kei enthralled with her adventures in the city as a spy for her merchant master. The neko proved to be an engaging storyteller, whispering about the scandals and backstabbing that went on with an uninhibited glee. Even Kimiko had an impressive history. She had been a streetwalker who was taught how to be geisha by a generous teahouse owner who happened to be an old consort of Lord Nobunaga himself. Momo could hardly believe that both girls were younger than she was.

She was especially surprised when a somewhat drunk Penken joined them, amicably putting an arm around her and Kei. He too shared stories of his youth as an adventurer in the great western nations of China and Korea.

"There," he whispered to Momo, his eyes glazing over in the past, "such sights one would see! My companions and I traveled into the Forbidden City and encountered the dragon overlord, Yun-Kai-Me. But he wasn't evil, oh no. He was a crafty beast, and ambitious in propelling the power of his nation, but he also helped us a great deal on our quest."

"You saw a real dragon?" Momo asked in awe. The other two girls exchanged glances and silently giggled, clearly used to this tale.

"More than that. Such adventures we had! Our leader, Lord Amano, once outsmarted a group of oni bandits with merely a song. We even journeyed to the cold north, where we encountered barbaric men with white flesh and sealskins. Of course," he chuckled, "the three of us managed to make peace with these strange humans." He wiped his runny nose and his face flickered from human to tanuki, as if he couldn't control it. "Then in Korea, we battled a nine-tailed demon that took on the shape of a fox, much like you can, Momo-chan!"

Momo felt uncomfortable being compared to such a demon, and her face must have revealed it because Penken suddenly apologized. "Forgive me, little one! Your kind is nothing like those western monsters. But you're a rarity too, you know. You're the first I've encountered in the past twenty years. Some say it's because the kitsune have withdrawn themselves from the rest of Japan, others that you've all blended in with society, working as teahouse boys and girls and as dancers. Whatever it is, it's the reason we've had to journey so far—" he stopped himself then, an abashed look on his face. "Forget a drunken fool's ramblings, Momo-chan." He tottered to his feet, using the two girls' shoulders as support, and joined a trio of guardsmen.

Momo looked at Kei. "Have you ever met another kitsune, Kei-san?"

The neko shook her head. "I don't know what Penken was going to say, but you're the first. What kind of powers do you possess?"

"I can shape-shift into a human of course. And I heal when I do." Momo thought back to when she turned her teeth into fangs against Gi-chan. This evening she had seen the old man and his oni companion across the camp, drinking with a couple of men and ignoring the girls completely. A disturbing memory of what Gi-chan had told her suddenly came to her. She looked over the two girls, and the image of that old man groping them nauseated her. If he ever tried anything again, she wouldn't let him get away with just an injured shoulder! *What else can I do?* Tanuki could create complete illusions. Could she do something like that too? "I...I don't really know what else."

Kimiko trilled a small laugh. "How exciting! You have a lot to discover, Momo-chan. I envy you!"

Momo remembered something she had read in one of her books. "I've heard that neko can produce gold coins from thin air. Is that true, Kei-chan?"

The young girl lit up in delight, and for a second Momo thought of Usagi again. Then the neko replied, "Oh if only that were true. You think I'd be stuck here?" She flopped on her back and stared at the stars. "I'd be somewhere far, far away."

The three of them lay like that in the open air as the quiet buzzing of the cicadas in the trees serenaded them to sleep.

*

"Dawn." Tanin held the word carefully in her hand as she kicked Kawaru awake. He squinted at the clear blue sky and then stumbled to his feet, instinctively testing the various knives and the poisoned needle hidden on his body. They had passed

the signs of the troupe's camp by the farmer's house long ago and had followed at a brisk pace for several hours more before finally stopping to rest. Tanin had permitted them more sleep than usual, feeling no need to rush now that their quarry was so near.

"It is time to prove yourself as a true Yan," a voice behind him said gruffly. Kawaru spun around and glared at Rinji.

"What are you implying?" he snapped.

Rinji ignored the open challenged and walked up to Tanin. She passed him the hard cracker that was the signature meal of all ninja and tossed one to Kawaru. The shinobi caught it and swallowed the dry food in two quick bites. He knew how he would prove himself. The fox girl and all her guardians would wash his blade tonight, and after that, his undisputed abilities would not be challenged by anyone. And if they were challenged – well, more fool those who still dared to stand against him!

*

The wagon wheels creaked incessantly as they made the slow grind up the mountain path. The horses panted in the heat and the troupe had to slow their pace down considerably so as not to overexert them. Momo woke up that morning feeling almost happy, but the high temperature quickly got to her. She felt a familiar distress as the sun burned through her fake clothes and baked her body. *Today, I will escape*, she vowed again, although with less heart than before. The kitsune found the idea of leaving her new friends and going into a voluntary isolation too painful to bear. As the day wore on she approached Penken, who was huffing considerably as he tried to keep pace with one of his men. He turned to her, not pleased at being interrupted in his conversation.

"Yes Momo-san? What is it?"

"Penken-sama," she began, "please, is there any way we can contact Haruhiro Takamoto, the silk weaver of Yubikawa village? He is my adoptive father and he must be very worried about me." The red-faced man paused and whispered something to the soldier. The other man bowed briefly and jogged up ahead.

"Walk with me, Momo-san," Penken said gravely. "It's time you heard the truth."

Momo ignored the words and persisted. "If you could send but one messenger back, or perhaps talk to a merchant heading the other way, just—"

"Momo." He handed her a wet towel. "Place this on your head." She obliged and he led her to the cook's wagon. They climbed inside, where pots and bags of rice swayed perilously in the uphill struggle. He sat cross-legged on the bare floor and waited until she sat down before beginning.

"Your father is dead." He bowed low in apology. "The Yan struck your house at the same time they attacked you, killing him and the apprentices. The tengu were foolish to lie to you at the time, but in their mind, they thought it would make your transition easier."

The wagon lurched suddenly and Momo bent over as a wave of nausea struck her. She let the towel plop to the floor as she fumbled for the door. She failed to get on her feet and instead slid to the floor, breathing heavily and staring at the blue boards.

"Momo-san, I'm so sorry. Aiken tried to defend Takamoto-sama but she failed you."

"What about Taku?" she managed to gasp between breaths.

"Who?"

"What about Taku!" The words came out in a vicious snarl as she lifted herself up on all fours and whipped around to face the tanuki. The whites of her eyes had a strange yellow tinge that seemed to burn toward him.

He faltered. "I…I do not know," he managed. "The tengu didn't tell me about him." A low growl emerged from the tiny girl's throat. Penken lumbered to his feet and eyed her cautiously. He felt like he was trapped in a room with a vicious animal. "Please Momo-san." He swallowed. "Please."

The kitsune darted out of the wagon on her hands and feet. Penken started after her and stared in alarm as the girl's body shifted itself into an orange and red fox, smaller than her human body yet infinitely more powerful in appearance. The fox scurried through the surprised humans and toward the rear of the camp. *She's trying to escape,* Penken suddenly realized. That was unacceptable. Lord Sharada had given explicit instructions on the importance of finding this kitsune, and failure at this point could have drastic consequences. He closed his eyes and tapped into his powers.

A stone wall suddenly sprang up in front of Momo. She skidded to a stop in surprise and tried to get around it, only to find herself enclosed by three more. By the time she had realized it was only an illusion, a man had tossed a net over her. Penken walked over and watched her struggle and snap. He shook his head regretfully as one of his men placed the wiggling form into a brown sack and tied it shut.

VII. Bloodshed on the Mountain

    Kenji Nakano gave a satisfied grunt as he arrived at the town square. The cage swung slowly in the air, hanging from the tower he had constructed just for this purpose. Inside the prison was a decrepit man, emaciated from days of starvation. Tattered clothes hung loosely from a once plump frame, and dirty whiskers were scattered over the sagging, sunburnt cheeks. Upon seeing Nakano the man scurried to the edge of his cage and thrust his hands pleadingly through the metal bars. The cage rocked at his sudden movement and the pitiful figure moaned in pain.

    One of Nakano's deputies bowed low. Nakano nodded and gestured at the prisoner. "Has he said anything new?"

    "No, Nakano-sama, he sticks with the same story. Perhaps some torture will set him straight?" The stocky peasant grinned eagerly.

    "No." The samurai found that distasteful, no matter how perplexing the merchant's story. Gen had insisted that he knew nothing of the shinobi's attack, but instead that he was merely a spy for yet another faction. Even if he spoke the truth, he wouldn't name his superiors and instead resigned himself to a slow starvation. "Please," Gen moaned thickly as his hands trembled against the cage bars. "She'll kill me if I say anything!" Nakano shook his head in disgust.

"Send me word the second he breaks," he instructed the peasant. It was time to head back to his house; Nakano's superiors required daily reports sent to them and he had to draft another dull account of the daily happenings in Yubikawa.

At home, Nakano marveled yet again at how efficiently his belongings had been sorted, how cleanly his rooms were swept. His old maid had never been so adept at the daily necessary chores of a household! The day after Haruhiro Takamoto and his three apprentices were found, Nakano took his old friend's son as his ward. At first, the samurai had dreaded the notion of caring for a mentally handicapped man, but he had soon found Taku to be more than capable of earning his own keep. The young man gardened, cleaned, and even cooked basic meals, all with an enthusiasm and capability that the samurai had never expected. Taku would hum tunelessly, with a placid smile on his face, while working, and then meekly retire to his room. Nakano soon was comfortable with leaving the large man home alone.

Strange, how one who does not possess the wits of a full man could fit here so well. Nakano had found himself growing attached to the large lad. Reaching into his pocket, he pulled out the candied peach he had picked up from the market and rolled it between his fingers. He entered Taku's room and found the man sitting contently on the tatami mat, intently carving at something in his hand. He looked up at Nakano's entrance and babbled happily before lurching to his feet. Nakano smiled.

"For you," he offered. Taku grinned in delight and shoved the candy into his mouth, chewing eagerly. Bits of powder flaked down his chin as he closed his eyes in delight. Nakano watched the large man eat with a strange sense of peace.

Taku suddenly grunted. He bent over, retrieved the object he was working on, and offered it to Nakano. The samurai paused and slowly took the wooden figurine. He had never taken the time to notice what Taku worked on in his spare time, but he knew the man could spend hours carving away. Nakano ran his fingers over the crude design, marveling at its stark beauty, formed with a childish simplicity. The small wooden fox was smiling enigmatically out at him and Nakano found himself smiling back. He offered it back to its creator a small bow. Taku only hummed to himself as his eyes went somewhere far away.

*

The hot darkness threatened to smother Momo like a

woolen blanket. No one had entered the cook wagon since she had been imprisoned in the cage, except a brief visit by a serving girl who had kept her distance. Momo tried again to shift her form, hoping to burst the cage apart as her mass increased, but the second her rippling flesh touched the edge of the bars it withdrew as if burned. She was a prisoner in this cage, trapped as a fox, stuck with strangers who clearly were not as benevolent as they had claimed. Despite it all, the young girl did not feel the least bit scared. Instead, rage simmered through her like a hot poison as mental images of Taku and her father slain and the betrayals of the tengu and Penken flashed through her mind. She seethed at the fate that the cruel gods had imposed on her.

This will not be, she thought angrily to herself. Her mind turned to the carving of Inari, the god of foxes, stashed away somewhere in the women's wagon. It was a gift from Banken and perhaps as foul as his promises had been, but nonetheless she mouthed a silent prayer towards it. If the god could siphon any of his strength down to her, now would be the time. She snapped at the thin wires of the cage and forced her teeth to grow as long as she could, but the thin metal held. She snarled quietly and spat out a wad of blood. They could not keep her here forever. If Taku had indeed been killed, then those tengu would have much to answer for. The thought of her innocent and loving brother lying as dead as that apprentice spiked a fresh wave of fury in the kitsune.

The wagon rocked to a sudden stop. Momo whipped her head around, ears alert. For a few seconds there was silence, then tinny desperate shouts popped in the air. She could dimly hear the scrape of a sword leaving its sheath, and then one of the shouts slipped into a high-pitched scream. A horse moaned like a creaking gate, and an explosion far to her left rocked the wagon slightly. They were under attack! She began to scrabble against the bars of the cage with renewed energy, whipping her paws against the metal until they bled.

"Momo!" The wagon door banged open and the sudden beam of light illuminated the form of Kei. She ran over to the cage and fumbled with the lock. "We're being attacked! We have to get out of here!" The rank stench of terror nearly overwhelmed Momo's senses. The neko grabbed a sharp knife and hacked the lock off with four quick blows. She barely had time to open the cage before the fox darted out. "Wait!" Kei cried, as the kitsune scrambled outside. "Wait!"

*

Kawaru felt like he was dancing. Tanin had ordered them all to work separately to increase confusion, and he preferred it that way. They had seen no signs of the tengu, but the strange nature of this circus and the whispered mutterings of a "kitsune" confirmed with no doubt that they were on the right track. He sent his image forth as he remained behind unseen and watched two men chase after it. With casual ease he chucked two knives at them. One found its mark but the other man, by sheer luck, managed to duck out of the way. He turned around in bewilderment as he looked for the source of the attack.

"Come at me then," sneered the shinobi as the soldier stumbled forward, jabbing his spear futilely into the air. Kawaru grabbed the haft and kicked the man in the stomach, sending him sprawling like a flopping fish. The spear now in his hand, he allowed his form to reappear before expertly twirling the weapon above his head before the gasping man and driving it into his skull. "Too slow," he laughed.

He heard the distinctive *twang* of a bow and rolled under an arrow that nearly impaled his side. He readied another knife and saw the shooter was a large and somewhat overweight two-legged tanuki. Despite the creature's soft appearance he was already fitting another arrow into his bow.

The shinobi exploded into action, charging the tanuki before he could get another shot off. The otherman only had a second to react before Kawaru's knife plunged toward his neck. Somehow, Penken shrugged off the weapon with his arm and as the knife hung in his meaty shoulder, the tanuki shoved Kawaru away with his free hand. The man used the momentum to backflip once and stood before him with a snide grin on his face. Then the young shinobi flicked out his sword, as deadly as a wasp.

A bolt of lightning caught Kawaru in the side and rocked him off his feet. He rolled three times on the dusty ground and lifted himself up to behold the figure of an old man cackling wildly. Gi-chan raised the staff over his head with both hands, and began the incantations of another spell. *A sorcerer?* Kawaru had never met one of those few, who could control nature's powers, and he certainly didn't expect to see one here. His ribs ached from the electric burst and he barely managed to dodge the second bolt. The electricity crackled furiously in the dirt beside him and sent white spots dancing in his eyes.

The old man hooted gleefully and slowly approached the ninja. Behind him Kawaru heard Penken grunt as the tanuki ripped his knife free from his arm. He summoned his chi again and disappeared from his opponents' sight. He then sent a double to charge at the tanuki, catching Penken off guard. The fat tanuki reeled back and knocked his head against the women's wagon with a heavy thud. He slid to the floor, stunned.

Gi-chan did not seem daunted by his enemy's abilities. He chanted something in an arcane tongue and sent a gust of cold wind hurling to where Kawaru had vanished. The ninja felt his bones ache fiercely in the arctic air, and his invisibility wore off as his concentration failed. *No!* He propped his quivering body up with his sword and watched helplessly as ice crystals clung to his blade. The weapon would not hold much longer.

The old man howled in delight and readied himself for a third bolt. As he raised his hands over his head, a long needle popped out through his jugular. It had been thrown with such precision that there was almost no blood, as the sorcerer slid first to his knees, and then face-first onto the ground. Kawaru looked up to see Rinji standing over him, his expression indiscernible behind his black veil.

"Get up," the older man said. He then vanished to rejoin the massacre.

*

The oni grunted as he blocked the cat masked *kunichi's* sword slice with his bracer. Tanin impassively pressed him forward, the bodies of his companions littering the battlefield. He barely had time to block another blow before being forced to wheel away from a sudden spinning kick. He straightened himself only to have to jump out of the way of another sword slice that would have opened his chest. Gorofuku already had several cuts on his arms and torso, all superficial, but the pain and loss of blood from the injuries were wearing him down.

She can't be a human! The entire morning had descended into pandemonium. Gorofuku was at the front of the troupe when he heard the screams, and he had turned to see a man clutching his throat as blood spurted out between his fingers. Another man was already dead on the ground, but of the attackers there was no sign. An explosion went off at the edge of the camp and the oni ran over there to see yet another one of his companions' charred bodies. In the short time he had gone there to investigate, this strange woman had appeared, waiting for him over the corpses of the men he had left behind.

He saw an opening and rushed at it, slicing with his long knife and hoping to end it in one blow. His weapon passed through the figure of the ninja, which shimmered and disappeared like some elusive mirage. The real Tanin was already behind him and she scored a brutal slice against his back.

The fresh pain filled the oni with a wild rage. He roared and spun around but the ninja was already gone. A soldier rushed up to aid Gorofuku, only to find his arm separated from its shoulder. The man fell to the ground shrieking and only then did Tanin permit her invisibility to wear off. She flicked the blood off her sword and silently regarded the oni.

Gorofuku considered his options. The woman was far superior to him in combat, but he was much larger. A single blow would end it once and for all. He steeled himself for the oncoming pain, and rushed at Tanin. As expected, she lightly leapt back while landing a blow on his muscled forearm. Rather then drawing back from the pain, he blundered forward and shot his good arm out. Tanin dodged the attack but not before catching a slice on her neck. For the first time, her blood misted the air in a fine spray. She rolled back and away before the damage could accumulate and rose to her feet again, regarding the oni with a new wariness.

That's right, you bitch, he thought to himself. His left arm burned where her sword had severed his tendons, but he knew how to beat her now. No matter how agile she was, Gorofuku was twice her size and immeasurably stronger. He advanced on her again.

Once again, Tanin sliced at him with her sword in a sharp whipping motion that was aimed at his other arm. Gorofuku steeled himself for the blow and then watched in amazement as the weapon passed harmlessly through his flesh. He had no time to react as Tanin's real blow, the blade's shadow, impaled him through the lungs. He struck out and missed as she calmly twisted the shadowy weapon and extracted it. Gorofuku fell to the ground choking blood, and his breathing grew heavier and slower. Before his brain shut down he made out the figure of the cat woman standing over him.

Tanin winced as she felt the oni's wound on her neck. That was close; another inch and it might have been critical. When she was satisfied that the oni was dead, she allowed her shadowy blade to fade away. No one had ever defeated her shadow strike, the innate talent that the old blood had passed on to her, in which the blade became the illusion and the shadow following it the real attack. Sudden movement to her right caught her attention, and she turned to see a small fox dart across the bloodied battlefield with two girls running after it.

*

There was chaos and death everywhere. One of the wagons was burning and the stench of oily smoke gagged Momo's lungs and watered her eyes. She stumbled across the gaping corpse of a man and, appalled, switched directions in her mad attempt to escape the carnage. The ground was littered with the bodies of the men she had been traveling with. The horses whinnied in terror and the burning wagon collapsed as the two hitched to it broke free of their harnesses and galloped off, hooves thundering like beating drums. The air was soaked with ash and blood, overwhelming Momo's senses as she aimlessly ran about.

"Momo! Momo!" Kei's pleading cry snapped her out of her disorientation. She paused and turned around to see her friends running to catch up with her. Kei's hair was tangled and wild, her skin stained and dirty. Kimiko followed close behind. "Momo-chan," Kei wailed, "don't leave us here!"

Everything seemed to happen at once. Kei stretched her hand out pleadingly towards Momo. The burning wagon tumbled to the ground, a smoking wreck. In the distance a man staggered, clutching his stump of an arm until some invisible force disemboweled him. And Kimiko sank to her knees, perplexed at the sai that had suddenly sprouted in her chest.

"Kei-chan?" the young girl whispered in a cry as soft as rustling leaves, and she fell on her side as her eyes glazed over. Tanin reappeared before the two others and regarded the fox before drawing her sword in one rasping motion. Kei screamed in a high-pitched wail of agony and fell over her dead friend's body. The desperate sound reached into Momo's brain and switched something on, something alien, something completely unnatural. The little fox's whites burned yellow and she bared her teeth in a snarl. A whisper of deep cacophonous laughter echoed in the back of her mind. The cat-faced woman swung at the kitsune with deadly speed, but Momo easily dodged the blade.

The smell of blood drew her on. She scrabbled on the woman's clothes, feeling the heat generating up and the throb of life trickling down as she dug her claws deeper into the cloth. Tanin tried to shake her off but then the fox leapt to her throat and buried her teeth in the bleeding wound. Momo savaged it viciously, felt her teeth grow long and hooked as she tore flesh.

The thrumming laughter in her mind egged her on and torrents of red poured down her jaws. This time she did not find the taste repelling; it had a satisfying salty flavor. She kicked with her hind legs off the falling body and landed neatly on all fours.

Once the kunichi was flat on her back, Momo darted forward to chew more on the neck.

"Momo?" A small girl's voice interrupted her. "She's… dead. They're both dead." Momo turned around and saw Kei sitting on the ground, clutching Kimiko's body like a girl holding a doll. She trembled as they made eye contact, and then her eyes rolled up as she fell over, unconscious. Momo ran to her. The neko's face was ghost white, and if it weren't for the slight movements of her chest she would have appeared as dead as Kimiko. Slowly her body shifted and melted, shrinking into the form of a tiny white cat. Momo wasted no time. Turning into her human form, she tenderly picked up her friend. Her thoughts were solid and clear as she carried the girl away away from the mountain path and toward the woods beyond it.

*

"*Unbelievable,*" Rinji signaled as he and Kawaru stared down at Tanin's body. The two ninja shared uncertain glances. Up until now, they both had thought her to be invincible. "*Who could have done this?*"

"Let's find out," Kawaru answered impatiently. They had finished killing off the last of the troupe, but there were still no signs of the tengu or the kitsune. The ninja was frustrated enough at his failure to redeem himself; Rinji's rescue only stung him further.

Rinji shook his head, already decided. "No, this is folly. We don't know who this troupe was, but there were no tengu or kitsune among them. Tanin's death was a great blow to our tribe and there is no sense in risking ourselves anymore. It's time we cut our losses and returned."

"What?" Kawaru hissed the word in complete acid. "You cowardly old fool! Twice now we've lost comrades. I retreated once, but I won't do it again!"

"You know nothing!" Rinji flew into a rage at the upstart's attitude. "Don't you see, you idiot? Yes, we lost two, and nothing was accomplished for it! This is a foolish cause that will continue to weaken the Yan. It's a conflict between daimyo, not us."

Kawaru laughed into Rinji's face. "You pathetic geezer. You're afraid of dying, aren't you?"

Rinji narrowed his eyes. "We are retreating, boy." Before Kawaru could answer, Rinji unsheathed his sword and pressed it against Kawaru's neck. "Listen to me well: you will learn how to follow orders, or you will not live to see the night." The two locked eyes for a moment. Then Kawaru flashed a wide grin and Rinji felt a sharp pinprick in his side. He stumbled back at the sudden pain to see Kawaru holding a tiny needle in his hand.

"You fool. You dare threaten a prodigy like me? You'll only hold me back, Rinji. The honor of the Yan may be dead to you, but I'll see it through, don't you worry." Rinji already felt the poison working through him and a violent convulsion in his stomach sent him tumbling to the ground. A second, stronger one made him swallow his tongue. The dying man grabbed feebly for his sword, but his strength was seeping away. Kawaru kicked the body repeatedly as Rinji's movements slowed down and finally stopped. When he was satisfied that the other man was dead, he ripped off Rinji's veil and spat in his face.

"That was fun," he laughed. "What next?" He turned to Tanin's body. With eager, trembling hands he detached the cat's mask from her head and threw it aside. The face underneath it caught him off guard with its plainness. Ordinary features only marred by the shock of death stared up at him. "How disappointing," he muttered. "I had thought you really were some kind of freak."

"So that was the needle you were going to use in Sato village," a voice behind him said. Kawaru nearly tripped over Tanin's corpse as he stumbled around. Tsukimi was looking down at Rinji. "Quite a painful fate you had in store for me," she added.

"What are you doing here?" Kawaru asked cautiously. The

kunichi had a strange light in her eyes, and her skin looked pallid in the descending sun.

"I followed you, of course," she answered. She stepped over to Tanin and reverently placed the mask back on her face. "I was only a half a day behind you, at the most."

"Why?" Kawaru stepped away from the woman. He was out of knives and she knew about the needle. He considered his options.

Tsukimi stood up from Tanin's corpse and regarded him. "Kawaru, you really are a fool. You think you can work alone? You think you are *so* talented, but in this world, there are those who would regard your abilities as child's play." Was she mocking him? Kawaru tensed up in anger.

"You speak of the dangers of working alone, but look at yourself, Tsukimi," he sneered. "It can be dangerous for a pretty girl like you to be in the wilds by yourself."

Tsukimi smirked. Yes, she was mocking him! *How dare she?* "Didn't you hear what I just said? Child's play, Kawaru, that's what you do. I want you to remember that well." She struck out like a viper with her bare left hand, and Kawaru barely had time to see the green light emerge from it before a blinding blast of cold fire seared his eyes shut. He fell, screaming, to his knees, clutching his burned face.

Tsukimi turned away from him. No longer concerned with the other, she regarded the footprints leading into the woods. She calmly stepped away from the wriggling form and darted in after her quarry.

VIII. Meetings and Partings

A light rain began to fall as clouds drifted over a lazy sun setting in the west. Droplets squeezed through the thick canopy of trees that enshrouded the forest, filtering through the branches to make their final landing on the thick rubbery ferns smothering the ground. Momo slipped on one gigantic leaf and almost dropped Kei's tiny cat form. Exhausted and cold, she set the neko down on the leaf and prodded her gently.

The cat grimaced as a few icy raindrops found their way onto her face, and she slowly shifted back into human form. Her lids trembled as she began to open her eyes. "No," she muttered quietly, and she shut them tight again.

"Kei-chan?" Momo asked. She stroked the young girl's hair away from her face and wiped moisture from her forehead. "Can you walk?"

The younger girl opened her eyes again and looked directly into Momo's. "Oh Momo-chan, you're back!" With returning vigor, she got up on her elbows and started to stand. "Where are we? What—" Her face went pale as she remembered. "Oh Kimiko-chan," she whispered. "Oh no." She lay back down on the fern and began to weep into her hands. Momo grabbed Kei and hugged her tightly. The neko stiffened at her touch at first, but then gave in and sobbed loudly in Momo's arms.

"I saw her Momo-chan, I saw her die. Why did that happen?" Momo tried to think of an appropriate response but could find nothing to say. She feared bringing up what she had done to the shinobi. Inside, she felt cold and terrified but she forced a smile for the younger girl.

"Come Kei-san, we have to move. We're still in danger here." She let go of Kei and stood. Shifting back into fox form, she tugged at Kei's sleeve with her mouth. The younger girl looked at her for a second, and nodded before transforming back into a cat. They moved quickly on four legs, navigating with natural ease through the ferns that had deterred Momo earlier, leaping over logs and sliding over the mossy ground.

Momo soon realized that Kei was lagging behind. She had years of practice over Kei in navigating through the wilderness, and so she slowed down to accommodate her companion. The rain eventually lightened up to a thin drizzle that didn't penetrate the trees. After an hour, Kei skidded to a stop and collapsed, making small whimpering sounds as she lay down on a bed of green moss. Momo turned around and nosed her a couple of times but the cat only curled into a shivering ball. Her fur was not as thick as Momo's, and the kitsune could see that the moisture had seeped down to her skin. Momo shifted back into human form and picked up the cat. She could almost carry her with one arm.

"Come on, Kei-chan," she urged. "I'll take you." She looked around to get her bearings. Darkness had fallen, but Momo's fox eyes were still perceptive enough to navigate the woods. The troupe had been traveling up a mountain path when they were attacked, and as the two of them had escaped north into the forest, she could make out the western slope that would lead them back down the way they had come. Going up the slope would also follow the main road, only taking them in the direction the troupe had been going. After a moment's consideration, Momo started down the slope.

She was relieved that she had finally managed the escape she had been planning. Once she reached the bottom of the mountain path, she would make for Yubikawa. Killing that shinobi had proven to her that her enemies were not invincible, and she had to find out about Taku. If she hurried she could still make good time in the failing light, but Kei was sleeping now, weak from the day's trials, and Momo could not leave her here. However, her arms were growing tired and she felt a gnawing ache in her stomach that reminded her she had not eaten since that morning.

Finally she found some semblance of shelter in a rock outcropping that jutted beside a trickling stream. Gigantic ferns grew freely, and the chirping of birds gave the place a sense of sanctuary. She crawled underneath the rocks and gently placed the sleeping Kei there.

"I'll be right back," she whispered, and transformed into a fox. Running down the stream, she felt freer then she had in days. The rage of being lied to and caged had sublimated into a sense of victory over those who had sought her harm. For the first time in her life, Momo felt capable. She had a fleeting fantasy of remaining in fox form forever, hunting and taking care of all her needs for the rest of her life. However, the few days she spent with Kei and Kimiko reminded her she needed companionship as well. How unfair that she would also have the need to interact as a human!

Her quick reflexes were more than a match for the fish that darted in the stream and she soon had one wiggling in her mouth. As always when in fox form, the kitsune swallowed it raw in quick bites, and then peered through the water for more. She ate another before remembering she was gathering food for Kei as well, and abashed, caught a third. She wondered if the neko would like it raw too as she triumphantly trotted back to her hideout.

A woman was there waiting for her, standing immobile in the misty drizzle like some kind of spirit. Her skin was unbelievably pale and her hair raven dark, but most striking of all were her eyes, narrow orbs topped by dark, intense eyebrows. Her head was bared and her hair tied up, showing off slender cheekbones. She was clothed entirely in the black outfit of the shinobi, similar to those of the cat-masked woman. The shinobi looked up as the kitsune arrived and waited, considering her silently.

The kitsune dropped the fish from her mouth and began to snarl. If this woman did anything to Kei, she would tear her apart! The kunichi did not react to the threat and coolly maintained eye contact. Finally, the shinobi spoke.

"You're from the circus troupe," she began. It was not a question. "Please, transform into a human. I would like to talk with you." Her tone was polite and gentle. Momo paused for a second, then reluctantly shifted.

Tsukimi shivered a bit as she was reminded of the dead tanuki back in that village, their bodies contorting and twisting, fur sprouting out as they met death. This was the opposite effect, but the resemblance brought back bloody memories. She stepped cautiously over to the small girl. The kitsune as a human was not an imposing figure at all; rather she looked young and innocent. Her hair was wild and tangled, framing a cherubic face with two round eyes that regarded her solemnly. Something in those eyes reminded her of Makoto. Momo took a step back as Tsukimi approached and her lips parted in a semi snarl. The kunichi stopped and indicated the outcropping.

"She's an otherman too, isn't she?" When Momo did not answer, Tsukimi shrugged. "I assume you two escaped the attack. Do you know where they were taking you?"

"Yes," Momo shot back fiercely. "Away. You're trying to kill us, so we were fleeing!"

Tsukimi sighed. "There is much going on right now that I don't understand. At first, when I heard of Makoto's death, I thought of nothing but vengeance. But then, witnessing the slaughter…and Kawaru…is more unnecessary death really needed now? My vendetta is my own, and not the tribe's." Momo had no idea what the woman was talking about.

"What are you doing here?" she asked.

"I want to understand," the ninja answered. "Tell me, what is your name?"

"Momo."

"Well Momo-san, I am Tsukimi. Please, answer this next question for me. Do you know where the two tengu are?"

Momo blinked and hesitated for a second. When she saw the kunichi's eyes narrow slightly she quickly answered, "They left a couple days ago. They didn't say where they were headed."

Tsukimi nodded, her own suspicions confirmed.

"What about you?" she pressed on.

Momo felt her anger spike. "That's none of your concern! My father's dead and my brother too, because of you!" The last word came out in an accusatory growl.

Tsukimi did not seem fazed. "Yes, a brother. I know of you, Momo-san. I know where you live, and what my people have done to your home. For that, I must apologize. I too lost a loved one that horrible night. Perhaps it's karma that things have happened this way. But, rest assured that your brother is alive. He is under the care of a man in Yubikawa village and he's quite well."

"Alive?" Momo said slowly.

"Yes, alive. I know this because my tribe has spies in your town. I know of Kenji Nakano, the samurai caring for your brother. But I wouldn't advise you to return there. My people have no more concern for the village of Yubikawa unless you are there. Their concern is you, Momo-san," Tsukimi said gravely. "But mine is not. My business is elsewhere."

"Alive," Momo repeated. The word rolled off her tongue in pure wonder. Tsukimi nodded slowly. Her dark eyes bore deeply into Momo's until she lightened it with a hint of a smile.

"Good luck, Momo-san," she whispered. "I wish you well." With that, she abruptly vanished. Momo made a small sound of exclamation and then ran underneath the rocks. There, Kei slept on peacefully. Beside her was a small cloth sack. Upon opening it, Momo found a handful of crushed herbs and six small balls of rice.

*

Momo awoke the next morning in excellent spirits. The rain had finally stopped and although the sky was still somewhat gray a promise of sunlight danced along the edges of the clouds. She stretched in her fox form and licked Kei a couple times in the face. She had spent the night cuddled up with the cat, keeping her body warm, and it seemed to do her friend some good. Kei's eyes fluttered open and she looked at Momo in astonishment. Momo rolled one of the rice balls over to Kei and the neko gobbled it eagerly. Between the two of them, they finished the kunichi's food quickly, and stepped outside feeling refreshed.

They both shifted back. Kei stretched her arms and let out a small sigh. Standing beside her, Momo was inches shorter, but she felt intensely protective of her new companion. She recounted to Kei the events of yesterday, and this time the neko took it all in. Her lips trembled a bit but she remained calm as Kimiko's death came up. When Momo was finished, Kei whispered a small prayer for their friend.

"She is in a better place," Kei said resolutely. "And I will never forget her."

"Nor will I," Momo said. The two girls bowed their heads

in a brief silence before Momo spoke again. "Kei-chan, I'm going to take you to the nearest village. I can leave you there." She almost bit her lip as she said the second sentence. Kei's eyes flew wide open and she grabbed Momo with a note of panic in her voice.

"But why, sister? Why?"

"I am hunted, Kei-chan," Momo said gently. "Those who attacked the troupe yesterday were after me and no one else. I can't risk your life with me anymore."

Kei made an angry face and hit Momo's shoulder. "Stupid! Don't you remember? All othermen are in danger, not just you. I'm going with you."

Momo considered that. She had never had a real friend before, one she could talk with, share her thoughts and feelings. She almost feared the complications and obligations that real companionship would require. But then she laughed quietly at her own silliness and took Kei's hands in her own.

"Kei-chan, nothing would please me more." The returning smile almost convinced her that she had made the right decision.

"Sister, where will we go?" Kei asked.

Momo let go of her and walked a few paces away. She thought of Tsukimi's advice the night before, while memories of Taku and his gentle nature played through her mind. *Kei is in danger regardless, but Taku will be unharmed as long as I am not near him. Big brother, take care. Forgive me for not coming back to you.* There were no questions left to debate. She looked east when the sun suddenly broke through the clouds, blinding her with its intensity. She turned around toward Kei, who saw her friend's outline illuminated behind a bright burst of sunlight.

"We head east," Momo said. She smiled radiantly, and Kei suddenly realized how beautiful her friend really was.

*

Penken groggily opened his eyes only to see the destruction of his troupe. One of the wagons was a smoldering wreck, and the one he was leaning against was torn beyond repair after the horses had kicked themselves loose. Bodies were everywhere, men he had laughed with, played dice with, drunk with. All slain. To his disbelief, even Gi-chan and Gorofuku were dead.

Why? Why did I survive? He knelt beside the body of Kimiko and stroked her head, unmindful of the wound that burned his shoulder. He would have remained there, perhaps until the sun set again, if it weren't for the sudden return of the tengu.

Banken's wings flapped mightily as he lowered himself onto the dusty road, Aiken not far behind him. They looked about incredulously.

"Penken! Thank the gods," Banken rumbled in relief. "When we saw the smoke, we feared the worst."

"This is the worst," mumbled Penken. "How can it get

worse than this?"

"What great force did this to you?" Aiken said.

Penken flapped a hand casually to the edge of the road against the forest. "Look for yourself. Two of them didn't make it." Banken inspected the bodies and then returned.

"One had her throat torn out, and the other seems to have been poisoned. We don't use poison, do we?" Penken shook his head. "It would seem that ninja was killed by one of his own men. A dispute, perhaps?"

"We'd best hope so," Aiken said. "Enemies this powerful would annihilate us all, if fully united."

"We *are* annihilated," Penken said. "There's nothing left here, nothing!" He pounded the ground weakly.

"The fox lives." Banken's three words stopped Penken.

"What makes you think so?" He turned around and looked desperately at the red giant.

"That ninja's throat was torn out by some kind of savage animal. Only a henge could transform its teeth so and I highly doubt the little neko did it. Besides, have you found her body?"

Penken shook his head, somewhat mollified. Banken's reasoning was indisputable. If Momo was alive then there was still some hope for them, and his men had not died in vain. He stood up, ashamed of his breakdown, and bowed low to the two tengu. "My two dear friends, what would I ever do without you?"

Banken grinned and then let out a booming laugh. "Enough, Penken. Let's go hunt for her."

Part 11
The River F

1. Festival of Lights

Obon lanterns flared to life, peppering across the smooth ebony water. The tiny lights danced like goblins' eyes across the bank as the unseen villagers carrying them slowly proceeded toward the murky Sano River. Hiroshi rubbed his hands to ward off the unseasonal chill and hastily shouldered the wooden pole on his shoulders. The singing and dancing would begin within the hour and he didn't want to miss the festivities so he tried to hurry, balancing the day's catch in two hanging buckets. Men and women from all across the country traveled to Kusama village to visit their relatives and loved ones during the festival. Hiroshi, who had just turned seventeen, was looking forward to catching a glimpse of the big city nobles and samurai – not to mention the beautiful women who accompanied them! The buckets swayed as he ran alongside the riverbank.

The slender boy struggled under the weight and his bare feet slipped on the cold mud. He toppled over as the fish tumbled out, their flesh glinting like rusty metal in the half moonlight.

As he brushed sweat from his brow he picked himself up and silently cursed himself. With no father and an ailing mother, Hiroshi would soon be the sole provider for the family. Grandfather Hidetora was still in charge but he was getting older and it was starting to show. Hiroshi wiped his gummy hands on his shirt and watched the lanterns by the riverbank bob as the first sounds of music wafted over. He morosely sighed as he scooped the fish back into their buckets.

A rustling in the nearby bushes caught his attention, but he assumed it was only a rabbit. Hiroshi picked up his pole again and trudged for the village, somewhat slower and abashed at his earlier hurry. The mud squished pleasantly between his toes as a quick burst of wind set him shivering. Lifting one hand, Hiroshi rubbed his face vigorously against the chill. When he lowered it, a young girl stood in front of him.

Hiroshi shouted and jumped back, spilling the fish again. He untangled himself from the ropes and struggled to his feet. The girl's eyes flickered down to the fish. She was short, scarcely taller than his grandfather, with a round apple face and black hair that spilled onto her forehead and over her eyes. A white dress hung loosely over her thin frame. Somewhat chagrined, Hiroshi struggled to say something.

"Are you here for the Obon festival?" he finally asked. Instead of answering, the girl began to sniff. At first, Hiroshi thought she was crying, but he realized that her nose was directed at the fish. Then he realized that although the wind was steadily blowing, her dress did not flap with it; instead it hung there like smoke, pulsating to its own hidden beat. *A ghost!* The Obon festival honored those who had passed on to the next life but Hiroshi had never expected to encounter one of those ancestors right here! The boy cried out in terror and ran, leaving the fish behind him.

Momo did not spare him a glance – there was no time to waste. She scooped up one of the fish and mashed the last of the herbs inside of it. If Kei wouldn't take this, then the kitsune didn't know what she could do.

Two weeks had passed since their escape from Penken's troupe. Kei and Momo had traveled through the dense forest, though very slowly as the neko's condition was rapidly weakening. They had stayed deep in the woods, using the sun as their guide as they crossed the mountainous terrain. Before long they had reached Okayama, a city as large and impressive as Kei had promised. The tiny figures of merchants and other travelers threading their way into a massive mesh of wooden buildings and paved roads sent Momo's head reeling. Who knew that so many humans could live together?

They had had their first argument then, with Kei insisting

that they find refuge there. The little neko was born and raised in that city and was all too eager to return to it. She told Momo she knew of merchants who would take them in, but Momo did not want to put their lives in the hands of any more strangers, human or otherwise. Besides, she had snapped at Kei, it would be very easy for spies to find her in a big city. It was better for them to stay away from all civilization.

Kei had grudgingly given in, but it was around that time that her health began to fail. One morning she woke up complaining of a headache and by that evening, she was racked with fever chills. The next day Momo found her curled up in her cat form. When the kitsune touched her, she felt a sickly heat radiating from her friend's body. Kei protested when Momo tried to get her to walk and finally the kitsune had to carry her. Kei's dark mood, still lingering from their fight, only seemed to worsen her condition. She fell into a hazy state of consciousness and soon could barely speak. After two days Momo began to fear for her friend's life and she tried to force her to eat some of Tsukimi's herbs. Kei would not take them, and they were out of food. When Momo found the river, she left Kei behind to try to fish. It was then that she had encountered the village boy.

She arrived back at their camp. The tiny neko was asleep again, her body tensed up and jerking fitfully in some kind of fever dream. Her whiskers quivered like strings on a shamisen as she flailed her paws in an imaginary run. Momo dropped down beside her and ran a hand over her head.

"Kei," she whispered soothingly, as she had used to do when her brother was sick. "I'm here, Kei. Please, wake up." Kei opened her bleary eyes and stared up at Momo. Although she could speak in her cat form, lately the effort seemed too much for her. "Can you eat?"

The neko shook her head mournfully and closed her eyes again. Momo struggled to fight back tears as she rubbed her hands in desperation. "Please," she said, "please Kei." She did not want her friend to die like this, cold and isolated in the middle of nowhere. She placed the fish under Kei's nose but got no reaction. The kitsune thought back to when they had met, how cheerful and full of life the young neko had been and how easily she had taken Momo under her wing. "First Kimiko, and now you," Momo whispered. *She can't leave me alone like this.*

Her ears, enhanced with the senses of a fox, picked up the distant sounds of music. There seemed to be a celebration going on in the village that bordered the river. She had no choice now; if Momo couldn't heal her friend then she would have to find someone who could.

*

"A ghost, Hiroshi? You're an idiot," sneered one boy. The others laughed uproariously.

Hiroshi shook his head, undaunted by the jeering. "I saw

what I saw," he said. "I feel foolish for running now, because I don't think she was a hostile ghost. Maybe she wanted to make friends."

"Maybe you wished she wanted to make friends," one snickered. "Are you lonely, Hiroshi-chan?" Hiroshi only shrugged sheepishly. He was a good natured boy, tolerant of the others' jibes.

"I believe you, Hiroshi-san!" Eizo piped up. Only twelve, the boy had not yet lost all of his baby fat, but his father was the mayor of the village so he hung out with the older boys whenever he wanted to. "After all, it is Obon. Maybe the dead did come. Anyway, it's pretty cold for late summer, isn't it? I bet the ghost brought the chill with her!"

Hiroshi smiled briefly at the younger boy, and then turned back to the others. "Speaking of Obon, we should go. I think the Odori dance is about to begin." One of the big festival events was the Bon Odori, a dance welcoming the return of the dead. The other boys nodded and clapped Hiroshi on the back – despite their teasing, Hiroshi was well liked among the group. They scattered for their houses.

Hiroshi clutched his coat against the cold wind as he walked home. Around him the villagers were setting up the festival's decorations. Although Kusama was not a large village, it was frequently visited by merchants and samurai, and both types of travelers were rapidly filling up the local inn. Hiroshi felt a slice of envy as he watched one well-dressed samurai strut by.

Like all the boys he loved the stories that were passed through Kusama, and lately there had been plenty colorful ones. Merchants gleefully told the gathered packs of boys their tales of war escalating in the eastern fiefs. One warlord was uniting the others, the merchants said, recruiting fearsome beasts from foreign lands to do his bidding. Some claimed Nobunaga was a savior, others a devil, but Hiroshi knew one thing: someday he would go east and find out for himself. He could not be a fisherman forever, mucking boats and slipping about in the mud. He would be like his grandfather, a warrior, serving under a noble samurai and slaying these fearsome foes, evil men and their demonic pets. The rumors whispered on; Nobunaga was coming, he was not coming, he was building a fleet to sail north. To Hiroshi it did not matter because the whispers all meant one thing: he would soon get to fight.

He passed the wooden inn, from which dim sounds of laughter drifted. A soldier lounged by the entrance, bathed in the weak lantern light as he embraced a young serving maid. Hiroshi quickly averted his eyes – he recognized the girl as a neighbor's daughter and wondered if his neighbor knew or cared what his girl did with strangers. Hiroshi had long ago vowed that he would never be like these coarse men, rude and ignorant of a woman's honor. Obon was a time of peace and reflection, not an excuse to chase after girls! Such behavior seemed an insult to their ancestors. When he was a warrior, he would treat women nobly, as any proper samurai would. Hiroshi hurried past the couple and slowed as he approached his house.

He lived with his mother and grandfather, the latter a well respected man in the village. Grandfather Hidetora was a stout man growing thick in the belly, though his arms were still corded with muscle. He had a stern gaze that frightened the younger children, though he was always quick to soften it with a laugh. Hiroshi loved him dearly, as his own father had passed away before he could remember. To him, Grandfather Hidetora was everything he strived to be: father, guardian, warrior, and man.

"There you are," Hidetora snapped impatiently. "Help me with these robes." His mother sat serenely by the fire pit, boiling tea. Hiroshi hurried over and helped knot the thick ceremonial obi that was instrumental to the Bon Odori. He then donned his own, a white woolen robe that dropped down to his feet. Hidetora stood and adjusted his obi, which was too tight around his midsection. He grunted in annoyance.

"Father, you eat too much," Hiroshi's mother chided. She was a gentle woman who had never once raised a hand to Hiroshi. Hidetora complained that she had made Hiroshi soft, but he had never hit Hiroshi either.

"Nonsense," Hidetora grumbled. "I eat just enough to honor Buddha. See?" He slapped his protruding belly for emphasis. "Just like the Brahmin, yes? Stop chortling!" he snapped as Hiroshi hid his mouth. "Come, let's go."

"Have fun you two," Hiroshi's mother waved. Hiroshi darted after his grandfather, who was already impatiently striding towards the town square. "Implying I'm fat," he snorted. "Your mother speaks out of turn sometimes!" His grumblings only amused Hiroshi more and the boy had to avert his face to hide his grin. "We indulge our women and children too much, and look at them! Dishonoring their ancestors so!"

"I didn't know you were an ancestor yet, grandfather!" teased Hiroshi, unable to resist.

"Their elders then!" snapped Hidetora. "You too, boy. No respect. And look at those arms! Those are fishermen arms if I've ever seen them. Not a day of combat on them." Hiroshi said nothing; he knew what was next. "In my day I fought alongside Katsurou Ashikaga, bastard son of the Shogun. I had the honor of defending him as a bannerman when he overthrew the villain Yoshizumi, his unworthy brother. I was there when the arrows found their mark and brought peace to these lands. And all for what? So I can end my days raising an ungrateful daughter and her lazy grandson? Ah, just finish me now, gods!" He rolled his eyes in mock exaggeration. His words contrasted his tone, which rang of feigned exasperation. To Hiroshi's ears, however, they rang of challenge.

"Just watch me, grandfather! I'll honor you yet. The Hidetora blood runs strong in me!" His grandfather raised a hand.

"Be glad you're lazy. Better lazy than dead. Trust me boy, you pray that peace is maintained and that these wicked rumors are just the whisperings of drunk men." Before Hiroshi could respond, an uproarious cheer sprung up. The town square was strung end to end with brilliant lanterns that alternated red and white. A makeshift wooden scaffold was raised in the center, built only for these three special nights. Other revelers had gathered, old friends and neighbors already drunk from sake and wine. Three musicians stood to the side, one playing on a flute and the other two beating drums. The dancers circling around the scaffold added their own beat with large wooden clappers. Hiroshi's mouth broke into a wide grin as he burst in a run.

"Slow down, boy! Let your elders go first!" Hiroshi ignored his grandfather's protests and joined the circle of dancers. He swung his legs in time to the flute and grabbed a pair of clappers. For a good hour he danced, letting the music sway his body. He sweat felt clean against his face as he exerted out his frustration. Call *him* lazy? Soft? He would prove his grandfather wrong. As soon as the autumn harvest was brought in, he knew where he was going.

The song ended and Hiroshi sat with his friends, laughing and passing cups of sweet wine. He felt lightheaded and strong, and he imagined himself astride a horse, carrying the colors of a noble daimyo. He would war and return in time for the next Obon. Next time he danced at the Bon Odori, he would dance a man.

The moon was out, providing just enough light to illuminate the river. Hiroshi glanced at the ghostly waves and suddenly shivered, recalling the girl from before. Was she here at the festival? He strained his eyes but could not find her. Other villagers lay in clustered heaps, talking and eating while the musicians played a softer tune. Some soldiers were there too, chatting amicably with the town elders. Hidetora was entertaining two of them, no doubt recalling stories of his past.

"Try this." A mug of something pungent was thrust under Hiroshi's nose. Sipping it he winced, feeling the fire in his belly. His friend laughed. "Sake from Hokkaido, Hiroshi-chan. Soldier's brew!"

"Soldier's brew?" Hiroshi quaffed half the cup and choked some out of his nose. There was more laughter.

"Hiroshi the soldier! Well, at least you can learn to drink like one," his friend said. Hiroshi managed a grin and passed the drink back. A few more rounds were poured and soon his head was reeling. The musicians started up another song and Hiroshi stumbled to his feet. "Let's dance!"

The boys put on a show, carousing merrily in the circle. Hiroshi locked arms with an elderly woman and a young man and they all danced frenetically to the rising and ebbing music. Red and white lanterns swirled by him, bobbing and blurring until they become one great streak. The man next to him suddenly had on a red tengu mask, the long nose jutting obscenely out at Hiroshi. The music grew high pitched and ragged, interspersed by jingling bells. Suddenly Hiroshi stumbled in a wave of nausea and he wrenched free from the circle.

His grandfather found him retching in an alley. He shook his head and smiled indulgently. "Time to go home, boy."

"I want to be like you," Hiroshi moaned between gasps. His grandfather patted him on the back.

"Well, you got that part down all right. Let's see what else we can teach you." With surprising strength and tenderness, his grandfather lifted Hiroshi onto his back. "Come, it's late."

The revelry continued in the distance but most of the villagers were stumbling home; it was only the first night and some had to be up early. "I won't envy your headache, boy,"

Hidetora said. "But I'm still dunking you in the river tomorrow." Hiroshi dozed on his grandfather's shoulder, snapping awake only to throw up again. "There you go," Hidetora said, rubbing his grandson's back. "Get it out before you see your mother."

"Hidetora-sama! Hidetora-sama!" Eizo, the chubby mayor's son, ran up to them. His face was painted in white streaks, as the younger children were apt to do. "There you are! Oh. Is he all right?"

"Just some bad fish," Hidetora said. "What is it?"

"They need you! There is someone at the village gate!"

"So? There's always travelers. Does your father need me now to assess every wandering soul who stumbles across Kusama?"

"No Hidetora-sama," Eizo bowed low. "But Father is drunk. My mother said to find the first elder I can to come see this girl."

"So I'm an elder now, am I? Let's go, Hiroshi," Hidetora grumbled. "On your feet, now. It looks like we can't go home yet." Hiroshi stumbled upright, blinking his eyes open. His stomach still felt queasy but he found he could think more clearly.

"What is it, Eizo?" he asked.

"A girl, Hiroshi-san. A girl in a white dress. But…oh, just come! It'll be better if you see what I mean." *A white dress?* The last waves of drunkenness fled as Hiroshi felt his innards lurch again. *What new development is this?*

*

Kei felt unnaturally light. Momo could feel the sharp edges of her ribs grinding into her arms and she knew her friend didn't have much more time. The human women surrounding her kept warily back. When Momo had stumbled into the village begging for a healer, they had assumed that she was the sick one. Unsure how they'd react if she told them the truth, Momo played along with the farce.

"Don't worry," one of the women ventured. She had a kind, if haggard face. "The healer will see you soon. She's the best in this lands, or so travelers have said." One of the other women nudged the speaker with an angry look, and she fell quiet. Momo understood that peasants were a suspicious lot, often cowardly and sometimes even treacherous. She silently wished she could get a doctor of noble birth, perhaps a samurai, to look over Kei, but it seemed she would have no choice now. *This is for you, Kei-chan,* she resolved. Nothing short of losing her friend would have driven her to try this.

"I hope she isn't contagious," one of the women whispered. Momo's keen ears picked up everything. "Perhaps we should get the soldiers to drive her out."

"Are we no better than animals? Maybe those in Okayama would resort to such barbarism, but do not forget our way!" hissed another. "We do not turn away the needy." The other woman snorted and folded her arms.

"Well, I'm going to get my husband. There's something unnatural about her!" she said. Before she could add to that, an older man pushed through the crowd. The others respectfully made way for him.

"Here, here she is," a boy said excitedly. "I wonder, maybe she has the consumption?"

"Eizo!" one of the women snapped. "Come here!" The boy grinned cheekily and melded in with the women before peeping out between their dresses. The others had formed a wide berth around the older man. He looked her over impatiently.

"Yes?"

Momo struggled to find the words. She had little experience dealing with strangers. The old man's imposing stare bore into her and her tongue stumbled until Kei let out a tiny moan. She thrust her friend forward pleadingly "She's sick. My friend is sick! Please, she needs your help. She…she's all I have." She dropped to her knees and cradled Kei tenderly. Some of the women began to laugh.

"A cat?" one asked.

"Ridiculous. You intrude on our festival for such a reason!"

"Who would waste time healing an animal?" The peasants'

words stung Momo's ears. She began to tremble with rage. She whipped her head up in an almost feral motion that set a couple of them back.

"She's my friend!" she shouted at them.

"Such impertinence!" one of the women snapped. "If you were my daughter, I would have you beaten and then married to a butcher. How dare you come here and spread your trouble!"

"Wait," the elderly man said, one hand in the air. "Buddha says that all things in life must be honored. If our village has the power to heal this animal, then I say let it be done. It is the edict of Jodo-Shinshu that we must preserve life when we can." Momo had no idea who this Jodo-Shinshu was, but she felt her knees quaver in relief as the man stepped forward.

"What is your name, girl?"

"Momo," she replied. She let the man take Kei into her arms. A small part of her winced anxiously. *What if Kei transforms? What if the villagers find something unusual?* But such matters were out of her hands now. If these villagers could heal her friend, then she was willing to take any risks necessary. The crowd of people began to disperse back to their homes and the old man motioned Momo to follow. A boy was beside him. Momo recognized him from the river.

"So you aren't a ghost," Hiroshi said. He managed to crack

a tired smile. Up close, the strange girl had an allure about her. He had watched her challenge the villagers and silently approved of her strength. *To go so far just to save her pet,* he marveled. They locked eyes for a second and Hiroshi wondered if she found him attractive or was just rude. Then without warning, she stepped toward him. Hiroshi stepped back; women did not approach men so boldly! She only came up to Hiroshi's shoulder, but for a moment she seemed a good head taller.

"I'm Momo."

Hiroshi managed a feeble laugh. "Twice now you've scared me. Are you sure you aren't a ghost?" When she didn't respond, he shrugged resignedly. His head pounded from the alcohol and he needed sleep more than anything. "I'm Hiroshi Hidetora. My family's house is not far from here. My grandfather is Kiyoshi Hidetora, the man who is taking your pet to the healer. Please stay with us while you wait for him to return."

"My pet." She did not say it like a question. Hiroshi thought he saw the hint of a smile on the edge of her lips as she followed him. *What strange wind brought this girl to our village?* Perhaps she was some kind of spirit after all.

11. Saima

Evening brought a sallow gloom that draped over Banken's mighty shoulders and sank down through his entire body. He stared into the great fire they had built for the night and watched the sticks crack apart and sizzle in the flames. Aiken sat across from him, her figure shimmering through the haze of orange flame and smoke as she roasted a brace of hares on her spear. The two had not spoken since they stopped for the night, but conversation had grown old and awkward some days ago. Banken managed to keep a frown from his face – he was not one to show despair even when it consumed him – but he snapped a wooden branch, thick as a man's arm, into tiny, fractured pieces.

Aiken ignored her mate and turned the hares over. Their skins were blackened and ashy while the meat inside remained pink, almost raw. That was the way tengu preferred their meat, but she felt her stomach tighten up at the prospect of eating. Worse, her chest was aching again. The scar from Yubikawa only helped remind her of the guilt that was brewing inside her, simmering like a hot broth. The two tengu were camped out at the foothills of Maruyama Mountain, a cold and snowy place even now in the heat of late summer. Impossible to scale for most humans, it would be an easy task for the two tengu to hop from one cliff to the next, ascending it in less than a day. However, both were too discouraged to continue their hunt.

"We should break camp early tomorrow so we can catch up with Penken," suggested Aiken, stiffly breaking the sullen silence. But when her lover snorted derisively as a response, her temper snapped. She slammed her spear into the mud with a thud, sending one rabbit flying into the fire, and stood. "Banken!" she hissed, "look at me when I speak to you!"

Banken paused in snapping his branch, then tossed the wood into the flames. "We cannot fail here, my heart." The calm and controlled tone of his voice stopped Aiken. "You know what that human lord expects from us. Like it or not, we tengu need Nobunaga's support. Without that, our people will be left to the mercy of the enemy. And we were ordered to find a kitsune."

"A kitsune! And now so much depends on the poor girl," Aiken muttered. "Surely we can do other things for these blasted humans?" It irked her that their chieftain had agreed to assist Nobunaga and his followers so readily. Though she felt little obligation towards the humans, she was compelled to obey her ladyship.

Banken shook his massive head slowly and flapped his wings twice before scooping up one of the blackened rabbits and consuming it in two mighty bites. Bones crunched and charred meat flew like spittle. Tossing the remains aside, he continued. "We must get Momo. It was bad enough that Sharada's men were slain by the Yan, yet that'll seem like nothing if we return without the kitsune. We can't fail a second time!" And that was what was most disheartening about it all. Despite their best efforts, despite moving at the fastest pace possible, the trail had lately gone cold.

The tengu had left Penken behind with a few of Nobunaga's soldiers some days ago. The tanuki was weak and soft and not suited for the rapid pace they would take. They used their mighty wings in short flights above the forest, searching with their eagle eyes for any signs of a fox or a girl. They had flapped until their wings ached and could not carry their weight anymore, and then they walked, charging through brush, sniffing the air and testing the ground. And yet, although they were competent trackers, it was becoming obvious that Momo had somehow eluded them.

Aiken bit into her rabbit. Despite Banken's frustration, it had not seemed to dull his hunger at all. He was already starting on his third while she finished her first. Tossing the remains into the fire, she sighed. "I don't know what we can do, my love. The little fox has escaped." Secretly she was relieved that Momo, whom she had grown quite fond of during their short time together, had somehow evaded them. She didn't know why Lord Sharada wanted the kitsune, but she doubted it was in Momo's best interests. Nobunaga's vassal had an unctuous quality about him, one that Aiken never trusted. She shook her head.

Having eaten, Banken felt new resolve course through him. It was time to propose to his mate the idea he had been playing with for the last few days. It wasn't a coincidence that he had led her to this particular mountain range. Aiken had not caught on yet, but now in the crux of their despair, he felt that she might listen.

"Aiken," he began, suddenly feeling nervous as he spoke. "I do have one last idea. See how we are at the base of Maruyama Mountain? Recall, if you can, who lives near the summit."

As predicted, Aiken's head whipped up and her eyes narrowed in sudden understanding. A low growl rumbled dangerously from her throat. Banken braced himself.

"No!" she snapped. "We are not going there. He isn't involved with any of this."

"But you know he could find her. Saima is a tracker, first and foremost. Don't forget that before things went bad, he could trace a sparrow's flight days after its passage. He would be able to pick up on Momo's trail, no matter where she is."

"You can't be sure of that," she said in a voice sharp with rancor. "Regardless, he is a danger. Lady Jinzo would punish you severely if she knew you tried to make contact with him. He is trouble, Banken, and I don't like how your sentiments have made you blind to this!"

Banken almost lowered his head at the accusation but he knew if he did, she would win this argument. It *would* be practical to leave Saima alone but, as she well knew, he had another motive to seek him out. "My brother has made mistakes, Aiken, I know. But he always had the best of intentions for us. True, he was misguided, but perhaps his time in solitude has changed him. Perhaps it's time to give him a second chance."

Aiken, who knew the depth of affection Banken held for his older brother, sighed. When Saima had been exiled from their tribe, her mate had fallen into a deep depression that had taken months to wear off. To this day, she knew he had never fully accepted the loss of his brother. But Saima was irascible, irrational, and prone to mad ideas. He was brilliant too, a prodigy who had once promised great potential. Tragically it was his brilliance that had led him down this path. She didn't want to bring him back.

"No Banken, and I stand firm on this. Saima is dangerous. If he felt needed again, he wouldn't hesitate to try to return home with us. It's only because he was so publicly humiliated that he voluntarily stays in exile."

Banken stood. "Aiken, I love you. You are my heart, and my life. But on this I must stand by my decision. Saima will listen to me. He always has, and he holds the same brotherly bonds with me as I to him. You can't understand this."

Aiken thought back to all the times they had gotten into arguments. Mostly, Banken would bluster and moan but in the end he would relent, as if he had secretly agreed with her opinion all along and only put up a show because it was expected. She knew of his attitude and indulged it for they often did think alike, but she could not think of a time when Banken so set his heart on something she utterly disagreed with. This relationship he had with Saima was something she was never a part of, the one aspect of her mate that she had never been allowed to share. She knew then that this had nothing to do with Momo or their greater mission. Banken wanted to see his brother for his own reasons.

"So you're right. You are your own being, Banken. I can't and won't control what you resolve to do. But know this, and know it well. In the years we've been together, when has my judgment failed you? When has our *people's* judgments ever failed *us*? Saima is on that mountain for a reason, and it is justified. I can't claim to understand the bonds of brothers. But I know what can happen if he is brought out of his exile. This is so foolish of you!" She found herself standing, and practically shouting the last. The two tengu stared at each other, glaring through the trembling flames. Sparks spat and popped numbly onto their skin.

Banken finally broke the gaze and turned around. "Go catch up with Penken, if that's what you want," he said in a cold voice. "But I'm finding my brother." He stepped away from the bonfire and over to his pallet. He lay out the blanket and crashed down on it with a thud, his back facing her.

Aiken couldn't believe this. *What is it about him that has such a hold over you? Over so many of our kind?* Yet Banken's decision was made, and she would follow. But she would not forget what had just transpired between the two of them. Something had changed, and she didn't quite yet know what that entailed for them.

*

Far to the east, over sloping hills and valleys, through dense forests and swamps, past countless little villages and rivers and roads, lay the sprawling capital city of Kyoto. Home to the emperor, the light of the land and direct descendent of the Sun God, Kyoto was long known as the center of Japan. Over a million souls populated the city, mostly humans, but it wasn't uncommon these days to see oni, tengu, and kappa walking through the busy city markets. Races that had once been mere rumors and whispers of the forest now openly mingled amongst humans as Lord Oda Nobunaga offered sanctuary to all their kind in the confines of the city walls.

 The city did indeed take in their kind, as a huge dry sponge would absorb all forms of liquid and blend them together into one damp mass. Kyoto churned with life, as Lord Nobunaga and his generals prepared for their next attack, pushing both east and west to the unconquered fiefs that still stood stalwart against the oncoming tide. The warlord's unspoken intention was to unite all of Japan under his rule, and nowhere was that more obvious than in Kyoto. The streets buzzed with rumors and stories, of the employment of mythical beasts and races that were even more fantastic than the ones that shared inns and broke bread with the humans. Intrigue dappled the streets, tales of assassins and enchantments and a covert underground organization that aided Nobunaga as much as his large armies did.

 It was through these streets that General Senichi Yoshida strode, his decorative black armor glinting under the hot sun. His skin was sticky and his beard itched terribly in the humid air, but he made an impressive show as he hurried through the markets with his men. Merchants and samurai alike scattered before him, as the characteristic black dog-shaped helmet was well known throughout Kyoto. He was one of the top generals under Lord Nobunaga, and known as the "Earth Dog" among his soldiers. Three oni marched with them, towering beasts of muscle and fang who could crush a man's head with one hand.

Yoshida ignored the stares and whispers around him and focused on the matter at hand. Frustration filled his every being, for the western advance had to be delayed yet again. It was his goal to see the sea on the west shore before his death, a testament to his dedication and love at his lord, but constant uprisings around the capital continued to delay him. The latest inconvenience was Nobunaga's own brother-in-law, a coward by the name of Asai Nagamasa, who had proven to be a traitor when he switched sides to support a rogue fief that still refused to serve the great warlord. Hoping to march west, Yoshida had suddenly and unexpectedly received orders to head east in order to stop this rebellion.

That was very well, but Yoshida was not about to leave his western front unattended. The market was behind him as he walked alongside a canal that led towards the outskirts of the city. Once, these buildings were considered slums which all but the untouchables avoided, but because of these canals, some newcomers had decided to make their home here.

"Take me to Lord Kaaro," he told the first kappa he found. He could never tell these creatures apart, squat green beasts with shells like tortoises and human faces with duck bills where lips should be. They were the rivermen, one of the first types of othermen to approach the humans. Kaaro, the leader of the one thousand kappa that currently dwelled in Kyoto, had taken the initiative to war together with Nobunaga. Yoshida respected the kappa as fierce and deadly warriors, but their unsightly features never failed to repulse him.

Even more disturbing was their complete lack of respect and protocol. For example, this particular specimen, a mottled brown monstrosity, simply leered at the general before loping off. If a peasant had showed such attitude towards the honored general, he would have sliced his head off without a moment's hesitation. But dealing with othermen required a certain tact, one that he did not possess in abundance. He envied those like Lord Sharada, who could charm even the most alien of life forms. Yoshida was not a patient man by any means, and it was hard to deal with such impudent creatures.

Well trained, the oni and soldiers behind him did not move at all while they waited by the riverbank. The buildings here were a combination of tightly packed wooden houses, ramshackle dry constructs that could flare up in a single spark, and newer, muddy huts half buried deep in the water. These latter were the dwellings of the kappa. Yoshida found their kind unreadable on many levels, but most of all their minimal societal structure baffled him. The tengu had some sense of hierarchy, although they treated their females as equals, and the oni were in many ways as disciplined and ordered as humans were. Only the henge, the shapeshifters, were a greater mystery than the kappa.

The arrival of four kappa interrupted his thoughts. One of them, no larger than the others but wearing an ornamental blue belt, was clearly Kaaro. Lord Kaaro often pointed out that he only wore the belt so that humans could tell them apart, as if that was some kind of joke among the kappa.

The leader sketched a bow when he saw it was Yoshida. "Lord General," he said in a raspy low voice. "I am honored that you came to see me yourself. Your messenger has explained everything." The other kappa shifted about, looking bored through lidded eyes. To the general, they seemed indolent and stupid, more animal than human, but he had witnessed their prowess in battle. Underestimating these beings was a mistake he only wished for his enemies to make.

"Lord Kaaro," he bowed. "If you could secure a western foothold before I return from this insignificant rebellion, I would be most indebted to you." One of the kappa flashed its teeth, but whether it was a grimace or a grin Yoshida couldn't tell. He kept his eyes fixed on Kaaro's, who at least maintained a respectful and downcast look.

The kappa nodded without hesitation. "Yes, yes. It sounds like a good plan. In the meantime, I wish you luck on your inevitable victory." Kaaro always spoke implacably, with the right amount of respect. This only bothered Yoshida more, as his subordinates didn't seem to follow their lord's etiquette.

Eager to get out of the sun and into a cool bath, the general bowed once more. "You will leave tomorrow. Your services to Lord Nobunaga will not be forgotten." He turned then, and motioned his men. With the aid of the kappa, his next great invasion in the west would fall to the simple task of striking at the weakest point. He was well satisfied that he would see the ocean soon.

*

The general marched pompously off with his men, unaware that one of the oni had stayed behind. Kaaro eyed the towering giant nervously and took a step back. "Captain Yugotaro," he said slowly. "I hadn't expected to see you here." His eyes bulged as the oni reached down and wrapped one meaty fist around his neck.

"You know what to do," Yugotaro said. "I trust you will complete my request?"

The other kappa cowered before the imposing figure. Kaaro bleated and nodded as he struggled uselessly in the steel grip. The oni bent down low so that the two were within kissing distance. "Do not fail. Even a dimwitted turtle like you should be able to set up a meeting with the other daimyo. Lord Sharada insists that we keep the alliances the way they are. Do you understand?" Kaaro managed a choked gasp of affirmation. His pale green skin was turning waxy. Satisfied, Yugotaro let the kappa go and thrust a small bag into his arms. Kaaro and his followers scampered off without a backward glance. The oni watched them leave and let loose a low chuckle.

He cared little for what General Yoshida wanted. As far as he was concerned, the fat general was a pawn in the middle of greater events. It still amazed him that so many of Nobunaga's men believed in the childish fantasy that the othermen were aiding them simply to unite Japan underneath their human lord.

*

The air was thick with the steam of the hot springs scattered about Saima's home. Aiken realized that for one who had tried to betray his entire people, Saima lived in comparative luxury. Tengu enjoyed the steam these baths gave off, and the naturally mountainous terrain suited their build and body types. They also coveted eggs and birds, two delicacies that were abundant here. She reflected that the humans' term for them, "mountain goblin," was not entirely undeserved. This hot, sulfurous place almost felt like home.

Watching Banken hop from ledge to ledge on the sheer gray mountain soured her mood once again. The fight of the night before was over, but his resolve in seeking out Saima had not faded. He only had challenged her once, with a questioning brow as they woke up, and she had simply nodded. He now moved rapidly, driven to find his brother after so many years.

It was no great secret where Saima dwelled; Aiken had been part of the party that had escorted the humiliated revolutionary to his place of shame. Returning here after all those years sent a chill down Aiken's spine and made her legs feel wooden and slow. Besides, they had been climbing all day, not even breaking for a meal. Leaping mightily from one ledge, she flapped her wings and nearly crashed into Banken as she landed. Surprised by his sudden stop, she slipped and fell on her hands. Her knees skidded painfully against the rocky slope.

"We're here," Banken said. He sounded nervous and unsure of what to do. Once again, Aiken secretly wondered what kind of hold Saima had over Banken, who was typically so casual, so confident, and so powerful. She did not like this uncertain side of Banken. He stood before the gigantic cave that was cut into the rock like a small human child quailing before a snake hole.

"Do we go in?" she asked. Banken looked at her and smiled nervously.

"Aiken," he said. "If I was wrong to do this, then I apologize." He looked like the old Banken again as he marched inside the cavern. However, Banken's heart was hammering mightily. How had his brother fared, after all those years in this place? Did isolation and darkness drive him further into madness? Would he be willing to assist them in capturing Momo? He resolved that if Saima was not, then they would leave him here without a second thought. *And if he tries to follow us?* Could he fight his own brother? This was a question he wasn't prepared to answer.

A sudden glint appeared in the darkness. He heard the sound of a pen scratching against paper, and as he drew closer he saw that the glint was actually the glow of an oval lantern. The flame inside burned green, giving off a sickly hue. The scratching sound abruptly stopped and Banken heard a chair scrape back. Someone rose and approached, not calling out a challenge but simply moving towards them. A second glow joined the first as another lantern was brought closer, and then he saw him.

Saima held a long leather whip in one hand, the lanterns in the other. His face shone green with the light and it broke out in mock delight as he gleefully snapped the whip once against his side.

"Ah, dear brother!" he exclaimed in a high pitched voice. "How unexpected of you to visit!"

III. New Companions

He led them to the back of the cavern where the stalagmites jutted up like giant teeth. The air was thick with burning herbs that suffocated the air. Saima's dwelling was sparse; a crudely crafted worktable stood in one corner but otherwise there was little else in the cave. Squinting in the sickly green light, Aiken could make out a quill and paper, bottles of ink, an elaborately decorated globe nestled in a bronze mechanism, and a narrow tube that she guessed to be a sort of foreign invention from far away. Underneath the table and thrown about in careless piles like discarded toys were a countless array of books and scrolls. The human books seemed ridiculously childlike compared to the massive scrolls that were rolled up and scattered among them. One such scroll was splayed out on top of the table.

Saima delicately set aside one lantern and pinched the flame out with two of his fingers. The other lantern's flame only weakly illuminated the room and Aiken could barely see the others' silhouettes. Saima's pale gray eyes gleamed dully as he tossed his whip aside and settled down on his padded straw bed.

"I was in the process of transcribing Lady Murasaki's diary. It's a fascinating tale about the court life of humans, five centuries ago. Funny, how so little has changed since then, while the rest of the world moves on." Saima gestured to the scroll on the worktable, and the carefully painted calligraphy that stood out sharply on the fragile rice piper. Banken gazed down at the other rolled copies of scrolls and the books.

"You've stayed busy," he began gruffly. "That's good to see." It seemed to be the wrong thing to say. Saima's eyes flared up and he waved contemptuously to his worktable.

"My life's work," he said with a sneer. "Even if you all are so ready to forget me, I intend on leaving something behind for our youth to read. Perhaps one will look beyond his mundane existence and pick up where I was forced to leave off." He laughed then, a sharp and derisive bark that stung their ears. "Unlikely of course. I'm sure you've come to burn my last treasures, isn't that so?" He fixed Banken with an accusing stare.

Banken flinched and took a step back, though he stood a good half a head taller than his older brother. Saima was oddly built for a tengu. His skin was a burnished dark maroon, making him look like carved wood saturated with dried blood, and his eyes were gray while most tengus' were black. He was short as well – an exceptionally tall human could match his height, if not his girth. Moreover, he favored his right hand, a trait normally associated with humans.

Saima walked over to his table and picked up his brush, appearing to dismiss the others. He resumed writing on the scroll with quick rapid movements, occasionally squinting at the open book as he copied the characters down. The tengu possessed a nimbleness to his writing that was also uncanny among the tengu. Most were clumsy at best when handling delicate tools, but Saima could use human craft with ease. Banken glanced at Aiken with uncertainty, and she made a motion towards the exit. Before he could respond, his brother spoke up again.

"Well then, do what you will. I have no time to entertain guests. Even one so exalted and respected as you, dear *brother*." The last word dripped pure acid. "Or go now, leave me. This isn't a good time. Perhaps tomorrow, or in a week, I might find it in me to put up with your stench and listen to your prattle. You two bring bad memories, so leave with them. Go, go, go." Saima waggled his fingers at the last without pausing in his writing.

"Brother!" exploded Banken in a pleading voice. "Already you bring up the past. Has it crushed you so much? The times change, as do tengu. Perhaps Lady Jinzo has forgiven–"

"Forgiven? Forgiven? *I* haven't forgiven the way her disgusting pet nearly popped my eye out. I feel the sting of his whip to this very day. I tried to save you all, and in turn you repaid me with this." Saima waved his arm about the dank cave.

Banken glowered and folded his arms. "Nobody forced you to stay in here. You could have left anytime you wanted to." When his brother didn't respond, he pressed on. "Saima. You attempted to murder a human lord. If you had succeeded, our entire people would have been driven out. You could have ruined our clan. It was right to exile you."

At this, Saima finally set aside his brush and turned around. Aiken thought back to when he had been betrayed by his friends and turned over to her ladyship for judgment. Back then his eyes had always shone with a bright fever that burned with his convictions. But now, after years in this dark cave, she could tell that the light had gone out. Now only gray steel faced them.

The small tengu turned to the sphere and spun it on its device. "Look," he said. "I purchased this from a merchant I crossed paths with earlier this year. He had obtained it from the southern island, where traders from all across the world gather. This is a globe, a map that curves completely across this sphere. I have not been idle in my exile, dear brother and sister. I have learned much, so observe. See how small our land is?" One finger stopped on a tiny cluster of islands. "See how insignificant it is compared to the rest of the world?" He spun it again and Aiken could make out large chunks of brown representing other continents scattered across the blue water.

"What's your point?" asked Banken.

"An entire world, and it is populated by *humans!* Look dear brother, and perhaps even you can see my reasoning. There are nations of humans expanding, conquering, too innumerable to count but they spread across the globe like flies on a carcass. I've read books describing humans, of different sizes and colors, but still human, who live their lives in entirely different fashions from the ones we share this land with."

Banken glanced at Aiken, who only shrugged. Saima watched them expectantly and then raised his eyes to the ceiling as if pleading to the gods. "Then I ask you," he said after a second, "*where are the tengu?* Where are our people? Why do we hear nothing of our exploits in other lands?"

Banken shrugged. "Perhaps we only populate this island. It is well known that oni do not live here, but rather dwell in the western continent, along with other strange creatures."

"Yes," hissed Saima, "but why do humans live everywhere? They are like vermin, consuming the land of the gods' natural creatures. Do you know of Emperor Jimmu?" Getting no reply, he continued. "That's the first god of the humans, so the story goes. But I have found something interesting: a document, written by the great Yanno." Aiken had heard of Yanno, a tengu who had lived hundreds of years ago. She knew that the historical figure greatly influenced Saima's own beliefs. "In it he describes how Jimmu, who is so often deified as a direct descendent of the sun god himself, is in truth a bastard child of some western Korean demon. It is all speculation, true, but think on it. What if man was a pestilence created by the gods to test the rest of all kind? What if they are the invaders that spread in their ships across the globe, the evil offspring of coupling demons designed to eradicate this land of all life?" His voice grew high with excitement.

"You're mad." Aiken said. *He is worse than before.* "Banken, let's go. There is nothing here for us."

"Yes go," Saima echoed in a mocking tone. "Go little brother, leave me now. I have no use for you. As Father would say, I have no time to deal with weaklings."

Banken froze. His body grew rigid and Aiken could see nearly every muscle standing up in a tight cord. At that moment Aiken wanted to go over and hug him. *Not here*, she harshly reprimanded herself. *Not in front of this creature.*

Her lover spoke with a sadness that nearly tore her heart. "Don't speak of him, Saima. Not to me. I came here for friendship as well as a favor but you seem intent in throwing my offerings of peace aside."

Saima cocked his head to one side like some greedy imp. "A favor?" His eyes glinted in the green light. Aiken remembered. *More than anything, he craves to be needed.* "Forgive me then," Saima continued. "Years alone in here have ruined my manners. Perhaps I spoke in haste. I can hardly refuse a favor for my little brother. Sit, and tell me what you've come for."

Banken shared an uncertain glance with Aiken. He considered, and for one hopeful moment she thought he'd leave. Instead he settled on the floor, his wings drifting down slowly, and began to speak. As Banken related the events of the past months, Aiken watched Saima with a growing unease. In the flickering room, beneath the dancing shadows of the green light, the dark tengu's eyes began to shine.

*

He spent the second evening by the riverbank, watching the fireflies. Hiroshi rubbed his tongue against the surface of his mouth and grimaced at the dry taste. Last night he was a drunken disgrace, and his friends had spared him no mercy that morning. In the distance he heard music and revelry but he had no stomach for it tonight. Fireflies dipped in the darkness and flashed their secret signals to each other. Hiroshi sighed.

He sensed as much as heard her approach. The ghost girl, he thought of her, though she had a name now. Momo. Like a peach. Her face was certainly round like one. Perhaps she tasted like one too – he couldn't resist the thought. Hiroshi's meager experience with girls was mostly watching the older boys strut around, swapping partners as quickly as mayflies. But not him, no. He would wait until he was worthy of a woman. Until he proved himself. But her eyes were so dark and she had so boldly walked up to him…

He stood and turned to her. Momo wore the same white dress, imperceptibly smooth like unblemished snow. Her face was ruddy, though, red and self-conscious. She looked frightened and he smiled to reassure her. Her eyes met his and then slid away. He tried to hide the hurt as he quickly bowed.

"Good evening, Momo-san. What brings you here?"

"It's loud in your village, Hiroshi." To hear his name in her soft voice! "I don't like so many strangers around me."

"Is it far from your village?" When she looked back at him he stuttered, embarrassed. "Forgive me! I didn't mean to be intrusive."

"Very far," she said with a tinge of sadness. "Very different too."

"How so?"

"Just more," she said after a moment. "More of everything. More soldiers, more merchants, more lights. More humans." She glanced across the riverbank. "Same fireflies, though."

Hiroshi smiled. "Is your cat all right?"

"Kei is fine, thanks for asking. She needed rest and food and that was it. I suppose she wasn't built to travel."

"That is good to hear, Momo-san. Will you be staying awhile then?"

Momo looked over and he could see the anxiety peeking from beneath her eyes. "I don't know, Hiroshi-san." Compelled by her fear, or perhaps just by madness, he impulsively reached forward and grabbed her hand. Momo stared up at him but did not recoil right away. When she did, she did not seem particularly angry. What did her eyes read now? He couldn't tell.

"You may stay here, Momo-san, please know that. We are hospitable in Kusama. We would never turn travelers away."

"Thank you, Hiroshi-san." A faint smile. "Perhaps we will."

Hiroshi felt joy bubble forth and he learned forward in a burst of enthusiasm. "That's good to hear! Tomorrow is the last night of Obon and we're going to send the lanterns down the river. Will you come and watch?"

She nodded and bowed low. "It would be an honor." Momo paused one more second and looked over the peasant human. He was a scruffy boy, thin and unkempt. Still, Momo found his earnestness compelling. This boy had an aura about him that reminded her somewhat of Taku. Of course, Taku couldn't speak and this boy had much to say.

She turned and walked up the hill, sensing the boy's eyes on her back. Unlike the stares of other men, she found she didn't quite mind. "Hiroshi," she said, trying the name again. It was a nice name.

This village was busier than Yubikawa had ever been. Momo was no stranger to Obon but Kusama celebrated it differently. The steady stream of travelers brought an energy and flow that she found overwhelming and yet sometimes invigorating. She watched a young boy chase after a girl with a paper dragon and smiled.

The smile faded as thoughts of the circus troupe came unbidden to her. The smoke, the blood, the screams all hit her like a hurricane and she darted for somewhere dark. Her skin tingled and beckoned her to change, but that would be madness here. Kei would have to recover, and soon, so they could escape back to the forest. Or maybe Kei should stay, unsuited as she was for the wild. The thought of being alone slowed Momo's steps.

One day at a time, she promised herself. Tonight she would feed Kei. Tomorrow she would go watch the lanterns float down the river. After that, she could think about leaving these people and their lights behind.

Kei was tucked away on the upper floor of the town's inn. Just as in Yubikawa, this inn overflowed with soldiers and their steel, though these soldiers hummed with an excited, joyous buzz. No one paid Momo any heed as she bounded up the stairs to the room that the old man Hidetora had paid for. Kei slumbered on with a peaceful expression on her face. Much to Momo's relief her forehead was cool and her whiskers no longer shook with nightmares. The young kitsune sat by her friend and stroked her soft, white fur for some time.

There was a knock on the door. Momo tensed as the innkeeper entered with a tray, Hiroshi's grandfather following closely behind. The old man let the woman set the meal down and then closed the door behind her. He turned to Momo.

"You are not what you seem," he stated flatly. As Momo's eyes shot open he waved his hand. "Forget it, forget it. I don't know and I don't care to know where you're from. War brings orphans from all over." Hidetora glanced over at the slumbering form of Kei, who to him looked nothing more than a simple cat. "Orphans and their pets," he added wryly.

Momo stood and bowed low, as her father had always trained her to do in front of human men. This Hidetora radiated power despite his age, and she could sense he was no fool either. "Thank you, honorable sir, for taking us poor ones in. May Buddha protect—"

"Buddha has enough on his plate," Hidetora said impatiently. "I'd imagine you to be the first of a wave of refugees from the west. Tell me, what bodes for our village? Do you know of anything?"

Momo froze, unable to think of a story. "I…" she began.

Her tongue felt heavy. "I…"

Hidetora eyed her critically. "I see you lost your wits as well as your way, young girl. Never mind. Stay for the festival, and we can talk after. Perhaps there will be work for you. The fields need harvesting and the rivers fishing. If you seek a home, you may find it here."

"Thank you," Momo said. "Thank you." She meant it from her heart. This man's generosity only convinced her she could not endanger these humans further. She would leave when she was ready.

"Fine, then," Hidetora said, standing. "Rest and come see me when you are ready. And," he added as he paused by the door, "do not cause trouble here." He raised his eyes inquisitively before stepping out. Momo watched him go and then turned to Kei.

"How can I promise that?" she wondered out loud. The sleeping neko had no answer for her.

IV. Returning to the Dead

She dreamt the same dream as the night before and was back in the cage. Rusty wires joined together like thick gray fingers and she scratched her paws on them, feeling her flesh tear and bleed in explosive agony. Behind her the heavy breathing of the sorcerer grew louder, ragged and tinged with phlegm. Turning back, she saw only darkness, but Momo knew the old man was close. She desperately tried biting through the wire cage but it held firm, as it always did, as it always would.

"You won't escape!" cackled Gi-chan, and he began to chant in a horrifying, strange tongue that scraped against her ears like a knife.

"No," gasped Momo and she stared at her bloody paws, willing them to change, to transform, to do *something*.

Suddenly she felt the rank hot breath of the old man against her ear. "Your friends have known me for some time now," he crooned. "You will find it rather…*interesting*." Momo whirled about in horror and tried to slip past, but the old man darted out like a snake and snatched her neck. Lifted harshly, she saw that it was not Gi-chan at all but her father who had grabbed her.

"Momo," Takamoto said, his firm voice tinged with contempt. "Why have you let this happen?" Momo tried to wrench free but her father's grip held. "You let us die," he admonished her. "You let us all die!"

"I didn't!" screamed Momo, and suddenly she was free and standing over the fallen body of the cat-masked ninja. Thick smoke and ragged screams choked the air and she realized she was back at the ambush on the mountain road. The prone black figure stirred and began to lift itself up, marble cat eyes staring right at her. Without hesitation Momo leapt forward and tore out the woman's throat, unleashing a fountain of bright jeweled red that sprayed high into the clear sky and pattered gently down like rain. As she stared at the ruined throat the white mask cracked and fell in half, and she saw that the face underneath it was Taku, glazed eyes wide with shock…

With a loud shriek she flung herself up from the futon, shivering in the icy cold sweat dotting her skin. She moaned and grabbed for the covers as her breath tore from her throat. *It was only a dream,* she tried to comfort herself as her breathing slowed. *It was just a dream.* But in her mouth she could still taste the woman's blood.

"Sister?" A small voice brought her back.

"Kei!" The neko was awake and blinking feebly in the wan morning light. She looked as healthy as the day they had met.

"Where are we?"

"We're safe, Kei-chan. This is Kusama village, a few leagues east of Okayama. We're in their inn." Even Momo found it a bit odd, speaking to a talking cat.

"Kusama," Kei said, nodding. "I know the place. Good fish."

"Oh Kei!" Laughing, Momo flung the covers off her and cradled the neko on her lap, stroking the smooth white fur. "It's so good to see you awake!"

"I'm hungry!" Kei said. "How long have I been asleep?"

"Let me tell you everything," Momo said. She related the past few days to her friend in between bites of salted fish and pickles, hand-feeding the neko, who seemed to enjoy the pampering. After they had eaten, Momo set Kei down. The neko tentatively stood and stretched, her furry paws sticking out. "Can you transform, Kei?"

Kei nodded. "I think so." Momo watched in wonder as the cat form rippled like light on water. She had a hard time focusing as the shape of the body rearranged itself and finally she had to look away, as if the sight might burn her eyes. When she looked back, her friend was in human form again, young and lean and with a cheeky smile on her face.

"Well, I'm back!" Kei exclaimed triumphantly. Her skin glowed as a faint blue dress formed over her body. Momo realized that Kei had always worn human clothes before, the finest that Penken's troupe could afford her. She never knew that nekos could generate their own images. Kei was pretty, the kitsune realized. Prettier than she was. Kei had her raven hair artfully done in a noblewoman's bun and her cheekbones were fine, in sharp contrast to Momo's pudgy, round face. Then she saw Kei's eyes.

"Green?" Momo cried, alarmed. "How can you pass as a human with green eyes?"

Kei shrugged. "Who says I need to? These are friendly lands, sister."

Momo shook her head. "You can't walk out like that! The humans here think you are a cat. My *pet*. They don't know what we are!"

Kei snorted indifferently. "And so? Who are they to stop us?"

Momo couldn't believe her. She glared at Kei. "Are you stupid? Don't you remember what's following us?"

Kei looked uncertain. "I don't know. How do you know they were following us? Maybe Penken was hiding some treasure. Besides, I thought they weren't going to bother us anymore."

Their concern is you, Momo-san. The ninja woman Tsukimi's words rang in her ears. Momo grabbed Kei's hands. "Please Kei-chan, you know that isn't true. That ninja woman said others are after me. It's dangerous to stand out so much."

Sulkily, Kei shifted back into her cat form. The little creature peered up impatiently at Momo. "So what now?"

Momo hesitated. "We have to keep moving. We will continue east, for Kyoto. If it's as safe as you say, perhaps we can find sanctuary there."

"Oh that's a good plan, sister!" Kei said happily. "You will love Kyoto, just you wait! The most beautiful and powerful people dwell there. They can protect us, I don't doubt it!"

"Protect me, Kei-chan," Momo corrected in a soft voice. "They don't want you." She found the next words hard. "I think it best if we part ways soon. Staying with me is only dangerous."

"Sister!" Kei snapped. "Don't talk like that. We stay together, as sisters do, okay?"

"But remember Kimiko…" Momo's voice was small. She could feel the guilt well up again.

"Exactly," Kei said. "That's why I'm staying with you. Momo-chan…you…you're all I have right now."

Momo fought to hide her tears, but in the end she failed. "I don't want to hurt anyone, anymore," she whimpered. "People close to me die. Everyone dies." Suddenly soft arms were around her and Kei, back in human form, hugged her friend.

Momo wept and Kei waited and eventually there were no more tears. Resolved, Momo stood. "Thank you, Kei," she said.

Kei's face turned feline and she wiggled her ears mischievously. "Hey, a fox and a cat working together! I sense a fable will be written about us soon."

Despite herself, Momo giggled. "Kei, you're silly."

"When do we leave? Tonight?"

"No," Momo said. She thought of Hiroshi and her promise to him. "We'll leave tomorrow."

*

"Tell me Banken, what do you think it means to be a human?" The three tengu were perched on a ledge that any but a tengu would find precarious. The view below was spectacular, with winding rivers and a canopy of green arching over the horizon, but Saima looked only at his brother.

"I don't know." Banken shifted uncomfortably. After Saima had joined them, they had not wasted any time in continuing their hunt. Saima suggested they start at the summit of the mountain, to better gain their bearings, but they spent half the morning ascending it and now Saima seemed content to just sit. "What are we doing here?"

"Patience, dear brother, patience," Saima said. "The Red Eyed Falcon does not stir just yet. Until then, can you answer my question?"

"I can," Aiken interjected. "The answer is, you provoke us with your nonsense. Now my question is, do you do it because you think you sound wise, or because you know you sound foolish?"

Saima grinned at the female tengu, his white sharp teeth glistening. "Dear sister, ever so apt with words. No doubt your tongue is as sharp as your blade."

"No doubt." Aiken eyed her brother-in-law carefully. "Well you remember that."

"To be a human," Saima continued, "is to create and destroy. These specimens seek to build and tear down faster than the most capricious gods. Their short lives are fraught with chaos." Saima stood and swept his hand over the landscape. "All of this, this land before us, is just a temporary dream, destined to be disrupted within a few short years. The gods took their time building their world but the humans will destroy it twice over in a lifetime and then build it anew. So they see fit."

"Where do you get these ideas?" Banken asked.

"I just keep my eyes open, dear brother." Saima snorted. "Now tell me this: what do you know of these lands?"

"These lands are free to our kind," Aiken said. "Lady Jinzo bequeaths her protection on all tengu. Under her guidance we are safe."

"Oh really?" Saima asked. He smirked. "Is that why you serve Lord Oda Nobunaga now?"

Aiken glared at him. "A temporary necessity."

"I doubt that. Humans have a way of sticking to your gums like an irritating sap, and Nobunaga is but an insect in a swarm. After him will come others, each with more demands and more treaties, until they swallow us all whole. This one country, this insignificant nation sweats over Oda Nobunaga, though he is nothing more than a frog prince compared to what is to come. I ask you again, what do you know of these lands?" Aiken glared at Saima. How she hated him! "These lands," Saima continued, "are owned by Lord Motonari, the western daimyo. He feuds with Lord Nobunaga and soon their armies will come to blows. Japan is fraught with these sorts of conflicts, my dear ones. It's a time of opportunity."

"What kind of opportunity?" Banken asked.

Saima looked reflective for a second. "'From Apollonius I learned freedom of will and undeviating steadiness of purpose; and to look to nothing else, not even for a moment, except to reason.' A great man once said that. A great human, I should add. And there is reason to follow in the steps of others, no matter the source."

"Again I ask, what are you talking about, Saima?" Banken was growing irritated. "Are we going to sit here all morning listening to your riddles, or are we going to find the kitsune?"

"He enjoys playing you," Aiken warned. "Don't let his prattle deafen your heart."

"I am merely thinking out loud, Aiken, nothing more. Humans are a fascinating kind."

"For someone who tried to defy them once, you certainly seem to love them now!" Aiken shot back.

Saima laughed. "On the contrary, dear sister. I love the tengu. That includes you, sister, despite your misgivings about me. Back then I was as foolish as Pompey, openly defying the inevitable. Since then I have learned something of subtlety. Never mistake admiration as love, just as you should never mistake love as pain."

"Riddles, again?" Aiken snapped. "I will hear no more of this."

"You won't have to," Saima said, suddenly standing. "The Red Eyed Falcon comes." A speck in the distance turned into a low-flying bird that soared toward them at alarming speed. Banken and Aiken flinched as the falcon shot between them and dived over the other end of the cliff. "Come quickly!" Saima called, chasing after it. Banken cursed as the other two stumbled up and followed the smaller tengu. They leapt off the summit and landed on a ledge cropping out right beneath them. A cave beckoned in the wall next to them.

"This way, this way," Saima said. "We only have a few minutes." The cave was cold and pitch black and Banken stumbled twice. "This is insane," Aiken whispered. She dearly wanted to return to Izakaiya, their home mountain where the day's worries consisted of cleaning and finding the evening meal. How did she end up on this mad quest?

"My lady," Saima said, abruptly stopping. The darkness bulged outwards as bright white light flared across the cavern. An elderly human lady stood with her back to them. Straight white hair fell down to the small of her back, and she was dressed in a simple brown tunic. She perused them with an irritated look on her face.

"Saima, isn't it? Well, speak then." Her voice was rusty, as if rarely used.

"My apologies, my lady," Saima said respectfully. "It is good to see you so well."

"I am tired," the woman said. "It is past midmorning and I need rest, so make it quick."

"Of course, of course. These here are my dear brother and sister. They have lost someone important to them and they need her found."

The woman sighed. "Have you a gift?"

Saima regretfully shook his head. "Only a promise. But it is one you will dearly treasure as much as any gold: the lost one is a kitsune."

The lady cackled, a cryptic sound that rattled the walls. "Oh! Ho ho, well then. That is gift enough, isn't it Saima? You never fail to surprise me."

"I had thought so, my lady," Saima said, bowing low. The woman motioned the three of them over. "Come then, sit on the ground. This will take but a minute." She withdrew a bundle of twigs from her garments and ran her hands over them. Without warning, the twigs burst into flame and smoke engulfed the narrow cavern. Banken and Aiken choked at the sickly sweet smell but Saima inhaled deeply with his eyes closed. In the glow of the hidden light, Aiken could see the ghostly face of the woman, wan and slick with sweat.

"Fire," she whispered in a low voice. "I see fire. Green soldiers march west and their hands mix with the blood of men. A river beckons the dead to return and they bulge and dam up the flow." Aiken groped for Banken's hand and found it. She couldn't help but tremble at the woman's ominous words. "A village celebrates their death tonight," the woman continued. "I see them sprawled out like candied dolls, eyes waxy with sugar. Your kitsune sleeps with them, Saima. She sleeps by the Sano River!"

"A village by the Sano River? It must be Kusama," Saima said. "It's not far, my friends. I can show you the way." He excitedly stood. "Thank you, dear lady, thank you!"

"Go," the lady croaked. She began coughing in the smoke.

"Leave me now. Find your kitsune and bring death upon this weary land." Banken and Aiken stood without hesitation. Saima bowed and retreated down the cavern, Banken in tow. Aiken started to follow when she felt a dry hand settle on her waist. She froze.

"Wait," the woman said. Aiken turned. She was twice the height of this creature and she could easily crush her skull with one hand, but the tengu found she couldn't break the stare. "In you I see death as well." The woman's red eyes flickered across Aiken's body and settled on her right shoulder. "Beware the green fire," she added after a moment.

"Green fire?" Aiken asked, but then the smoke surged forth and engulfed her. Choking and staggering, she darted through the corridor and out to the sunlight.

"There you are!" Banken exclaimed. He ran forward and hugged his mate. "You terrified me! Brother, what in the gods name was that?"

"Your answer," Saima said. "The kitsune is in Kusama village, you heard the lady's words. Was that so hard?"

"Can you trust such witchcraft?" Banken asked, stroking Aiken's head.

"Of course, brother. It is a human error to dismiss that which cannot be confirmed by the laws of man. You had a question for me and I had it answered. Be content with that."

Banken sighed. "I'll be content when that kitsune is back with us," he muttered. "Come my heart, let's find this village."

The three tengu bounded down the mountain in silence. Aiken stared straight ahead, watching Saima carefully. *Beware the green fire,* the woman had warned her. Of course that referred to Saima and his green flames. She hardly needed a warning for that!

*

The third and final night of the Obon festival had a melancholy tinge to it. Most of the villagers gathered by the riverbank, staring reflectively into the water. Children clutched their relatives' lanterns and shivered in the cool breeze. Kusama village was alive with the spirits of the dead.

Hiroshi stood with Momo some distance from his grandfather and mother. The elders wore sly smiles that made him uncomfortable. Ignoring them, he showed Momo his father's lantern. It was actually a candle with a paper cover over it. He had etched his father's name on the top. "I never knew him," he said. "But I heard he was a good man."

Momo nodded. "My father's dead," she said. She surprised at how easily she could say it now. Takamoto was also a good man and she would always think of him like a father, but she also knew that she was never actually a daughter to him. In truth, she wasn't sure what he had thought of her.

"I'm sorry," Hiroshi said. "If I had known, we could have

made a lantern for him too." Momo simply shook her head. Hiroshi smiled at her and set his lantern on the small wooden boat. The current picked it up and carried it down the river, chasing after the other lights. The two of them stood there for some time, watching the flames flicker and vanish in the ebony waters. "Let's walk," Hiroshi said after a minute.

They made their way up the river, away from the crowd of villagers. "I wanted to show you this," Hiroshi said as they came across a large boulder. "This is the head of Lord Sano, the deity who watches Kusama village." The head was a perfect gray stone, as unblemished as a newborn's skin.

"In the ancient days, before men ruled with swords and ships, our lord Sano was a god of these lands," Hiroshi began. "Sano-sama was a great and just god, and many people flocked here under his benevolent guidance. They built the beginnings of Kusama village, and all prospered."

Momo felt the stone with her hand. She watched Hiroshi, taken in by his words.

"However," he continued, "a dark oni warlord named Karumadona invaded this land, and he brought with him a legion of evil beasts and demons. They burned the rice fields and slaughtered Sano's people. At first, Sano petitioned to the Sea God, for help, but Susanou was too busy to bother.

Running out of options, Sano-sama challenged Karumadona to single combat, to settle the matter once and for all.

"They engaged in a terrible wrestling match. Karumadona tore off Sano's head in one mighty blow, and it fell here." He nodded at the stone. "But Sano loved his people, so he stayed alive long enough to strangle the life out of Karumadona. When the oni expired, a great fish leapt out of Sano's neck and jumped into the river. Now Sano lives on, as a fish, our guardian and protector in the water."

Momo pushed hard against the stone. It didn't feel like a head, or even bone. As far as she could tell, it was solid rock. Still, she shared a smile with Hiroshi. *Villagers do love their legends.* "One thing makes no sense, Hiroshi-san," she said gently.

Hiroshi looked at her curiously. "What do you mean?"

"It doesn't make sense at all, Hiroshi-san. I'm sorry, but don't you know? Humans can't turn into fish!" She suppressed a giggle with one hand.

"I know," Hiroshi said quietly. "It was just a story." Did she hurt his feelings? She looked over him carefully.

"I'm sorry," she started to say but her words were cut off as Hiroshi stepped forward and gingerly pressed his lips onto hers.

V. A Fable Retold

The peace party slowly wound their way up the dusty road, and the waiting kappa grew restless as the day's heat intensified. Normally, they would be soaking in the cool bogs and rivers that were their homes this time of year, but these were hardly normal times. Their leader, Lord Kaar, squinted his watery eyes and made out fifteen humans approaching on horseback in all their armor and glamour. Their captain had insisted that they meet on this public road, but Kaaro preferred that anyway. *Better to allow others to watch,* he thought with a smile. He uncapped the large water jug that was necessary for all kappa traveling by land and poured a healthy quantity of it over his skin. The wetness rejuvenated him for the work ahead.

Ten kappa lounged about, appearing lackadaisical in the late summer sun. Kaaro grinned as he looked proudly over his men and wiped mucous from his nose. He was the brightest of the bunch and could be appropriately cordial to the humans, whom the kappa recognized as a touchy lot. His submissive attitude had taken him and his band farther than the other kappa tribes who were still were squalidly waiting within the slums of Kyoto. Still, it would be good to be able to vent some of his frustration towards humans.

A small goblin flew ahead of the peace party and landed, waddling awkwardly on two legs. Unlike his larger cousins, the snow tengu was barely as tall as a human child while his skin was blue and his leathery wings a pale white. Though most, like this one, had the typical long nose that the red tengu had, a few snow tengu possessed large, brightly colored beaks as if they were birds. Kaaro cared little for the natures of other races, but he did wonder why the humans in Kyoto never bothered to contact these othermen. *Probably because they are as useless as nipples on a fish.* The little creature puffed up its chest as the humans caught up to him and arranged themselves into formation. It spoke in a high, regal voice.

"Lord Kaaro. As promised, I have brought you Lord Tanaka. The noble captain extends his welcome to your kind, and hopes that all may prosper in our new alliance." Kaaro flicked his eyes up and looked over the humans. They bored him, typical humans armoring themselves with words and false courage. The large banner of a boar flapped impressively in the wind but that only irritated him. Humans and their symbols!

Instead of answering, Kaaro nodded curtly and stepped past the little creature. The tengu blinked, wiped sweat off its brow, then turned and bowed to the one Kaaro assumed was Tanaka. The captain spurred his horse forward, making a great deal of noise in the process.

"Lord Tanaka, may I present the honorable Lord Kaaro, of the Kyoto tribe. His kappa seeks an alliance with our noble eminence," the goblin piped.

Tanaka, heavyset and bearded, nodded and dismounted. "It is good to see that others have heard our call. Oda Nobunaga is not the only one who extends friendship to othermen. Our master would greatly appreciate your assistance in our fight against him. It is an honor, Lord Kaaro." The man spoke kindly and bowed low. As he bared his neck, the kappa unlimbered the massive scythe on his belt and beheaded the man with one swift chop.

The blood spray splattered across him, warm and wet. The other kappa sprang into action and hurled themselves onto the soldiers. Although most were mounted and seasoned warriors, it made little difference once the kappa closed the distance. The burly rivermen killed quickly, tearing at man and horse alike with their long scythes and sharp claws. Horses screamed and men shouted, first in anger and then in terror, as limbs and bodies piled up. The blue goblin gaped up at Kaaro with his mouth wide open and quivering.

"You…you…" he stammered. Kaaro lashed out his fist and wrapped it around the tengu's neck just as Yugotaro had done to him. He lifted the creature, trying to keep the flailing wings away from his face. Holding him away at an arm's length, the kappa sneered, "I most honorably apologize. We weren't here to parlay." The tengu tried to speak but then Kaaro squeezed his fist. The neck popped like a cracking chicken bone.

Afterward, Kaaro saw to the dead. "Scatter their bodies about and position them more gruesomely," he instructed. Yugotaro's orders had been explicit. He reached into the bag the oni had given him and withdrew the items inside. In one body he stuck the type of bone knife that the mountain tengu favored. On another he laid trace amounts of tanuki fur. Here and there he dabbled, until it seemed a great host of othermen had swept across the humans. He came across the blue goblin body and regarded it for a minute.

"What should we do with that one?" one of the others asked.

"Burn it," Kaaro finally replied. "It has no use here." The kappa looked disheartened and Kaaro suppressed a grin. "Fine, it's yours then."

The kappa grinned toothily and carried the little creature off. The kappa leader nodded in satisfaction after they were finished. The smell of roasting tengu stirred his hunger, and it was past time they caught up with the others at the Sano River and ate.

Laughing and jesting, the kappa packed up. They left the bodies where they had arranged them, like broken rag dolls strewn across the road.

*

The two of them walked along the Sano River in silence. Momo felt increasingly awkward as the sun lifted above the thin range of clouds and dappled the forest with light. *He should not have been so forward.* Her head ached from lack of sleep and she had considered leaving in the night, but Kei was not yet fully recovered. That morning, before the rest of the village even stirred, she heard a tentative knock on the door. Hiroshi invited her for another walk and feeling embarrassed, she hesitatingly agreed.

This was all so confusing! He had offered to show her the best fishing spots on the river, but that premise was as thin as a spider's web. She didn't want to ignore his eager looks and clumsy gropes for her hand but she certainly did not appreciate the sudden kiss from the evening before. Were all human boys so rude? What disturbed her more was the heat that lingered afterwards, tingly and warm. She could still feel his wet mouth on hers.

She looked at Hiroshi as he stumbled on ahead. His ears

were almost too big for his skinny head and his body was skinny and ungainly. Yet…his eyes were so warm and kind when they looked at her, and he did have the nicest teeth. Yes, what he did was very inappropriate, but she found she did not completely mind. Only, what did that mean for her now?

Hiroshi stumbled in the mud and glanced at her furtively. She knew he sensed something was amiss, but he bravely kept up the charade. "We're almost there," he reassured her for the fifth time. "It's darker than I remember."

"It's early," Momo muttered. She should be on the road now, leaving Kusama and this boy's nonsense behind. Staying around could hurt far more than one village boy's feelings.

"Yes, yes, you're right. Ah, there it is!" Hiroshi pointed to a point the river where the waters eddied around jagged rocks. "The fish migrate along here but the water is shallow. Sometimes you can even scoop the fish with your hands! Isn't that something?"

Momo, who scooped fish with her teeth quite regularly, couldn't help but giggle at his attempts to boast. Of course Hiroshi misread the signs and stepped closer, one hand reaching out for hers. "I thought of you last night," he said suddenly in a quiet voice. "I had trouble sleeping."

"As did I," Momo responded, without thinking. Hiroshi's eyes widened.

"So you thought of our kiss as well? I'm sorry Momo-chan,

but I couldn't resist. You have this allure about you and I fear I am powerless before it!"

Momo let out a squeak and then hastily turned her cheek as Hiroshi moved his face forward again. Rebuked, Hiroshi took a step back and looked over her. "What is it?"

"Hiroshi-san," Momo said carefully. She had no experience with this! She avoided looking at him, in case she might do something foolish. "I'm sorry. I don't feel it is proper that you kiss me."

The hurt was evident. Hiroshi stepped back, hands dropping to his sides. "I see." For a brief wild second Momo wanted to go to him but she held back. If she was weak now, it would only hurt more later. "Is it how I look?"

"What?" Momo couldn't help but laugh. "You look fine, Hiroshi!" *It's what I am,* she wanted to say, but that wouldn't answer any questions. Finally she settled with, "I'm not ready."

"Is that true?"

"Yes." Momo said it easily, because it wasn't a lie. "I don't feel ready for that. Do you understand?" To her relief, Hiroshi's face broke into a smile. She found herself staring at his smile a little too long and turned her face down before he could see her blush.

"I suppose so. Ah, Momo-san! You are truly are amazing, did you know that? There are girls in my village who…but never mind that. You know, I am glad you are like that. I think that is why I like you. Oh forgive me, Momo!" Hiroshi bowed low in his babbling. "I was so rude last night. To assume…to assume that you were thinking…" his words faltered.

Momo bowed back. "It's fine, Hiroshi. A simple misunderstanding, and one that we have cleared up. I hope we can still be friends." She felt like a fool saying it.

Hiroshi nodded. "I can settle for that. Perhaps one day you will feel differently?"

Momo only shrugged, not wanting to reveal the truth. "Look," she said, changing the subject, "it's past dawn. And we stand by a riverbank. Perhaps we'll catch a glimpse of the Green Man."

"Who is that?" Hiroshi asked.

"The Green Man dwells in halfway places. At dawn, by beaches and riverbanks, where east meets west. He guards the poor folk. Animals and children and villagers." Usagi's words came back to her. "He never judges, only protects. Perhaps he is watching us right now."

Hiroshi laughed. "Now who is telling tales, Momo-san?" He turned and looked back at the river. "Have you ever seen this Green Man?"

Momo thought about it. "I don't know," she said after a minute. "But I'm sure that he's seen me." She smiled sadly, eyes watering without warning. *Are you there, Usagi-chan?* "Let me stay here alone for awhile, Hiroshi. I want to think." *Please watch over Taku for me, okay? And Father, if you are listening, I hope you are not too disappointed with me. I'm sorry I never became the apprentice you wanted me to be. I'm sorry I was not a good enough daughter for you. Please forgive me, all of you.* The Green Man was silent in response.

*

Hiroshi left Momo by the riverbank feeling more embarrassed than ever before in his life. Foolish boy! Foolish, foolish boy! How could he have acted so stupid? All his life he had promised himself he would never behave as so many other village boys did with their girls and then there he was, kissing and slobbering like the rest of them! Truly he was not yet a man, for he had some seasoning to do. After this harvest he would war through the winter and come back a hero. Perhaps then he would be worthy of someone like Momo.

Firm resolve gave way to fiery passion. Oh Momo! The taste of her lips, like milk and honey, still clung to him. Last night had been more than fretful and he awoke this morning in a fog. He had envisioned the two of them walking down the river, kissing and touching and perhaps more than that, and now the reality of the situation shattered his heart into two. He cursed and punched a nearby rock, bruising his knuckles.

"War," he growled to himself. "Turn me into steel, turn me into a warrior. Win me Momo's heart, and I will give my all to you!" A couple of younger boys ran up to Hiroshi but one glare at them sent them scurrying. He nodded to himself, feeling powerful. *Let my enemies tremble!* Hiroshi strutted down the road and towards his house.

Grandfather Hidetora sat there with a guest. The unfamiliar man smelt of leather and horses and Hiroshi immediately perked up. No doubt this was what he would become by next year! Clearly a soldier, the man had soot on his unshaven face and battle-hardened features. His hands were calloused and bloody and a long spear was laid across his lap. Hidetora sipped tea and motioned Hiroshi over.

"Come and sit, boy," he said. "Do you remember your cousin, Arata?"

The man looked indifferently over Hiroshi. "He was still a child the last time I rode through," Arata said. "You have grown."

Hiroshi puffed his chest. "Thank you, Arata-san! It is good—"

"Never mind that," his grandfather interrupted impatiently. "Your cousin has come with grim news. Some of his fellow soldiers were found dead by what appears to be a great host of monsters. Tengu and kappa, tanuki too by all accounts. It seems the stories of the othermen are true."

"What do you mean?" Hiroshi asked.

Arata snorted. "Have you been deaf to the rumors? Oda

Nobunaga, may he be forever damned, has hired a sorcerer to do his bidding. This sorcerer in turn has employed demons and terrible beasts to serve the warlord and now they have invaded these lands."

Hiroshi looked at his grandfather. "Tanuki? Aren't they our friends?" He had only seen tanuki once, when two of them had passed through Kusama as merchants. That was some years ago and he could barely remember their faces.

"It appears not, boy," Hidetora said. "These othermen are no friends of ours. Some daimyo have ordered them to be killed or driven out of their lands. It appears their concerns are warranted."

Hiroshi's cousin nodded briefly. "It is so. Our lord had taken efforts to parlay with some of the creatures but it seems those efforts were fruitless. Soon all of Japan will go to war against these creatures."

"So what now?" Hiroshi tried to quell the fear that rose in his throat. *I am no coward, grandfather! I will fight, Momo, just you wait and see.*

"Nothing," Hidetora said. "We pray the worst does not come this way. Arata said his men were slaughtered a five days' march east of here. That is far enough that we may be overlooked."

"So we do nothing?" Fear gave way to anger. "We sit here

like cattle, praying the wolves do not show up? What kind of action is that?"

"A wise one," Arata said. "Othermen are dangerous. They use magic and strange illusions to deceive our very senses. They can transform into your best friend and slip a knife in your back while you sleep. Keep yourself safe, boy. Farm your land and fish the waters and feed the soldiers who will fight to defend you. That is your best path right now."

"I will be a soldier, cousin!" Hiroshi spat. First Momo and now *this*? Did everyone here think him a silly boy? "I will fight!"

Hidetora looked over his grandson. He was hardly sixteen, still skinny and unfilled. "You will not," he said. "You must watch over your mother."

"Oh, so I am a nursemaid now?" Hiroshi glared at his grandfather and stood. "I am a Hidetora," he announced. "And I will honor your name." He left the house without looking back.

"Wait!" Hidetora started to say, but Arata placed a hand on his shoulder. "He has fight in him, grandfather," he said. "Perhaps I can take him with me."

"I don't know," Hidetora said. He thought back to his own callow youth and the tragedies that had awaited the young boy who had once rode from his village with a host of soldiers. That young boy had been fortunate enough to become an old man, but countless others whose bones still littered the Tokaido road had not. Hidetora slurped his tea and stared at the leaves on the bottom of the cup as if they could give him answers. *Those are fishermen's arms,* he had mocked his grandson, then oblivious of those words' impact. "My grandson believes I think him a fool. If only he knew the truth." He coughed and stood up. "The only fool in this family is this old man right before you. Thank you for coming by, Arata-chan. I will think on your offer."

"I will be at the inn," Arata said. "And I leave in two days. Your presence would bring a great boost of morale among the men, honorable grandfather. You know you're quite the legend among the garrison. I'll saddle an extra horse if you decide to ride with us."

"Better me than him," Hidetora bowed low. After the younger man had left, Hidetora began cleaning up. "Better me than any of these boys," he said sadly, to himself.

*

"Yellow," Kei said and watched her outfit turn yellow. "Now red." Her clothes rippled and shifted appropriately. The neko sighed and flopped onto her back. Where was Momo? Weren't they supposed to leave this morning? The nerve of that girl, making Kei stay cooped up and then vanishing! She was angry. She hated the squalor of this room and her lack of fine clothing. She hated not doing anything and being bored all the time.

At least Penken knew how to treat a lady. The fat tanuki had garbed her and Kimiko in the most daring fashions and best hairstyles money could buy. A kept girl had to look her best, and even though Kei could make a few cosmetic changes on her own, they paled before the makeovers she had gotten back in Kyoto!

Now this. Stuck in a room and forced to lie about as a cat. Well, she would have no more of it. No doubt Momo-chan was out having fun on her own. Kei was hungry and she needed money. Just one night of work and she could hire a wagon to take herself and Momo straight back to Kyoto. Then she could show that little country kitsune exactly what she had been missing her whole life!

"Pink," Kei said, and giggled as her form changed once more. When she was done she was outfitted in a slim kimono that showed off a slender but seductive figure. Green eyes flashing, Kei opened the door and went downstairs.

VI. Broken Bonds

Kaaro watched smoke waft over the water and grunted in satisfaction. "Good enough." The current carried the splinters of smashed boats down the river and out of sight. Bodies lay sprawled on the mud where they had made their final stand. The kappa went to work, burning the small encampment to the ground. One kappa offered Kaaro a hunk of meat from the spit and he eagerly snatched it. Killing was hungry work.

"Report," he said between bites. The leg was thin and scrawny, devoid of any fat. He would have to go fishing later.

"All dead," Daru said. The heavy-lidded kappa blinked water from his eyes. "We caught the skiff that ran off and drowned the humans. We are done here, Lord Kaaro."

"Not done," Kaaro said. "Make it look like tengu did this. Slice the necks and arrange the bodies as if they fell from great heights."

Daru grunted. Kaaro's second-in-command looked stupid and spoke slowly, but was no fool. "Beg pardon, lord."

"Yes?"

"What is this for? What gains are there in killing humans? I grew up hating no human."

Kaaro snorted. "Humans have no love for kappa and you know that well. We are merely striking first."

"And making it seem like others are doing the killing? I see no purpose."

"And you have no need to," Kaaro sneered. "That is why you do not lead us. Or are you questioning me?"

Daru shifted his feet uncomfortably. "No lord. Only curious."

"A poor trait to have, Daru. Best drop it."

"Yes lord." The kappa bowed low and relayed Kaaro's orders. The kappa lord strolled down to the firepit and cracked off another joint of meat. War was in his blood, he had realized over the past few days, and he loved this sort of carnage. Peering down the river, he grinned eagerly. There would be more to kill soon enough.

*

Momo watched the fish flicker and skip down the river current and envied them. If only she could join them in the murky water and just swim away from all this foolishness! When did life get so complicated? She hardly felt like the same girl who peddled her father's wares in Yubikawa village.

"So much has changed," she whispered to herself. People

were dead and others would die too if they caught up to her. She missed Taku and she missed her father. She even missed those apprentice boys, whose names she could never get right. They all meant an earlier time, perhaps not a happier time but one where she knew her place in the world.

And then there was Hiroshi-chan. Why did he pick her, when there were so many human girls who lived in the village? What was so special about her? She had never pictured herself kissing a human, let alone liking it. She had to leave Kusama village and soon, but now she found herself coming up with reasons not to go. What kind of madness was she falling into?

The sun had fully ascended and she sighed reluctantly. Whatever lay ahead of her, she wouldn't find it just sitting here. It was past time she returned to the village and found Kei. Her fantasies were only that – just fantasies. She would only hurt Hiroshi and the villagers if she hid out in Kusama. If those black robed ninja descended upon them, she had no doubt what the outcome would be.

Her hearing picked up a familiar breathing and her heart froze. Momo quickly dived into the brush and waited. It only took a minute for the large red tengu to catch up to her.

"Momo," Aiken said, bobbing her head respectably. The female tengu bore the scars of her earlier battle but otherwise looked about the same. Her oily black hair was artfully done up in a majestic warrior's bun. "It's good to see you again."

"Is it?" Momo asked. She eyed the tengu suspiciously. "What are you doing here?"

Aiken sighed and spread her hands out to show she was carrying no weapon, yet Momo looked at the deceptively small axe haft dangling from the tengu's waist. She remembered how long those weapons could extend. "We've been looking for you, Momo. Do you remember my promise to you?"

"As long as I'm with you, I'm safe," Momo said. "Those were generous words, Aiken."

"I meant them," Aiken said. "I can never beg your forgiveness for leaving you like that. Penken Satsumoto, the leader of the troupe, had called my mate and me away on an emergency. We had expected to leave you for only a day or two."

"I know Penken," snapped Momo. "He tried to use me like some carnival wench after you two left! He wanted to sell me to human men! Is that the protection that you promised me, Aiken?"

Aiken's eyes bulged slightly. "What? Penken did that? I promise you I had no—"

"Or was it when the Yan attacked?" Momo continued, unable to keep the sneer out of her voice. "Or when you lied to me about my father? Tell me one thing, Aiken. What is it you exactly want from me?" The last words came out in an animal hiss.

Aiken regarded the kitsune carefully. *She's changed so much in so little time!* Momo's eyes no longer had that fearful look to them. Instead the kitsune seemed angry, on edge, and ready. Aiken suddenly realized how capable the kitsune would be in taking care of herself. "By your path," she said carefully, "it would seem you are traveling east. Would I be wrong in assuming you are going to Kyoto?" After Momo reluctantly nodded, Aiken smiled gently. "That is where we wish to take you. Would it be so amiss to join our paths?"

Momo looked at her. "Kei and I are fine," she said, and then cursed herself for mentioning the neko. "We don't need your protection anymore."

"I know," Aiken said. "I am hoping we can travel together as friends. Four are better than two, and othermen are growing less welcome in these lands by the day. You could do well to have two tengu on your side."

Momo appeared to consider it. She stared carefully at Aiken, watching for signs of deception. The tengu shifted uncomfortably under her scrutiny. "You never answered my question, Aiken," Momo said. "Why did you come after me?"

"I…" Aiken paused. *I don't know.* She suddenly felt wretched, agreeing to this task without questioning its reasoning. When Banken and Aiken had first received their orders, they had seemed noble enough. Extract othermen who still dwelt in persecuted lands and deliver them to Kyoto, where they would be welcome. But there *was* more to this than that, wasn't there? Why this kitsune? "Momo, I…"

Before she could find a response, a large net crashed down onto Momo. "I got her!" Banken cried triumphantly, landing next to the writhing figure. "There!" The net's weights kept the struggling form of the kitsune down under a tangle of heavy ropes.

"Banken!" Aiken shrieked. "She was considering joining us! There was no need to strike first, you arrogant fool!"

"My heart," Banken protested. "it's better we catch her now before she gets away again!"

"Was this Saima's idea?" Aiken raged, her fury enveloping her. She took a step towards her mate, who took a step back. "What madness did he wrap you into?"

"Look, can't we discuss this later?" Banken hissed. He eyed the net, which had grown curiously still. "Let's secure the kitsune."

Aiken folded her arms and glared at Banken. "You do it then."

Banken shrugged, his jaw set in a stubborn grimace. "Fine.

At least we can go home now." He stooped over to pick up the net. Without warning, it bounced up and wrapped itself around his face like a spider web. Banken stumbled to his knees and clawed at the tangle as an orange flash darted into the woods.

"Oh very good, Banken" Aiken sneered. "Well done indeed! There goes your little fox." She couldn't help but feel a flash of admiration for Momo. *How did she throw off that thing? It must have weighed at least twenty stone!* "What now?"

Banken cursed and tore the net off his face. He wouldn't meet Aiken's eyes as he blundered noisily after the kitsune. Aiken watched her mate go, disgusted with the whole affair.

*

The men loved her. Kei relished this kind of attention, the looks and stares, all for her! How easy these humans were, pliable like dough and all too eager to turn their hard earned money her way. She slinked over to one soldier who had the clink of gold on him and traced a finger along his cheek. The innkeeper and the serving maids watched on in stunned silence. Kei snickered – let them be jealous!

It only took a few minutes for propositions to fly and she snatched one from the wealthy looking soldier. She tittered at the collective groans from the others. "Don't you worry," she promised. "There will be plenty to go around."

Of course, she wasn't *really* doing anything. The humans wouldn't ever have to know the anatomy of a neko, and they wouldn't notice anyway. Let her trick their senses and play into her charms. In the end, Kei was a good deal wealthier and just as pure.

She led the man by his belt, moving ever so seductively. In Okayama she had grown up watching women ply men with subtle gestures and looks but she found it to be a weary waste of time. Men didn't need to be teased – they only needed to be satisfied. The man grunted with effort and Kei fixated on his jingling purse. Perhaps he would fall asleep after, as men were apt to do, and she could make off with the entire bag! "Not bad for five minutes work," she whispered under her breath. She could then find a wealthy merchant to give her and Momo a ride to the capital in style!

They stumbled into Kei's room and the man groped for her eagerly. "Now, now," Kei teased, taking a step back. She let her kimono fall, revealing the alabaster skin beneath. "Do you like me?"

The man nodded eagerly. "You are beautiful, girl. Do you live in this village?"

"Just a passerby, my lord," she said in a high singsong voice. "Lost and looking for someone to keep me warm for the night. Could you do that?"

The man already had his armor off and his shirt over his

head. Kei laughed at his eagerness and helped him with the buttons. "My, what a strong man you are!"

The man nodded. "I fight for Lord Motonari. Tomorrow I must ride east and protect these lands." He grunted and looked at her as she shed the last of her garments. He didn't even notice as the illusory clothes faded into nothing behind her naked form. "I could use a girl on my travels. Would you be interested?"

"Maybe," Kei smiled. She put her arms around the man's neck. "Let's see what you can do, first."

They had barely begun when the door exploded inwards. The old innkeeper stormed in, broom in hand, followed by a trio of older, armed men. The woman stared at the couple with her mouth agape. "Whore!" she shrieked, her face dissolving into wrinkles. "I won't have this at my inn!"

"What?" the man cried. He fumbled for his clothes.

"You!" one of the other men said. "What are you doing here? The captain will hear of this, rest assured!"

The naked man shrieked at that. "No! Please, I was just having some fun, can't you see that? Please!"

"You wench! You slut! We take you and your sick pet in and this is how you repay us? I will see you beaten!" the innkeeper screamed over the other men. She began thwacking Kei's naked bottom with the flat of her broom.

"Ow, ow!" Kei cried. She ducked out of the room, her clothes reassembling around her body before she was completely downstairs. She ran past the gaping mouths of the humans and ducked into an alley. She quickly shifted into her cat form.

"Gods, what a bore these people are," she huffed as she trotted back out. The village was alive with running adults and staring children. "What's the big deal with all of that, anyway?"

*

"What is this?" Hiroshi asked. He had gone to the inn to find his cousin and listen to some stories about the war, but instead found the common room packed with people. The innkeeper was shrieking at an officer who patiently listened while avoiding the flecks of spittle from her toothless mouth. Hiroshi saw Eizo with some of the other boys and waved to him. "Hey, Eizo-chan! What's going on? Did something happen?"

Eizo pumped his thick legs over. "Oh did it!" His eyes shone with excitement. "You know the girl we took in on the first night of Obon? The girl in the white dress, what's her name?"

"Momo," Hiroshi said, his heart starting to hammer. "What happened? Is she all right?"

"More than all right," Eizo grinned. "Apparently she was entertaining some of the soldiers in the inn. Took one of them to her room right in front of everybody! So some other men drove her out and old lady Yama is furious! She thinks the soldiers attract that sort around here."

"Momo?" Hiroshi's heart plunged down to his stomach. *I'm not ready,* she had told him. Her voice had sounded so earnest, so sincere! Could it really all have been a lie? He dug his nails into his palms.

"Hiroshi-san? Hiroshi! Hey, are you okay!" Eizo's eyes grew wide as moons as he watched blood drip from the older boy's hands.

Hiroshi turned away, his eyes brimming with tears.

VII. Desperate Measures

Momo slowed down as she reached the outskirts of the village and shifted back into her human form. She was angry, far angrier than she had first realized. "It's funny, Taku," she whispered to her brother, hoping her words would somehow find him. "I finally find some creatures who are as unique and special as we are, and all they want to do is hurt me." A dull ache in her head was slowly escalating into a throb. Her legs felt wobbly and not completely under her control, and her senses were heightened and sharp. She felt like she did back on that mountain path, when Penken had casually mentioned that her father was not alive after all, that the tengu had lied to her.

"Those tengu," she hissed. She hated them more than ever! She hated Banken and his false bravado, his big frame hiding a coward's heart. She hated Aiken, with her poisonous words that sounded so sincere, so motherly at first. She hated the whole damn circus troupe and the pack of lies they carried with them.

Funny, how only the ninja woman had given her any grain of truth with her words.

The atmosphere in Kusama hung still with an unearthly air. People went about their business, but they seemed to avoid her as she walked through the village. Old ladies who had once smiled at her now ignored her, and a gaggle of children stared at her as if seeing her for the first time. What was going on?

She made her way to the inn. It was time to get Kei and move on. There was something wrong here that extended beyond the tengu and she didn't want to stay and find out what it was. Yet when she stepped inside, the innkeeper pointed at her and shrieked, "Get out!" Momo stared at her, aghast.

"What do you mean?"

The woman grabbed a broom and shook it menacingly at her. "You whore! How dare you show your face around here again? I'm calling the soldiers." Momo turned and fled. "Don't ever come back," the woman screeched after her. *Has the whole world gone mad?* She hurried through the village, looking desperately at the villagers' faces. Where was Kei?

"Kei!" she called out "Kei, where are you?" The villagers hardly spared her a glance. Two soldiers playing dice stood and one of them mimed an obscene gesture while the other laughed uproariously. Momo shot them a glare and scrambled by them. *What is going?* "Kei! It's me, Momo!" She heard someone else call out her name. Before she could turn and see who it was, a hand shot out and dragged her down an alley.

"What are you doing?" Hiroshi hissed. The boy looked haggard, his hair in a tangle and his eyes bloodshot. He reeked of anger, sending a spike of terror through her.

"I have to go, Hiroshi," she whispered. "Ow! You're hurting me! Please, stop that!" Hiroshi released her arm.

"You have some nerve," he said. "Coming back and strutting about like that. You know they're looking for you?"

"What? Who?" For a second Momo thought the tengu had gotten to the village but then Hiroshi said, "The elders! My grandfather is with them. They are furious with you, Momo. As…as am I." He glared at her. Momo could smell his disappointment.

"What do you mean?"

"Don't think I didn't hear about you! You must think me an idiot." Hiroshi rubbed his eyes. "Not ready, you said. Not ready for what? I would have been good to you, Momo-chan. I swear it." The boy turned away. "But no, I guess I was mistaken about you. It wouldn't have mattered."

"Hiroshi," Momo said softly, reaching one hand out. "I don't understand."

"No!" Hiroshi cried, wrenching free. "Just go, Momo. Get out of here. You've ruined the Obon, my family's reputation, and most of all, my heart. Just leave here now!" He shouted the last and ran from the alley as Momo sank to her knees.

"What did I do?" she whispered in a small voice. The rage that had sustained her earlier gave way to grief, and she let the tears fall from her face. Of all the betrayals she had been forced to endure in the last few weeks, somehow this one was the worst.

*

The tengu argued over the cook fire, keeping their voices low under the crackle of flames. Aiken vented to Banken, who fruitlessly tried parrying her words with first apologies, and then angry barbs. Saima sat off to one side, eyes flickering from one to the other as he silently chewed on his fish.

"You've gone mad," Aiken whispered, barely able to restrain herself from shouting. "We need to return to our tribe. This isn't our business anymore!"

"Return with nothing?" Banken hissed. Large splinters were all that remained of the huge trunk in his hands. Saima briefly considered handing his brother more wood but thought better of it. If there was one flaw Saima knew that he himself had, it was acting too brashly, without careful thought to the consequences. Last time he made that error he had found him exiled from his own clan, nearly executed for his crimes. If

Banken hadn't been his brother, Saima had no doubt what his fate would have been that day.

He watched his brother now as Banken pounded his fists onto the ground in frustration. "Our people are depending on us, Aiken!"

"To do what?" Aiken shot back. "Find a girl who happens to take the form of a fox? What use does she have to our tribe, Banken? Tell me that exactly!"

Banken growled and for a second Saima thought he would stand and strike his mate. Of course he didn't, but the cords on his neck stood out, as thick as vines. Banken had some of their father's temper in him, though it was checked by his loving heart. Not like their father, who had beaten Saima bloody many times over when the tengu was but a whelp. Their father hated Saima the day he was born, oddly colored and stunted as he was. Some tengu were known to leave the weak and deformed out to die but Saima had clung to life, proving by the narrowest margins that he could sustain himself in the wild. In fact, he had spent his entire life proving to others that he was worthy of his kind. Yet he was never good enough for his father.

"I thought so," Aiken said with a hint of triumph in her voice. "You know, I'm glad the kitsune escaped. We don't deserve her friendship, let alone deserve to be her guardians. Which is what you claim we would be doing, isn't that right?"

Banken glanced at her sheepishly. That familiar gleam of

guilt was in his eyes again. Saima knew that gleam all too well, appearing whenever Banken accomplished some great feat that made their father swell with pride. In his youth no one could throw farther or fly faster than Banken and everyone knew that he was destined for greatness. Everyone, that is, except Banken himself. The younger tengu always adored his brother and hated how easily he surpassed Saima in everything that mattered to anyone.

"I promise you, my heart," Banken said in placating tones, "I will protect her as I protect you. I stake my life on it! The Yan are still after her, and only we tengu are strong enough to fend them off. We're her best hope for making it to Kyoto."

Aiken scrutinized her mate. Her own temper was dying as quickly as the flames in the pit. Whatever differences they had, they always forgave each other so quickly. Saima found it annoying; it was time to interject.

"I agree, dear sister," he said as he stood. The other two tengu startled at him, as if they had forgotten that he was there. "Momo desperately needs our help."

Aiken glared at him. "And I wonder what you want with her, Saima," she said. "I recall that mountain witch getting particularly excited when you mentioned the word 'kitsune' to her."

Saima shrugged. "An oddity to be sure, but what do I know of mountain witches?"

"You seem to consort with that one fairly well!" Aiken shot back. Banken's mate was all too bright and that vexed Saima. Even before his public exile, she had never truly liked him. *That will have to be dealt with someday.*

Banken made a calming gesture with his arms. "Please, let's not argue anymore," he said. Saima was amused at how quickly Banken was in defending both his mate and his brother. *More of this, and he'll likely split into two!* He had to suppress a grin at the thought.

"Our people kept me on that mountain for three years, Aiken. It's only natural that I grow familiar with some of the denizens, just as neighbors grow accustomed to each other's presence." Saima shrugged, a harmless gesture. "I'm merely in agreement with Banken. We shouldn't give up the hunt so quickly."

Banken nodded. "Saima speaks true. We are too close, my heart. I will not waste the lives of Penken's men for nothing. Momo will be in the best care once we have her."

"So what do you propose?" The ice had not completely melted from Aiken's voice but she seemed resigned to the decision, at least for now. Saima tossed the fish bones into the fire.

"We have little recourse, I must admit," he said. "If Momo

has fled Kusama village then our hunt becomes that much more difficult." The other tengu nodded. "But I think it unlikely that she is far away."

"What do you mean, brother?" Banken asked.

"Aiken mentioned there was another with her. A neko, correct?" Aiken reluctantly nodded. "From what you have told me of Kei, there is another way to get to Momo." Saima grinned. He loved this sort of intrigue. His brains always beat other tengus' brawn and he found that others were often drawn to his ideas, as if his thoughts and dreams were infectious. Sometimes he wondered if he was born in the wrong form.

"Saima, what are you suggesting?" Aiken asked with narrowed eyes.

"Collateral," Saima said, stretching his wings. "You two make camp by the river. I'll find you tomorrow morning." He started to walk away.

"Brother, wait!" Banken called. "Where are you going?"

"Even if the kitsune hasn't fled yet, we haven't much time. Just wait and see what your older brother is capable of, Banken-chan!" He used the human title playfully and watched with glee as his brother faithfully sat down. *Good dog.* Banken would listen to him and obey, as he always did. Saima walked through the forest in better spirits than he had in years. He cared little for this hunt but it was good to get out and observe the world once more. Besides, who knew what kind of opportunity might be waiting for him? Saima had learned the value of waiting while in solitude, and he was not adverse to continue waiting until the gods deemed that he was ready to shine.

*

Evening gave way to night and most of the patrons were already gone, but Hiroshi remained to drink with his new friends. The soldiers were not much older than he was, but they had seen war and regaled Hiroshi with tales of fighting. Hiroshi found solace in their warm companionship and bottles of cheap sake. He had already consumed more than he had at the Odori dance, and yet felt better than ever. Here he could just forget about his troubles, forget about his family, and most of all, forget about Momo.

"Join us tomorrow," an older boy urged, not for the first time. "Protect your people as you find honor in the battlefield."

Again, Hiroshi found himself declining. "I'm so sorry, but I can't just yet. I have to finish the harvest and train a bit. Then I'll be ready."

The soldier waved his hand dismissively. "Peasant! I was two years younger when I first left my village. What's keeping you behind? Afraid to leave mommy?" The three laughed loudly and Hiroshi lowered his head as his ears turned red. Perhaps it was time to turn in for the night. He started to rise when the soldier clapped him on the shoulder, roughly pushing him down.

"Hey, where do you think you're going? The night's not over yet, and we have more drinking to do. Here, a toast to you then, mommy's boy!" He poured a healthy amount of sake into Hiroshi's glass.

Hiroshi pushed it away. "N-no thanks. I think I've had enough." The three boys regarded him with cold eyes and one thrust the glass back at him, spilling drops onto the wooden table.

"We said drink, boy. You think we're playing?" Hiroshi wiped sweat from his forehead. Putting on a tough face, he picked up the glass and downed it in one swallow. The men cheered him on.

"That a boy," whispered a man Hiroshi had not noticed before. He was older than the others, a hardened veteran with knowing eyes. He sat down with them and Hiroshi picked up the foul scents of tobacco and alcohol on his breath. "Come with us. Tomorrow we march east. The demon lord's forces are waiting to do battle, boy, and we know you want to prove yourself a man. There isn't time to waste, so make your choice." Feeling sick and head roiling, Hiroshi shivered. He didn't like how they looked at him.

"What is this?" Grandfather Hidetora's voice broke through the tension. The four soldiers glanced sullenly up at the old man.

"None of your business, grandpa," the veteran said. He casually flicked a cup off the table, shattering it on the ground. "Go clean that up." Without warning, Hidetora grabbed the veteran with both arms and flung him effortlessly across the room. The man bounced and rolled headfirst into the bar.

"Clean yourself up," Hidetora growled. He turned to the three younger boys. "Any of you want a go?"

The boys looked uncertainly at each other. "Kiyoshi!" the innkeeper cried. "Don't cause a mess in here!"

"We were leaving," Hidetora snapped. He uprooted Hiroshi and dragged him for the door. The veteran was just picking himself up, cursing while the other soldiers stared on in silence. Once outside, Hidetora dragged his grandson into a nearby alley and slammed him against the wall. "What the hell are you doing, boy?"

"Leave me alone!" Hiroshi snapped. "Why are you so concerned about me?"

Hidetora slapped him across the face. "How dare you speak to me like that? Where is your respect? I should have left you to those soldiers, who would have tied your drunken bottom to a horse's saddle. You would wake up halfway to Kyoto!"

Hiroshi began to cry. His grandfather set him down and

spat. How did his grandson turn out this way? He was such a happy boy once, carefree and good to his mother. Now this, consorting with dangerous folk and dreaming mad dreams. Of course, Hidetora suddenly realized, he himself was no different when he was the boy's age. He impulsively pulled his grandson into a rough hug. "Not yet, lad. You aren't ready yet. Tomorrow we'll talk and if you really want to fight, I will not stop you. But we do it my way, the right way. No running off with these soldiers, plunging headfirst into some front line to die. I will contact some people and see you get the proper training."

Hiroshi hiccupped between sobs. Hidetora pushed his grandson back and stared at his face. The boy's crying continued, heedless of his words. "What is it? Why are you like this?"

"She hates me, grandfather. She rejected me to go sleep with those men. Why? I don't understand!" Rivulets ran tracks down Hiroshi's dirty face.

"Momo?" Hidetora sighed. "You truly liked her, didn't you?" In truth, the old man was relieved that the grief came from such a familiar source. "Women," he snorted as he patted his grandson on the back. "Well, that's a whole other issue, isn't it? This won't be the first time you cry over one."

"But what is she? Is she just a prostitute like Yamma-san thinks?"

Hidetora paused for a minute and considered what he had heard earlier that day. *Green eyes,* they had described her. Momo didn't have green eyes, did she? Other things were inconsistent. Yamma was convinced it was her, but the old bird was getting on in her years and blinder than she'd care to admit. The soldiers at the inn had described her differently…her height and the shape of the face. Reluctantly, he voiced his suspicions to Hiroshi. "I don't think…it was her, Hiroshi. It was another girl. Maybe someone a soldier smuggled in, I'm not certain. But the description didn't match Momo."

The crying abruptly stopped. Hiroshi stared at his grandfather in wonder. "You mean…"

Hidetora nodded. "I believe that Momo is innocent."

"Oh! Well that is good. That is real good, Grandfather!" It was like the sun broke through the clouds. Hiroshi embraced his grandfather. "But…then, oh, I have to talk to her! I'm such a fool, Grandfather, I am! I have to find Momo, have you seen her?"

"Boy!" Hidetora called after the running lad. "It's dark, are you daft? Wait until tomorrow!" But Hiroshi was already long gone. Cursing and shaking his head at the exuberance of youth, Hidetora stepped out from the alley. True, Momo wasn't the same as that other girl but she wasn't what she seemed either. There was something wrong with this whole situation, and Hidetora found himself worried, both for his grandson and for the fate of this small village that seemed to be at the edge of some invisible storm.

*

The sentry posted at Kusama's gate shivered in the chill air of the dawn. He shifted his grip on his spear and silently thanked the sun god for once again banishing the night. He was cold and weary from another uneventful shift in this backwater village. Most of his fellow soldiers were up north, in Okayama City where the people were preparing for an attack from Nobunaga's forces any day now. Only a handful was garrisoned here, mostly boys unblooded in war. This particular sentry had never seen bloodshed himself, let alone any of the terrible othermen that were rumored to serve the demon lord.

Thus it was with the greatest courage that he stood his ground as the red tengu misted out of the early morning fog. The creature was large and muscular, every vein and tendon standing clearly out in the wan light. He had a vicious grin on his face and his beady eyes flickered over the guard. Trembling, the man raised his spear.

"Halt!" he squeaked, his voice cracking high.

"Good morning, friend," the tengu said in what almost sounded like an amicable growl. "I've come seeking refuge. Have you any space in this humble village?" The guard fumbled for words and finally stammered a command to wait. Saima watched the man scramble through the gates and sat patiently on the soft, muddy ground.

VIII. To Maruyama Mountain

Kei awoke in an unfamiliar place with unfamiliar creatures nestled beside her. She yawned and stretched before padding over to the saucer of honey left by the door. The other cats had already licked it clean and the neko grumpily peered at their sleeping forms. *Greedy little bastards,* she thought. They had fought over the fish that the old innkeeper had tossed them the night before, and apparently eaten everything else while Kei slumbered on. Still, it amused her to return to the inn and get fed by the very same woman who had earlier thrown her out.

But Momo hadn't yet returned and that worried her. She had hoped that the kitsune would be back in the room, but it was rented out to an unfamiliar man and his wife. Still unsettled by her friend's absence, Kei left the sleeping cats and went down to the kitchen where a serving girl was heating up a bowl of rice porridge. The neko meowed and the girl smiled and set down a dollop for her. After Kei had breakfasted she resolved to search the village for Momo. She wanted to apologize for breaking form and then get away from this place. Kusama village was proving to be far more trouble than it was worth!

Her cat form let her easily pass by the innkeeper, who was already up and sweeping the floor. The old lady smiled indulgently at Kei who cheekily stared back at the woman. "Old bitch!" she wanted to say, but that would certainly be a mistake. Instead she meowed again and slipped outside.

Soldiers were everywhere, rugged men who clutched their weapons and rushed about. Kei watched them go, bemused by the flurry of activity. She followed a trio and stared in shock as they reached the town square. A tengu sat there, surrounded by more than two-dozen men. Spears were pointed directly at the mountain goblin's chest, but he seemed unconcerned.

"I've come here to pray," the tengu said firmly. "I have no quarrel with humans, or with anyone for that matter. I am but a simple creature of the gods, come to pay homage to Lord Sano. I have journeyed far and I am weary. Is there no hospitality in these parts?"

"We are a peaceful people," an old man responded. He was short and barrel-chested, with thick, muscular forearms. "If you are what you say you are, then you are welcome."

"Foolish," a nearby soldier whispered to his companion. Kei strained her ears to listen. "Goblins serve Nobunaga, don't these peasants know that?"

"We can't act without our captain's orders," the other man said. "We must keep watch."

"Well, I'm sick of playing wet nurse to these ignorant peasants," the first man sneered. "Let's kill it and be done already."

"I will stay until tomorrow and then leave," the tengu was saying. He stood as the soldiers drew back and bristled their spears at him. "You need not fear me, good humans. I understand your concerns but I'm not going to harm any of you. I swear on all my gods and yours."

"Good enough," the old man said. He raised his voice. "I will not allow this creature to be harmed! Let him continue his pilgrimage in peace!" The crowd seemed to settle at that, though the soldiers remained. A captain pulled the old man aside and began arguing with him, in tones that Kei could not hear. The tengu merely sat back down like a stubborn mule and turned his back to the spears. He lowered his head and prayed in a low, earnest voice as he withdrew a blank scroll and began scribbling on it.

Kei stared at the tengu, intrigued by this sudden turn of events. She always liked tengu, who were a fun, jolly breed. Two of them were Penken's friends and she wondered if this particular one knew Penken as well. If so, perhaps he could provide them safe passage back to Kyoto! Kei navigated her way through the humans and climbed up onto a thatched roof. She sat and waited, tail flickering in anticipation of an opportunity.

*

Momo's dreams were feverish, rife with images that played over each other in rapid succession. She dreamt that she was a worm, boiling and screaming in hot water as her silk unraveled around her. She dreamt she was at the circus with Taku, hoisted on her big brother's shoulders. Only this circus was bathed in blood that ran down the streets in red streams. Momo cried to Taku of the danger but her brother babbled on, oblivious. Then the circus tents and people sank into the ground and the sky turned a deep yellow as the tinny music warbled into a deep, ominous buzz. A woman's laughter suddenly echoed, high and cruel. Momo hurtled through the air toward its source and found the woman waiting for her, irises burning bright and orange. The woman crooked a finger and hairless men with no teeth appeared out of nowhere and pushed Momo forward.

The dream broke apart but was followed by another one. Banken swung a net onto her and barely missed, but Aiken was waiting behind him with her own net. Unconcerned, Hiroshi sat off to one side with a bucket of fish. As Momo struggled against the tengu, Hiroshi took a fish out and scaled it casually with a knife. "Momo," he said in a calm voice as she screamed for help, "You've ruined the Obon, my family's reputation, and most of all, my heart. Do you hear me Momo? Momo? Momo? Momo?"

Momo awoke alongside the riverbank, nestled under the head of Lord Sano. The morning was unseasonably cool, a hint of autumn right around the corner. Momo stared gloomily at the mud, wishing she could just turn into an insect and burrow deep into oblivion forever. "I'm halfway between here and nowhere," she whispered to herself. "And I'm so tired of it." Her headache from the day before had not subsided and she could feel the pounding tempo increase alarmingly fast. It would be a bad day.

"Momo?" The kitsune started as she realized the last remnants of her dream were not a dream after all. "Momo, where are you?"

Hiroshi's earnest voice surged new life into the small kitsune. She scrambled out from underneath Lord Sano's rock and quickly shifted into her human form. The dress had just settled over her body when Hiroshi stepped out from the trees. "Momo!"

"Hiroshi!" Momo ran forward and hugged him fiercely. Hiroshi hugged back and for a moment, the two friends just held each other. Finally Momo broke free. "I thought you were mad at me!"

"I was, Momo, I was. I'm so sorry." Hiroshi looked sheepish, his boyish face reluctant to look at her. "A girl was seducing the men at the inn and people said it was you. I assumed too quickly. I'm sorry."

"What?" Momo punched Hiroshi on the arm. "You think I would do such a thing? Hiroshi-san!"

Hiroshi shrugged. "I don't know."

"Boys can be stupid, can't they?" Momo said. Despite her words, she found her headache suddenly gone. "Well, I guess I can forgive you now."

"Thank you Momo," Hiroshi said with an embarrassed grin. "Everyone knows it wasn't you, so you can come back to the village. Will you come?" He extended his hand. Momo hesitatingly grasped it.

"I suppose for awhile. But I must go soon, Hiroshi. I can't stay long." She had already guessed who the other girl was. *Kei, you halfwit,* she thought furiously. She would have to search the alleys and the houses of every villager to find the little neko.

"We will talk about that," Hiroshi said. She could sense his disappointment but didn't know what to say. They should have left Kusama days ago. Dallying with this boy had only given her pursuers time to catch up to her. Momo wanted to reach out and grab him, hug him tenderly and tell him the truth. Tell him what she was, what Kei was, why they were running, everything. But that could never happen.

"Okay," she finally responded. She wasn't sure what that meant. Could she truly stay here, where this boy accepted her so easily? Could she live in Kusama village? Somehow, the thought seemed both exhilarating and terrifying at the same time.

*

The chant was actually a sea ditty that an old sailor had once taught him. The sailor was a tengu as well, one who had fled his life of servitude to roam the seas as free as a wind god. At times, Saima still envied that tengu. Yet he was not one to toss away his duties so casually.

He could feel the spears hover around him as he wrote. It would only be a matter of time before the soldiers disobeyed the villagers and struck him down. Some would call it madness to so openly confront the humans but Saima was never one to disregard madness. The greatest achievements were accomplished by the most daring souls, and only those who failed who were labeled "mad." As for those who succeeded…

He finished etching the tiny letters onto the scroll and stretched, letting the sun play across his wings. He knew the effect that had on humans, who distrusted that which had anything more than two arms and two legs. He flapped them mightily and tested their strength. When it was time, he would be ready.

"I think I will walk," he casually said to no one in particular. He strode past the circle of soldiers, who broke apart as he stepped through them. Even though he was considered short by some, he still towered over these insignificant creatures by a good margin. The men closed rank behind him and followed as he made his way down the village. Saima critically eyed the buildings, noting how low the roofs were. This village was not adequately prepared for an attack from humans, let alone tengu who could easily fly from roof to roof and set the dry straw on fire. He would have to think on that.

The kitsune was no doubt long gone, but the neko was different; she would not flee this village so readily. Saima kept an even pace as he casually walked through the village, waving at peasants who scattered as he approached. He had no interest in their kind. It was the ones who did not scatter that interested him.

He saw the girl leaning casually against a large, two-story building. She wore a purple dress that seemed a bit too new and a bit too fine for these parts. She stared cheekily up at the tengu with none of the fear or uncertainty that humans typically exhibited. As Saima neared her, he could see that her eyes flickered green.

"Good morning, young girl," he said in a low voice. The girl grinned broadly.

"Good morning, tengu."

Saima tapped one thick finger against the building, making a thudding noise. "Would this be where you humans serve breakfast?" The girl giggled, one hand over her mouth. The soldiers had fanned out again, blocking any opportunities to escape. It didn't matter anymore. "You see, I'm supposed to meet some friends here."

The girl looked up at him, her irises sparkling emeralds. "What friends? I might know who they are."

"Oh, I think so, young girl. I think you know them well."

Saima stepped forward and smashed his elbow against the crown of the girl's head. She crumpled into a heap as her form writhed and reverted back into its natural state. The men shouted and their sergeant started barking orders. Without looking back, Saima unhitched his whip from his belt and struck at the sergeant, wrapping the fine tip around his neck. The man's words were cut off as he staggered against the taut whip, choking and fumbling for his sword. Saima jerked his arm back and in one fluid motion, the blade at the end of the whip drew against the sergeant's neck. He fell gurgling in a spray of blood.

Somewhere, a woman screamed. The soldiers only stood in shock for a moment, but it was a moment too long. Saima cradled the neko's quivering body against his chest and flapped his wings, giant beats that made audible thumps through the air. He dropped the tiny scroll at his feet as he effortlessly soared above the gaping humans, quickly flying beyond any bowman's range. He bounded once off a thatched roof, collapsing it as he landed, and then was up and over the gates of Kusama village. "Too easy," he said triumphantly to the unconscious form of the neko as he flew towards his brother's camp. "It's all just too easy."

*

Not again, Momo thought, breaking her grip from Hiroshi. *Not again.* The crying and the commotion echoed the violence that had trailed Momo wherever she seemed to go and she could only stare straight ahead as Hiroshi took off running. "Who is it this time?" she whispered out loud as she ran through the village, past the screaming children and the soldiers. "Who suffers now?"

She had her answer at the inn. Hiroshi's grandfather waited for her, his features grave and as hard as stone. He handed a scroll to her.

"Read it," he said. "I will not lie and pretend I haven't."

Hands trembling, Momo unfurled the scroll and stared at the crudely written characters. It took a moment for her brain to process what was written before her and when she did, her heart went cold.

"We have the neko. Come find us on the summit of Maruyama Mountain. Banken and Aiken." She crumpled the scroll in her hands and dropped it at her feet. Hidetora frowned at her.

"A man died today. I don't know what you are or what you have done, but you must leave."

Momo looked evenly at the old man. He was completely justified in banishing her. "I will."

Hidetora nodded. "Go in peace then, but do not ever return. You bring an ill wind with you, girl."

The old man was correct in every way and Momo bowed low to him in respect. "Thank you for your hospitality, sir. I will do as you wish," she said as formally as she could. Then she turned without a backward glance – Maruyama Mountain would be at least a two days' walk from the village. If she shifted, she could make it in half that time.

She could feel the villagers' stares as she walked and she dared any of them to speak up. Her eyes blurred, but not with tears. Instead, a strange yellow light pulsed in from the edges of her vision. She could hardly contain her true form and feared that she might suddenly shift in front of everyone. She hungered desperately for her fox body and she could already taste the exhilaration it would bring when she darted straight for the tengu and found their thick, meaty throats with her teeth.

"Kei, I will find you," she whispered, barely containing her rage. She cleared the last edge of civilization and stared at the forest ahead of her. Her senses were peaked and alert, ready for what was to come. She could smell the fresh moss on the riverbank and she could feel the gentle breeze coming from the mountain, still tinged with a hint of ice. She would follow that breeze straight up Maruyama Mountain. Momo tensed as her body started to shift.

"Momo!" Momo uttered a curse and hastily reverted. The yellow light bayed as it was stuffed back, sending waves of pain through her head. Hiroshi came stumbling out of the village. "Momo, wait!"

"Hiroshi," she said, grimacing in pain. "Turn back. This isn't your concern."

"It is," he said firmly. Momo turned around and saw that he had two packs with him. He tossed one to Momo. As she caught it, she heard the slosh of water. "Maruyama Mountain is a short hike. I've gone further than that with my friends when we went camping. I'm accompanying you there, Momo-san."

Momo looked over the boy. "Don't be a fool, Hiroshi. Don't you know what tengu are?" When Hiroshi didn't answer right away, she stepped forward. Her headache gave her a vicious edge to her voice. "They are treacherous demons, gigantic winged goblins that can lift a man high in the air and drop him to his death. If, that is, they don't decide to crush his skull or slice his neck first. Tengu are dangerous, Hiroshi. Stay away from me and from all of this."

"So you think you can fight one?" Hiroshi snorted. "One girl against two tengu? I find that notion somewhat strange."

"They want me, Hiroshi. They just want me, not my friend. If I offer myself to them, they will let her go."

Hiroshi looked over her. He could see her eyes were somewhere far away, that the whites had a sickly, yellow hue to them. "Momo, I know your friend is no ordinary creature. And...I know you're no ordinary girl. But let me come with you, at least to the base of the mountain. I know places where you can stay, people who may be able to help you. At the very least, we can come up with some ideas on the way." *Come back here, Momo,* he wanted to say. *Don't leave me just yet.*

Momo turned her head so he wouldn't see her wiping the tears that suddenly sprang forth, unexpectedly and unwelcomed. "I'm not worth it, Hiroshi," she said after a minute.

Hiroshi stepped forward. "Let me decide that. Besides, who said I'm going with you? I might just be off to Maruyama Temple to see the priest and ran into you by sheer coincidence. I hear he serves wonderful dumplings to weary travelers!" He grinned cheekily.

Go away, Momo wanted to say, should have said. But she couldn't force the words out. "Dumplings sound good," she quietly said, inwardly cringing at her decision, knowing how foolish it was. "You can come with me, at least to the base. But know this, Hiroshi...this is dangerous. And if something should happen to you..." She paused, feeling the words too painful to speak. "People get hurt around me. They do," she finally finished in a small voice. *They die,* she wanted to say, but the words froze in her throat.

Hiroshi grabbed her hand and gave it a brief squeeze. "Well, my mom always said I was a lucky boy. Maybe my good luck will cancel your bad luck. Isn't that worth trying?"

Momo's vision cleared as the last traces of the yellow rage dissipated. Despite herself, she managed a small laugh. "Hiroshi-chan, I really hope you're right about that."

Hiroshi grinned. "Me too. Anyway, I was getting a bit cramped in that village. Thought I might stretch my legs a bit. And…" he reached into his pack and withdrew a hatchet. Though used to cut wood, the blade looked exceptionally sharp. Momo frowned. "Hiroshi!"

"Just a precaution," he said. He shouldered his bag, feeling more a warrior than ever. "Come then Momo, let's go before my grandfather finds out about this. We still have more than half the day's light with us!"

Momo nodded and they started to walk. For a moment the trees beckoned her to cast her human skin aside and dart for the confines of the forest, but she shook that hunger off, for now at least. The tengu would wait, whether it took her one day or two to reach them. Better to go as a human, with words and reason, then to charge at them like some mindless beast. Despite their treachery, Momo still believed that Aiken at least would trade

Kei over without harming anyone. She would surrender to them, and let the gods decide what fate awaited her in Kyoto. No more running, and no more fighting. She would go in peace.

Side by side, the two companions winded their way through the forest as the summer heat gave its last nod before the coming cold.

Part III
Vendetta

1. The Hunt Resumes

    Tsukimi scaled the large oak tree and gingerly tested her footing on the thickest branch she could find. To her relief, tbe branch held firm. This vantage provided a good view of the forest around her, but she wouldn't be relying on her eyes just yet. She closed them and pressed one ear carefully against the solid trunk, gathered her chi.

    It only took a few minutes before the sounds around her – the rustling trees, the twittering birds, the autumn breeze – faded into silence. She focused her senses through the trunk, letting them trickle down the tree and across the ground. First, there was only the steady pulse of the tree itself, slowly thrumming with its own life. Then, the tiny vibrations of squirrels and hares darting through the brush. She could pinpoint their exact location around the base of the tree as she took in the sounds of the earth. Then…

    Yes, there it was. A heavier vibration, steady and careful. To a normal ear the footsteps would have been undetectable, but

Tsukimi had been trained in the arts of the Yan for well over a decade. She listened to the light footfalls until the man sprang up and found purchase on his own tree branch. Her hunter was not unskilled.

She withdrew two throwing knives and balanced one in her hand. The wind stirred and rustled the leaves about her, warning her of what was coming. Like lightening, two shuriken thudded into the tree by her ear, one pinching off a lock of hair as it passed. Tsukimi ducked around the tree and dropped to the mossy ground. She still did not know the man's location, but the shurikens' direction was obvious enough. He had struck too soon, blindly, like an overeager bat.

Tsukimi ran across the ground and grabbed an overhanging branch. She let her momentum carry her up as she flipped over and landed firmly on another tree. The branch swayed precariously but held her weight and she waited for a second to let it settle. Then she deftly climbed to the very top and peered out of the canopy of leaves. There he was.

A black figure darted swiftly from the smaller tree. Tsukimi aimed and threw her first knife. It hit its target across the chest but it was not a mortal blow; the man staggered yet maintained pace as he dove through the brush. Tsukimi jumped back onto the ground and drew her sword. The hunted was now the hunter. She pursued him, easily following the wounded man's trail. The droplets of blood soon ended but she could hear his labored breathing, hot and ragged. Abruptly the breathing stopped and Tsukimi skidded to a halt.

He came from above, as the Yan were trained to do. His blade was in an overhead position, a slash designed to perforate a man's skull. She met his sword with hers and sparks sizzled at the impact. The man skidded back and for a moment the two studied each other. The assassin's face was shrouded completely in black, his eyes all but invisible underneath the tabi cloth. A dark spot was spreading across his shoulder and blood dripped freely from the wound. He readied his sword in a traditional Yan stance and signaled to her.

"I found you first, traitor."

"So you'll be the first to die," Tsukimi responded, deftly maneuvering her fingers while balancing her sword between them. She gripped her weapon with two hands, a clear indication that she did not want to talk. The man grunted in understanding and charged. Of course, the trick was a familiar one to Tsukimi, who had used it more than once herself. The body double shimmered as it swung harmlessly at Tsukimi while the real form lurked behind, an invisible yet deadly shadow. Tsukimi sent her own double forward to meet them while she strategically retreated a few paces. As expected, the assassin reappeared behind Tsukimi's double and struck. Her copy

vanished in a puff of air.

Tsukimi threw a knife but the man sensed it and rolled out of the way. Without pause, he sprang, and she only just brought her sword up in time. Though she could tell he was no master swordsman, she had clearly underestimated his determination! She blocked two more blows before sweeping a low one of her own that forced the man to leap high. *Too high,* she thought as she jumped up to follow him. Her leap was more calculated than his, and she managed to score a hit against his thigh as they landed. He then tried to fake a left but she followed and slashed again, this time splitting his face wide open. The man unleashed a howl of pain and fell to his knees as blood poured over his eyes.

"A waste," Tsukimi murmured. To his credit, the man did not flinch as she brought her sword up. One quick blow and it was over. She studied the corpse and pulled off the mask – no one she was familiar with, thank the Buddha. The Yan had few friendships within its own tribe but Tsukimi had acquaintances, battle partners she would hate to have to turn on. Of course, they would all turn on her now.

Traitor. Any who escaped the Yan tribe were ruthlessly hunted down and murdered. Tsukimi herself had once taken part in such a hunt, chasing down a defector who had fled for the north. She did not care about any of that now. Makoto was dead and there would be more blood to shed before she was ready to give up her own life. Sheathing her sword, Tsukimi looked to the east, where she had last tracked the tengu. It was time to resume the hunt.

*

Kei awoke to flickering green demons. She briefly cowered from their shimmering forms as they danced on the massive cavern walls until she remembered where she was. Groggy, she tested the bruise on her head. It still ached, a constant reminder of her carelessness. Stupid girl! What would Momo think of her now, chained up like this?

The water bowl had been refilled and the neko eagerly lapped it up. A shackle around her hind leg kept her in her cat form but she preferred being in it anyway. Somehow, the idea of facing Banken and Aiken as a human was too painful – a real reminder of what had happened to her. The tengu had once been her friends! Why were they treating her like this?

"Penken," she whispered in a soft voice. She thought of the cheerful tanuki, his kind face and gentle words. He always had a moment to spare for Kei, his favorite of the girls. He wouldn't have let the tengu treat her like this! Was he dead, killed by the ninjas like the rest of the troupe? Was he watching over her right now like some a chubby spirit?

Voices argued in the other cavern, low and inaudible. Banken and Aiken were fighting again, as they had been ever since Kei first woke up. Banken had come to her twice, both times trying to start a conversation, but the female tengu had not yet paid her a visit. Obviously Aiken was too angry to see her now.

"...disastrous!" Aiken's final word echoed through the cave. Kei heard her storm outside, with Banken's footsteps following behind. Then there was quiet, with only the green lantern light and its shadows keeping Kei company. She settled onto her paws.

A sound. Kei was alert again, every inch of her body tensing up. Was it Banken and Aiken, returning to the cave? No. It could only be…Kei started to tremble. A torch appeared first, a slender green flame that accentuated the shadows, stretching them into giant, twisted forms. Then a new shadow, a tengu's shadow that paused by the entrance.

She had not been introduced to her third captor, the one they called Saima and she never hoped to see him again. He was different than the others, colder somehow, and far more cruel. She did not like the way that he stared at her with his beady little eyes. Banken's eyes were similar, but they looked comical, like some goofy clown that had escaped the circus. On Saima…they were so small, so sinister. She watched as he set his torch down and squatted before her.

"Alone again," he said after a minute. His voice was smooth, almost human. It carried none of the gravel of the other tengus. "How're you doing?"

Kei turned her head away. For all she cared, he could think of her as a simple cat.

"Not talking, are we?" Saima said. "Well, we'll see how long you can keep that up."

Kei had closed her eyes but she popped them wide open as she felt Saima's hand on her paw. "So small and fragile," he said quietly. "How do you change it? Show me."

"I'll show you," Kei snapped, unable to maintain her silence. "I'll turn it into a claw and rip your ugly nose right off!"

"I'd like to see that," Saima responded evenly. "I confess, I *am* curious about the magic that binds your form together. How do you manipulate it?"

Kei put her head back down so that she didn't have to give this creature the dignity of a response. For a moment Saima's hand remained rested on her paw, and then after an almost amicable pat he stood. "I'll find out," he gently said. "We will have plenty of time to spend together, Kei-chan."

The neko closed her eyes and waited until the tengu had left. Then she let the tears come. "Oh Penken," she whimpered in a scared, small voice. "What's to become of me?"

*

"What is to become of us?" Hiroshi asked, his expression

aghast. Momo reached up and entwined her hands in his. She had seen it before, the memory all too fresh in her head. She wished her mind would shut off the images but instead, like some cruel jest of the gods, they replayed right before her eyes. Bodies, at least half a dozen, floated down the Sano River. Their flesh was bloated and white but still fresh, and they did not carry the stink of rot just yet. It was curious how bloodless their wounds were, washed clean by the running water.

"This isn't good," Hiroshi finally said. Momo could only nod. The river snaked east, where the war was escalating. For bodies to wash this far downriver could only mean…

"You should go back," Momo said firmly. "Your village might be in danger."

Hiroshi shook his head. "No, we must find your friend first. We'll go back after we rescue her."

There'll be no rescue. Momo had no intention of risking Hiroshi's life. She would plead for Kei and give herself over to the tengu. It was a simple plan, and this boy was risking everything with his bravado. She had to do something about him, but she didn't know what just yet. "Hiroshi-chan," she said gently. "Your grandfather is probably worried about you."

Hiroshi turned and faced her. He could feel the heat emanating from her body, and her hand felt cool in his sweaty one. How could she understand his need to do this? How could any girl? He impulsively stroked her cheek, and then started walking before she could react to it. "The path to Maruyama temple moves away from the river. We won't find any more bodies." His voice came out a bit deeper than he had intended it to be but he was strangely happy about that.

Momo shook her head and watched her friend. The axe he used to hack out the trail looked like a child's toy. She had seen real weapons, the giant axes of the tengu and the vicious, cruel swords of the Yan. The bodies in the river reminded her of how dangerous the outside world was. Perhaps even just a month ago she would have found Hiroshi's attitude charming, maybe exciting. Now she knew better, and she could only pray that he would learn the truth quickly and not end up like those bobbing and drifting down the river.

*

The trail had grown cool but was not yet cold. Tengu left notoriously large campfires behind, a testimony to their love of heat. It only took one charred pit to point Tsukimi in the proper direction.

"Maruyama Mountain," she whispered to herself. It was so obvious – hot springs and high places. To tengu, it would be the perfect sanctuary. To a Yan such as herself, such a mountain was only a minor inconvenience. Tsukimi permitted herself to make camp early that night. Now that the quarry was in sight, it was time to rest and wait. Her time would come.

11. A Night in the Temple

They spent the rest of the day in awkward silence. Their spirits had been quashed by the sudden appearance of the bodies, and by Hiroshi's growing affront at Momo's repeated insistence that he turn back. For her part, the kitsune began to resent his blind rashness. How did he expect to battle two gigantic tengu? She recalled when Banken slew one Yan and drove off another. The mountain goblins were fierce warriors and if the tengu had been with the troupe when the Yan had attacked again, she might still be on her way to Kyoto. Fighting them was sheer lunacy.

She sincerely regretted letting him come with her. It was only in a moment of weakness that she allowed him to slip past her defenses. Stupid boy with his stupid kiss! How could have she let him come? And yet, how could she have turned him away? The boy didn't understand the gravity of the situation, not truly. He never saw the ninja flashing in and out of existence, slicing helpless victims apart in great spurts of blood.

He never saw the tengu with their long weapons and cruel faces. He was just a silly village boy, one who dared kiss her when she had least expected anything of the sort. What would be the cost of all this?

Hiroshi charged ahead, swinging his axe occasionally to drive off a vine or branch that had grown across the trail. In truth, the boy felt foolish leading this girl toward the temple. He didn't know what he wanted to do, except he didn't want to let Momo go on without him. The priest at the temple was a kind man and he always offered Hiroshi advice when he had visited in the past. Perhaps he would think of something.

They were relieved when the forest finally gave way to a massive clearing. Nestled in the center was a bright, red temple sitting behind by a carved, wooden gate. A small green garden adorned with stone lanterns was off to one side, where a clean-shaven man dutifully watered the flowers. Beyond the temple, looming like some giant beast, was Maruyama Mountain. The path was well-tended, stone gravel snaking around the temple and up towards the mountain. The priest looked up, saw Hiroshi and gave a friendly wave.

"Hiroshi-kun! I had not expected to see you so soon after Obon. And who is this friend of yours?" The man was younger than Momo had expected, with a friendly round face. His head was bald and shone with sweat in the dimming light, and he was dressed in bright orange robes. "I am Hasegawa, a humble servant of Oho-Yama and groundskeeper of this temple. We don't often get strangers here." He bowed low before Momo. She took a liking to him immediately.

"I am Momo Takamoto," she said with a bow. "It is an honor to meet you, sir."

"The honor's mine!" the man replied with a wink. "Come in and wash up. Hiroshi often comes by with his rapscallion friends, but I think this is the first time that he's brought a real lady with him. Ah, Hiroshi-kun! Blushing as always! Well, come on then." He bustled up the stairs, leaving the two behind. Momo smiled at Hiroshi's burning face, their previous awkwardness momentarily forgotten.

"He *is* friendly, isn't he?"

Hiroshi nodded. "He grew up in Kusama. He's not much older than us but he took on the duties of priest when the previous one died. If we're lucky," he added in a conspiring whisper, "he'll slip us some sake with dinner."

Momo glared at his back. So much danger just around the corner and here he was, talking about sake? She looked over to the mountain, so close now. She strained to see the summit, where the tengu waited, and for a moment considered shifting into her fox form and running up the path. But then Hiroshi called her name and she turned back to the temple, reluctant to leave her friend behind just yet.

*

Steam rose from the springs of Maruyama Mountain and to Banken, it seemed that the hell itself erupted from the earth; a suitable atmosphere for Aiken's mood. He watched her now out of the corner of his eye as she bathed in the hot waters, completely ignoring his presence. Her contempt was palatable and it shamed Banken more than he was willing to admit. How he longed for the days before the meddling humans arrived, when he and his tribe would dally in the cliffs, hunting, drinking, and dancing while the sun and moon shone above! Those days seemed so remote from their current predicament; hiding away like bandits, threatening an innocent little girl! Banken felt sick to his stomach.

He couldn't bring himself to admit that he was frightened of Nobunaga, more frightened than of any other human he had met in all his years. Most tengu regarded humans as irrelevent, curious and amusing at times but far removed from tengu affairs. But the warlord had accomplished something no human had in centuries, uniting the various human tribes under one banner. What was once the amusing spectacle of squabbling humans had merged into a real danger, one that Lady Jinzo and the other elders did not miss. They had tasked Banken to serve as one of the representatives of the Akasaka tribe sent to appease the human lord while the tengu elders planned their next move.

But Aiken did not care for the politics that simmered just below the surface of everything they did. His mate lived a life of honor and dignity and was not suited for this sort of work. She should never have come with him on this mission. How could he look her in the eye when this was all over?

Saima emerged from his cave, languidly stretching his wings. Banken looked cautiously at his brother. Here was one who walked a different path; a tengu who was not afraid to get his hands dirty. Banken had desperately hoped that Saima had changed for the better in his exile, but he could easily see that nothing was different — if anything, Saima seemed more convinced of his mad ideations than ever. He didn't know what he would do about his brother once this kitsune business was settled.

"She sleeps," Saima said casually. He leaned against the mountain wall with his arms folded.

"Is she well?" Banken asked.

"As well as can be expected. She cries occasionally and doesn't speak. If you ask me, I'd suspect that she was vexed with us." Saima grinned and Banken was again taken aback by his casual cruelty. Could his own blood truly be so hardhearted? Banken wanted to slap his brother, plead with him to feel some empathy for the little neko. But he knew all too well that his brother would rebuff his attempts.

"I don't want her hurt," he warned. "Remember that."

Saima shrugged. "Physically she's unharmed. Emotionally? I don't suspect you'll be invited to any neko parties soon."

Banken sighed in resignation and turned away, feeling even more miserable about this whole affair. The little cat girl was dear to Penken, and Banken had few hopes that his old friend would take the news kindly when he learned of what they had done. For a moment, the tengu regretted sending Penken away – if the tanuki were here, none of this would have happened. How did everything spiral so out of control? Once he thought his quest was noble, teeming with adventure and the great deeds that the elders had always predicted for him. Banken grabbed his spear.

"I'm going to hunt," he announced. He leapt off the edge of the cliff, away from the knowing eyes of his brother, the angry stares of his mate, and this whole damned mess. At least in the air he still felt clean.

Aiken stepped out of the springs as soon as her mate was away. She shot Saima a single look that dared him to say anything, but the other tengu ignored her. Her heart still ached from the last quarrel, in which words that might never been forgotten were said. She knew Banken's tendency to act brashly, blundering through something because he believed the ends would justify the means.

No more. She would put up with this no more. She stepped into the cave, which had been rearranged for their prisoner. Banken's and Aiken's pallets lay near the entrance, conspicuously far apart as they had been for the last few days. Saima's large bed was nestled in the middle. In the back there was a bed of straw and a chain that had been embedded into rock. Kei lay there, slumbering quietly. Aiken marveled at how easily the neko slept, even in these trying times. Gods knew she herself hadn't rested well in weeks.

She sat on her pallet and closed her eyes, letting the soft breathing of Kei lull her to sleep. It would be dark soon enough.

*

The priest served them rice porridge and barley tea and for a little while, Momo felt almost at peace. The interior of the temple was vastly more decorated than its humble outside suggested, with brilliant brass images of the mountain god and ornate lanterns that lined both ends of the walls. The wooden floors were remarkably clean, if uneven and pitted from age. Momo was strangely comforted by the creaking sounds the wood made as they walked across it, which the priest described as "nightingale songs," purposefully designed so to warn him of any intruders. "Of course," he had chuckled, "should any bandits come the best I can do is sneak out the rear entrance!"

"Why don't bandits come?" Momo asked.

The priest shrugged. "They fear desecrating the temple. Oho-Yama is an angry god, after all! Besides, his servant lives on the summit of this mountain and she has promised her protection to me." Hiroshi and Momo shared uncertain glances with each other. "*Servant?*" Hiroshi mouthed. Momo shrugged back.

"I grow yams in the back," the man continued happily. "There's a spring nearby that the elders of Kusama occasionally bathe in and I make a good living off of them. Overall, not a bad way to spend my days!"

"I suppose not," Momo said. The rice porridge was delicious and the pickles just the right texture. She felt guilty, imposing upon this man's hospitality, but the sound of his happy chatter and the beautiful decorations lulled her. Before she knew it, the sun had completely set.

"Please excuse me," the priest said as he collected their dishes. When the two were left alone, Hiroshi nudged her. "Aren't you glad I brought you here? He's a good man."

"He is," Momo said. "It's peaceful here. Who is this Oho-Yama that he keeps speaking of?"

"You don't know?" Hiroshi asked. "Oho-Yama is the

mountain god, the big brother of the sun god. There." He rose and pointed to a large looming statue of a human. The statue's eyes were painted dark red, absent of any pupils. In one hand he clutched a pair of pine branches. "He's a protector of humans."

Then he won't be able to help me, Momo thought. A bell tolled in the other room and Hiroshi rose. "Come, let's pray for your friend." Momo followed him into the main hall, where the priest was kneeling before another carving of Oho-Yama. Incense drifted, its smoke stinging Momo's eyes. The priest rubbed his prayer beads and chanted in a quiet voice. Hiroshi, obviously familiar with the ritual, joined him.

Momo hung back. She suddenly did not like this strange human god with his empty red eyes. There was something sinister about him and she felt unwelcome, a foreigner in the wrong place. The others seemed to take comfort in the prayers, but Momo yearned for the simple Shinto shrine that her father had kept by their house. She smiled when Hiroshi motioned her over but did not move.

Afterward the priest showed them to their chambers. Momo was discretely led to the women's side, a seldom-used room that smelled faintly of mold. After the others had retired, Momo unrolled her futon and lay back, staring at the crisscross beams on the paper ceiling. *How did it come to this?* She listened to the crickets and found comfort in their lullabies, a dim reminder of a time when everything did not seem so strange and uncertain.

*

Hiroshi waited until the priest was snoring. He stirred in his thin blanket, shivering. It was cold in this temple, colder than he had remembered. Just a ways away was a hot springs, bubbly and rich with sulfur. He wondered if Momo would be willing to go for a quick night swim, and then hurriedly banished the thought. This was no time to play around.

In truth, the trip had not gone the way he had hoped. He had imagined them traipsing through the forest, singing songs and laughing together, but of course that was just the ridiculous notion of a silly boy. Momo's friend was in danger; this mysterious other girl who had shown up unannounced and then seduced one of the soldiers. He wanted to ask Momo who she was but was afraid of intruding further. *It's presumptuous enough that I even came along.*

Momo seemed distracted, and when she did pay attention to him she seemed mostly irritable, like he was some unwelcome dog following along. Yet when he had first caught up to her, she had seemed so happy to see him! Clearly she wanted to him to come along, at least then. How confusing!

Irritated and restless, Hiroshi slipped out of the bed and stepped back into the prayer room. Oho-Yama loomed over him, an impressive deity if he had ever seen one. Along with

Lord Sano, Oho-Yama was the guardian of Kusama village, so Hiroshi turned to him for help.

"Great lord, please give me guidance," he whispered as he knelt before the statue. The ground was cold to the touch. "Show me the way I am supposed to go.

"I fear my heart may burst from love and yet there is nothing I can do about it! She does not return my affections, but I can see she does want my company. I want to prove my worth and help her in whatever she needs. Is that foolish, Lord? Please, Oho-Yama, tell me that what I am doing is right. Or if I am being foolish, give me a sign!"

A gust of wind rattled the temple and Hiroshi startled. He turned and saw that the entrance to the temple had been left slightly ajar. He nervously rose and shut the door – no wonder it had been so cold! Feeling embarrassed, Hiroshi bowed once more to the god. He then looked toward the room Momo was in.

The taste of her mouth was long gone but the memory of it lingered like honeyed candy. He had never kissed a girl before and he still did not know what possessed him to kiss her so many days ago. She was so frustrating! She had gently rebuffed him the next morning and yet now they shared glances that were growing longer and longer and holding hands more frequently. Hiroshi was not completely blind to the signs. Perhaps she was awake, waiting for him. "Life is short, Oho-Yama, and any day now I may ride to my death. Surely you would allow me to see if she is asleep?" He took the god's silence as assent.

The nightingale boards squeaked in protest as he tiptoed over to the women's chambers but the priest slumbered on, oblivious to the warnings. His heart pounding mightily, Hiroshi slid the wooden door open. He paused then, mouth dropping open.

Momo was awake, but she was hardly waiting for him. Instead, her head was in her hands and her skinny little shoulders shuddered in sobs. She looked so fragile and pale in the dim light, like the little spirit he first encountered during Obon. Hiroshi immediately went to her and put his arms around her. Momo clutched his shirt and cried.

"Hiroshi-chan," she whispered after a minute. "I'm…I'm so scared."

Hiroshi held her tighter. He had no words for her, but rocked her in silence, letting the sobs continue. After a few minutes they had stopped. As if in a dream, he gently cupped her chin in one hand and turned her face up. Her face was wet and her eyes red, but her mouth was open and ready. He leaned forward and kissed her tenderly. She kissed back and the two folded onto the bed.

They lay there for some time, just kissing and touching each other's faces. Abruptly, Momo broke it off and smiled at him.

"Thank you, Hiroshi-chan."

"Thank me? For what?"

"For staying by my side. Why do you like me so much?"

Hiroshi shrugged. "You're just easy to like, I guess."

Momo laughed, a light sound. "I think you are too. I guess that's why I'm so comfortable around you."

"It's not because I'm brave and strong?" Hiroshi asked. He meant the question in jest but the words had the opposite effect on Momo. Her face grew somber and her eyes fixated onto his. "Hiroshi," she gently said, stroking his cheek. "Stay with me tonight, all right? Just for a little while."

"I will," Hiroshi said. They kissed again, more passionately than before, but then Momo stopped them. She snuggled into his arms, almost as if she were a child, and closed her eyes. Hiroshi watched her for a minute, marveling how easily she fell asleep. He marveled at everything, how capricious the gods were, how randomly splendid and exciting these last few days had been! He felt lighter than the Sun God as he lay with this beautiful girl in his arms, the two of them on the verge of some great journey. Hiroshi felt like he would never fall asleep, but then he did, quickly and without warning.

He awoke to a cold draft. For a second Hiroshi was disoriented, but then he realized that the window was wide open. Stumbling and yawning in the dark, Hiroshi shut the blinds. It was only when he turned around and saw the empty bed did he realize that Momo was gone.

III. Lingering Shadow

The autumn breeze was a cool welcome to Kaaro and the others as they set up camp along the riverside. As kappa always did, they dug themselves deeply into the mud, down to where the pools sucked their flesh eagerly, allowing them to sink their weary bodies into the dankness. They had followed the river for nearly a week but pickings were slim – the humans on the coastal embankments had fled, warned of the kappa by the bodies that had floated on ahead.

A low horn sounded once, signaling the return of his men. At last! Daru and the others had finally come back from the northern rivers. Kaaro surged out of his mud bed and ungracefully waddled upright. He shook the last specks of mud off his shell as the other kappa rolled back over into sleep. Daru swam upstream with an agility that would surprise most humans. He surged onshore in one fluid motion, as graceful as a diving bird.

"We found no roads leading west," Daru said as he bobbed his head to Kaaro. "The city of Okayama stands strong, fortified with many humans. I don't see a way through." He snorted once, blowing water out of his nostrils. Kaaro sneered.

"Idiot! Okayama is garrisoned with over one thousand soldiers and at least ten thousand other humans. You really were thinking that the twenty of us would fight them? Tell me something I don't already know." They needed to quickly pillage and instill further fear into the locals, causing chaos that would aid Lord Nobunaga's armies when they finally marched. Idling away in the mud would not please Sharada, nor his pet oni.

"Lord," Daru said. "We did encounter someone who claims he would help us. Taja wanted to spill his guts but I stopped him. He wants to speak to you, Lord Kaaro."

"We take no human prisoners, Daru!" Kaaro snapped.

"Oh," Daru said after a moment, as if he had to think about it. "But this one isn't a human." Intrigued, Kaaro motioned Daru on and followed him down the river. Daru's party waited for them, arranged in a circle. In their center was a giant mountain tengu. Despite being surrounded by kappa scythes, the red goblin merely stood there and calmly looked Kaaro in the eye as he approached.

"Ah, Lord Kaaro," he said, bowing low. The creature's human-like manners made him seem somehow impudent to the kappa. "It is an honor to finally meet you. If you would be so kind to call off your men, I believe I can be of service to you." Kaaro didn't like this tengu's tone. He considered splitting the creature's skull right there, but finally decided against it. He waved the others aside.

"Who are you?" he asked.

The dark tengu bowed a second with a flourish. "I am Saima. I was peacefully fishing down the river when your men accosted me. Doubtless I was very distraught, but not when I heard about your mission."

Kaaro unhitched his scythe and pressed the blade against the tengu's neck. Saima was small for a goblin and Kaaro large for a kappa, so he only had to look slightly up into the creature's eyes. "What do you know of our mission?" he hissed.

The tengu finally seemed to understand his situation as his manner changed abruptly. "Nothing, Lord Kaaro, nothing. Only through conjecture have I guessed that you are skirmishing with and killing humans. Is it true then that Lord Nobunaga's war has begun?"

Kaaro snorted. "Killing humans is right. Killing any being that is pledged to the lord of these lands, actually. Tell me why I shouldn't slice your throat right now."

"I serve no human, Lord Kaaro," Saima said. "I serve othermen. And I think I can help you."

"The ugly bird man is useless," one kappa laughed. "Finish him!" Kaaro thought for a moment and sheathed his blade. "Explain yourself, but do it quickly."

Saima grinned. As he related the details of Kusama Village to the kappa lord, he couldn't help but reflect that fortune took him in odd directions. What was almost a catastrophe might prove to be something else entirely. When Kaaro's face lit up as Saima finished, the tengu knew that a moment of opportunity had arrived.

*

Kei realized that the trouble with sleeping all day was that at night she was restless. She lay on her side, breathing steadily as she watched the huge slumbering forms of the tengu across the cave. The goblins had finally snuffed out those accursed green lanterns stinking up the air, but Kei's cat eyes could easily discern their shapes in the thin moonlight. Banken and Aiken lay scattered on opposite ends of the entrance but Saima was noticeably absent from his bed. Kei hated them all. How cruel to keep her chained like some lowly beast! How long were they going to do this to her?

Again she tried constricting her form so that her foot could shift through the shackle, but being confined prevented her body from changing. Kei knew that henge were sensitive to the external environment; clothes were often a chore to shift through, which was why most preferred their illusionary garments, and so the small shackle on her paw was enough to keep her body stuck.

She flopped on her back, furious at everything. She should have run when Momo first disappeared in Kusama. In truth, she should have run a long time ago, back to Okayama where she could have plied herself and lived comfortably off the foolish humans. If only Momo had agreed to stay! She was a pretty girl – though not as pretty as Kei – and the two of them would have run the city, much as Kei did long ago. She thought of the food and clothing waiting for her in the big cities as she waited for sleep.

After a while she finally dozed and she dreamt she was by the ocean, a place she had only heard of. Seawater lapped serenely on her bare ankles, and Kimiko was working her needles. In the distance, Penken wobbled on two hind legs, comically drunk as always. Birds screeched at each other overhead.

The dream popped when she felt someone's presence. It could only be one of the tengu. Kei started to hiss until the creature put a giant hand over her mouth.

"Be silent, it's me." Aiken's gravelly voice was nearly inaudible. "Stay still." Kei craned her neck back and watched as Aiken gingerly snapped the chain from the rock. It cracked loudly and they froze until they could hear Banken's soft snores. "Forgive me, Kei. Know that Penken had nothing to do with this," Aiken whispered.

Kei nodded, her eyes wide. She hesitated for a moment, trying to think of a reply.

Then Banken's voice cut through the air. "Aiken, is that you? Has Saima returned?" His eyes were pinprick stars as he rolled to his feet.

"Get out! Go, Kei, go!" Aiken hissed. To emphasize her words, she shoved Kei on the rump. "Go now!"

"Ho, where are you going?" Banken bellowed. "Aiken, stop her! The neko's escaping!" He was already on two feet, agile as an eagle. Kei darted for the corner of the cave but Banken deftly sidestepped and grabbed at her tail. He barely missed, his fingers clutching at strands of fur. Kei jumped onto the desk, scattering books everywhere, and leapt out of the cave with a single bound.

She could hear Banken coming after her, his breath frantic and ragged. She stumbled on the ledge, claws vainly trying to find purchase on the smooth rock. Everything was so *steep!* Kei leapt down the cliff, skidding and spraying rocks everywhere, and felt her ankle twinge in pain. She landed on all fours, gasping heavily. Tears of frustration brimmed as she looked around. She had fallen to another ledge, a narrow outcropping that extended out into nothingness. There was nowhere else she could go.

Banken's heavy form landed in front of her, a net in one hand. "Little neko," he rumbled, "I don't want to hurt you."

"Then let me go!" Kei shot back. Banken shook his head.

"This pains me, I swear to all the gods. But it must be done." He raised his arm, net ready. Yet as he aimed, a knife suddenly sprouted out of his elbow. The weapon looked like a tiny needle in his massive, muscled arm, yet Banken bellowed in sharp pain. He dropped the net and spun around.

Kei could barely make out the black clad form that had materialized behind the tengu. Like a wave, the figure surged forward and scored two strikes on Banken's abdomen. Banken roared in response and swung at the figure, who slid between his legs. Up close, Kei recognized the outfit of the Yan ninja. Terror washed through her body.

The Yan vanished as Banken turned and punched down into the rock. A spray of rubble erupted from the ground and for a moment the ledge swung, as if it might dislodge from the face of the mountain. Kei saw two more knives fly, both aimed at Banken's face, but he had already taken out a metal fan with his other hand and he easily deflected them.

All went silent for a moment. Banken circled around uncertainly, his chest heaving. The two shallow gashes on his side shone wetly. His eyes rolled like a mad dog's and sweat dripped from his body, as thick as raindrops. She saw the shadow before Banken did as it abruptly extracted itself from a mass of boulders. "Behind you!" Kei managed to shriek. Banken whirled about and sliced his fan horizontally. Whatever was behind him ducked, and a flash of green fire exploded against Banken's stomach. He howled in agony, the cry echoing like thunder.

"Banken!" Aiken thudded onto the ground. She had her massive axe in one hand and she expertly thrust it past Banken's side. It gave them some time, and she grabbed Banken's shoulder, shoving him back. "Retreat!"

Banken shook his head and stood firm. For a moment, the two tengu were side by side, bodies heaving in unison as they scoured the area for the attacker. "I think it left," Aiken finally said after a minute. Banken grunted in response. "We have no time," Aiken continued. "We must flee. Can you fly?" Banken nodded. Hoisting her mate onto her shoulder, the two tengu bounded off the ledge, leaving Kei behind. She lay there, paralyzed with fear, when Aiken unexpectedly returned. The female tengu picked up the shivering neko and looked her in the eyes.

"I'm so sorry," she said, pupils as cold as iron. Then she leaned forward, and flung Kei off the ledge.

*

The scent of blood was in the air. Or it would be soon, of that Penken was certain. The human city of Okayama was in a flurry as soldiers patrolled the streets, samurai strutted down with the airs that only their pathetic, rotten kind could possibly muster, and prostitutes eagerly plied their trade to all. There was a frenetic energy to these people, as if they knew death was just a day or two away and they needed to live life as quickly as possible.

Penken had seen it all before: humans, with their mucking about, always so quick to kill each other off. They could burn in the hells for all he cared. Bleary-eyed and well into his fifth glass of sake, Penken raised a toast to himself and drained his cup. The alcohol sapped the last of his memories away as he sat there, numb to the world.

The past few weeks had been bad. First there was the ambush on the mountain roads. Then an errant pursuit for the kitsune, culminating in his realization that he was just too fat to keep up with the others. The tengu had been kind about it, but Penken was horrendously shamed by his ineptitude. He had arranged a caravan to take him back to Kyoto, but found he could not bear to return there like a beaten dog. Lord Sharada had been explicit in his instructions, and failure did not seem like a good thing. Instead, Penken slipped away to Okayama, the nearest city that had both taverns and enough people to hide him forever.

He tried to remember the names of the dead and found that he couldn't. Did that happen with age? Did the dead slip away from you one by one until you were left alone on the shore, waiting for your turn? He could only remember the girls. Kimiko, Kei. Momo. Her name stung worse than the others. They had taken her under false pretenses and Penken had let her down. Just another girl in a long line who Penken had disappointed.

"Another round," Penken said. The bartender, a homely old lady, clucked her tongue disapprovingly as she took his glass. "You are number seven hundred and twelve!" Penken laughed as he pointed at her. "My seven hundred and twelfth disappointment! He nearly rolled off the stool as he chortled, wondering where that number came from.

"Some tea, please." The soft feminine voice perked up Penken's ears. He looked over and saw a slim, tall woman, as willowy as a tree branch. She had no bust to speak of, but her skin was an exotic mocha color that hinted of foreign blood. Curiously, her hair was auburn, very unlike the Japanese humans Penken was accustomed to. He had seen red haired humans in China before, but this woman had features that were completely unique. He could only stare at her like she was some kind of vision.

"My lady, you are exquisite," he finally managed to say. "Please, join me for a drink?"

"The tea was for you," she responded. She spoke in clipped, hasty tones and Penken could see that her mannerisms were awkward and not Japanese. *Definitely a foreigner.*

"No thank you, my dear. Sake will do just fine."

"I think tea is best, Penken Satsumoto." Penken's throat went dry when she used his name. He stammered a hasty apology and stumbled off the stool, but a a cool hand touched his shoulder. "No need to run, tanuki. If I had wanted you dead, you would have been a long time ago. Sit, and drink some tea."

Penken obligingly sat back on the stool. "Who are you?"

The woman smiled. "My name is unimportant. Sit and listen, Penken. I know all about you, and what you have done. It is time for you to make amends."

"What do you mean?"

Leaning toward him, the woman grinned widely. He didn't like the way she stared at him. It was a hungry stare, as if he was a tasty morsel for her to consume. "I have news of Momo, the kitsune you took in. Listen, and listen well, Penken Satsumoto. This concerns you more than you could ever have imagined." Up close, the woman's eyes were a distinctive blue, another trait he had never seen before. As she spoke her words, a flash of yellow abruptly skipped across them. Penken suddenly felt more sober than he had in days.

IV. Bloodmoon

The headache was back. It had announced its presence with a dull whine early in the dawn and had accentuated into a sharp pain thundering from the back of her skull, toward the front, where it threatened to burst out through her eyes. Momo gritted her teeth and kept running, grimly focusing on the dusty road ahead of her. Maruyama was steep and not fit for human travel, but Momo persisted, leaping where she couldn't run and scurrying up the steep slope. She was making good progress and hoped she'd reach the summit before noon. It was time to finish this.

A shriek echoed above and Momo skidded to a halt, her fox ears pricking up but it was only a small brown falcon, cruising lazily above her. Momo grinned at the creature, feeling a kinship with the wild animal. Despite knowing what was coming, she felt fiercely alive, ready for the oncoming trials.

The falcon shrieked again and Momo barked back at it, a high, excited yip that echoed against the canyon walls. She threw her head back and let loose a wild laugh, a high sound no fox or human would ever make, the manic rush in her body egging her on. The pain in her head was becoming almost unbearable but she took it in eagerly, letting it saturate her thoughts and empty her. Hiroshi was now a speck in her thoughts, a momentary pause before the oncoming madness. She quashed his memory with the pain and resumed running.

The sun slowly ascended, casting gold light upon the red mountain. Momo continued on, paws exploding as she leapt across the ground. The path ended at one point but Momo simply scrabbled up the rocky cliffs, leaping from ledge to ledge until she found a second path jutting outwards. The air grew colder as she climbed and her breath started coming out in small warm puffs.

Another shriek. Momo skidded to a halt and looked up to where the falcon was waiting for her, perched on an overhanging tree. The falcon's eyes were a solid red hue, akin to the statues of Oho-Yama. She grimaced at the creature, wondering what it wanted. After a moment the falcon took off and circled once over Momo's head before diving down. Momo watched the creature as it swooped against the mountain and caught an updraft that let it soar high and away. Then the pain in her head reminded her of her mission and she resumed climbing.

Her limbs were starting to ache with a pulse that matched

the throb in her temples. Though the pain had initially energized her, hours of running were taking their toll, and now she felt sapped of strength. In addition, she was hungry and thirsty, having taken in nothing since the night before, and the mountain was devoid of sustenance. She began to wonder how much longer she could maintain this pace.

Several rocks jutted over a ledge high above. She passed underneath it without notice until a small scattering of pebbles pattered down in front of her. That was just enough warning for Momo to dodge the giant rock that smashed right before her, spraying the air with dust and grit. Momo choked and darted left, avoiding another boulder that nearly crushed her. Smaller rocks fell about as Momo scrambled back from the avalanche. One jagged rock bounded right for her, and Momo couldn't avoid it. She stared right at the rock in horror as her headache suddenly escalated, and something seemed to explode from her head. At first she thought the rock had hit her, but then she realized that shards of the boulder sailed harmlessly around as a cloud of dust enveloped her. She coughed and fell, and as she did she caught a glimpse of a small brown figure behind the swirling dust, impassively watching.

The avalanche finally passed and Momo scrambled to her feet. She bared her teeth and snarled as the falcon spread its wings and touched down lightly. Her snarl faded as the bird shimmered and suddenly took the form of an elderly old woman.

"Splendid!" the woman cackled in a grating voice. "Your aim was true and your powers are ripe. Oh, it was marvelous!"

Momo let out a squeak. The woman was filthy, her skin brown and covered in dust. If this creature was some kind of henge, then she should be able to make her clothes look like whatever she wanted, but her tattered robes were stained a rusty red. The woman's pupils were visible but the whites were a discrete red, more bloodshot than even the worst drunk's. White and gray hair foamed from her face but was cut short, barely extending down past the nape of her neck. The woman bowed. "How rude of me. I am Fenghuang, guardian of this mountain. You are trespassing, my dear." When Momo didn't reply, the woman shook her head in irritation. "You have a voice, yes? I know what you are, little fox."

"I…" Momo started.

The woman shook her head impatiently. "Oh come then. I can see you need something to drink. Follow me." The woman walked to the edge of the cliff and jumped down, skidding across the slope. Momo saw her bare gray feet, calloused and horned, and shuddered to herself. For a moment she considered fleeing but then the woman's reedy voice called up. "If you don't follow me now then I'll come find you!" Momo quickly obeyed.

At the bottom was a small, sulfurous pool. The old woman cupped her hands into the water and drank deeply. "This will purify you, kitsune. Oh, and how is the head?"

Momo realized her headache had receded into a dull thump. "Better. But how did you know—?"

"Never mind that," Fenghuang smiled. Her mouth was completely toothless. She scooped some water into a skein hanging by her side and shook it once. "Change and drink this. We will talk like civilized creatures."

Momo reluctantly shifted into her human form, her white dressed shimmering into existence. The woman thrust the skein at her and Momo uncorked the bottle and tentatively sipped the liquid. To her surprise the water was sweet and cool, completely unlike the sulphurous black liquid bubbling in the pool. The old woman cackled with delight at Momo's surprised expression. "Now tell me, why are you on my mountain?"

Momo wiped the water from her lips. "I apologize, lady. I've come to rescue my friend."

"Ah, that little bakeneko?"

Momo never heard of the word but recognized the end of it. "She's a neko." Fenghuang impatiently waved her on. "She was kidnapped by the tengu, if you didn't know. They are holding her as a trade for me."

"Ah, so that's the missing piece," the woman said, sucking in air. "I had wondered why the mountain birds were roosting on my summit. Pesky critters, aren't they?" She regarded Momo and smiled. "Very noble of you, little one."

"She's my friend! And what are you, anyway? Are you a guardian of Oho-Yama?"

The woman snorted. "I have no use for your gods, kitsune. It's only the living who interest me. Like you." She took a step closer to Momo, who took a step back. "Don't be mistaken, kitsune. This is my mountain. But I serve no Japanese god. I am a refugee of my own people, my own clan."

"Are you henge?" Momo blurted, unable to contain herself. Fenghuang grinned toothlessly.

"Hardly. I was born a human girl, and I will die a human woman. You think the so-called henge are the only ones with powers, girl? I am a Bloodmoon sister, of the Josean dynasty. You do not understand yet, girl, but our lineages are closely linked, yours and mine."

"How so?" Momo stammered.

The woman laughed. "So ignorant! Oh, if only my sister could see this now." The woman took another step closer and her eyes clouded a thick red as her voice took on a deeper tone. "Show me that power, kitsune. I want to see your power." She crooked her finger at Momo. The pain in the back of the kitsune's head leapt forward like an eager dog. Momo whimpered and fell to her knees. Her body began to change, but somehow the woman's voice slowed it down. Fur sprouted from her skin, but her body remained human and her back arched painfully as her spine shivered between its two forms. "You are exquisite, little one. I want to taste it," the woman's voice whispered. Dry hands caressed Momo's back.

"P-please," Momo stammered. "What do you want from me?"

"This," the woman hissed, an icy voice. The pain in her head hummed and a low buzzing noise resounded in Momo's ears. The buzzing abruptly gave way to a clacking laughter that rattled in her skull. Tears streamed from Momo's face and she hunched over, quivering as her body continued its slow morph into her fox form. "There, there," the voice said. "Let me sip from it."

The pain flowed toward Momo's eyes, and a yellow light glowed from within. The old woman cupped Momo's head in her hands and stared intently as the yellow light streamed forward in a slender trickle. She drank it in for a second, her face greedy, enraptured, and then she abruptly broke it off. Pain exploded in Momo's skull and she fell as the witch pushed her and stumbled back, coughing and laughing.

"Marvelous. Oh, so marvelous! Kitsune, I have not felt that power in ages. To see it again was like…visiting an old lover."

The woman wheezed and caught her balance. Momo blinked away tears and realized she was back in fox form. Her headache was completely gone. She leapt to her feet and tried to run, but felt a paralyzing force held her down.

"You have not disappointed me, kitsune. You were blessed by my sister generations ago, but her power still runs through you. Thank you." To Momo's astonishment, the woman bowed low before her. "You have earned your passage here. Go now." Momo felt the paralyzing force lift. She wasted no time darting away, her paws scrabbling up the rocky hillside. She returned to the original path, where the remains of the avalanche were still scattered about.

Despite what had transpired, Momo felt stronger than before. Her headache was gone, and the water had invigorated her. After sniffing the air and ensuring that she was alone, Momo resumed climbing the mountain. Whatever the mountain witch had wanted from her, she had seemed satisfied, and there was no time for questions. Kei was waiting.

*

The Bloodmoon sister watched the kitsune flee and waited until she was out of sight before falling over, retching. The little fox's power was even more potent than she had anticipated! As Fenghuang lay there catching her breath, she allowed a wide grin to spread across her features. She hated this land, almost as much as she hated those whom she had left behind, and it delighted her to see Hyuang-nah's legacy so perfectly preserved in these wild creatures. Her kind would bring destruction, of that Fenghuang was now assured, and she was delighted that she would witness the fall of this cursed country.

V. Reunited

"He might still be alive," growled Banken as he sifted through the remains. Aiken stayed silent. *Sometimes things resolve themselves on their own*, she reminded herself. "There is no evidence of blood," her mate continued. The tengu was still disoriented from his wounds, though none were serious enough to slow him down. A large cotton bandage was wrapped around his waist where the ninja had sliced and burned him, but he stomped about, heedless of it and the stitches beneath. "I don't think that Yan bitch got to him."

Saima's whip lay where it had fallen, distinct with the katana blade attached to its end. The ground was trampled with the feet of an army but Aiken recognized the footprints; webbed feet that sank heavily into the mud could only mean one thing. "Look," Aiken said, picking up a green vegetable. "Cucumbers, the river kind's food of choice. They passed through here recently."

"I know it was kappa!" thundered Banken. "I can recognize their tracks anywhere. Blasted creatures. Filthy river beasts. They are no better than animals, to do this, to…" His words trailed off as he sputtered with anger and sank to his knees.

Aiken went to his side. She wrapped her arms protectively around Banken's head and pressed her nose against his matted hair. Nothing she could say would comfort her mate now, and she feared her words might betray her, reveal her true heart. Thank the gods he did not realize how the neko had escaped. Perhaps now they had a chance to start over and live their lives in a better way. Thank the gods Saima was gone as well; that tengu had brought nothing but suffering after they had unleashed him from his exile.

"We'll find them," Banken rumbled, dry eyes looking up at Aiken. He lumbered to his feet and extended his axe. "I *will* save him." The butt-end of his weapon slammed into the mud as he flexed his wings. One hand found its way to Aiken's and he squeezed it for strength. "Come, my heart. The tracks clearly lead toward that human village. Let us hunt. Perhaps we will find my brother, the kappa, and that Yan in one lucky stroke." As he strode off with his weapon in hand, a cold shiver ran down Aiken's spine.

And what would you say, my love, if I thought it would be best if we missed all three?

*

Kei lay in the branches until dawn. Aiken's aim had been true; what Kei had thought was her final plummet turned out to be a somewhat rude but nevertheless lifesaving crash into a thick copse of trees. One paw was bleeding and she had scratches all across her body, but she was at least safe for now.

As light returned to the mountainside, Kei gingerly descended the tree onto a spiraling dirt trail. She could see a distant temple at the mountain's base and she made for it, padding along quietly. Her throat was parched and her stomach rumbled uncomfortably. How she hated the outdoors! The neko looked forward to a hot bath and a full meal, both which she expected the local priest would provide.

Her spirits lifted as the day progressed and Kei grew increasingly confident that she had escaped at last. The Yan ninja was after the tengu, not her, and Aiken clearly wanted to let her go. Furthermore, no one seemed to be following her. Assured of that, Kei began planning out the next few days. She would hide in the temple and rest, perhaps assume a human form if it served her better. Then off to find some merchant who would take her – as a girl or a cat – to Kyoto. There, she would nestle herself back into the hub of activity and forget about the madness of these last few days. Maybe Penken was there too. She giggled, picturing the fat tanuki's expression as she padded into his home. She would sit at the table and demand sweet cakes as if nothing had ever happened. That was a good day to look forward to.

A heavy panting sound stopped her daydreaming. Some kind of hungry animal was approaching and it sounded quite large, like a bear or a wolf. Kei hurriedly dove into the brush and peeked her head out.

An orange blur whizzed by, almost indistinguishable. Kei barely blinked it was already past her, racing up the mountain trail. Stunned, Kei crawled out of the brush and back onto the road. Whatever it was, it was clearly in a hurry. Straining her eyes, Kei paused…could it be?

"Momo!" she shrieked, a high narrow voice that echoed across the canyon. The orange figure paused and Kei could clearly see the kitsune now. "Sister!" She ran toward the figure of the fox, who had already turned around.

"Kei!" Momo cried. Her voice was muffled as Kei tackled the fox and wrestled her onto her back. "Hey, ouch!"

"What are you doing here?" Kei cried. She buffeted the kitsune's nose playfully. "What in the gods' names are you doing here?"

"Looking for you!" Momo replied. She shoved Kei off with her hind legs and scrambled onto her feet. The two girls looked happily at each other. "Oh, it's so good to see you safe. Did those tengu hurt you? Where are they? Did you escape?"

"Hold on!" Kei said, laughing. "I'm fine, everything's fine. But sister, there's no time to waste; we must leave this mountain. It's still dangerous."

"I can believe that," Momo said, her expression growing serious. "But no, you first, Kei-chan. Please, tell me everything!"

Kei related the last few nights to Momo as they hurried down the path. The kitsune hissed in alarm when Kei mentioned the Yan ninja but then nodded when she heard how the woman had gone after the tengu. "I know who she is," Momo said. "And I hope she teaches them both a lesson."

"Not Aiken, Momo," Kei interjected gently. "Aiken saved me."

"I don't care," Momo said harshly. "She's as bad as her stinking mate. They can both die for all I care."

Kei said nothing to that. There was something different about her friend, a restlessless that Kei had not seen before. To change the subject, she pointed to the temple. "I was heading there, sister. I bet the priest would be more than happy to serve a wandering pilgrim girl and her pet cat!" She giggled at the thought.

Momo grimly shook her head. "No, Kei. We head east, right now. We have hurt these good people more than enough. It's time to leave."

"To where?" Kei asked.

Momo skidded to a stop. "I don't know, Kei. What do you

think?"

Kei smiled. "I think you should see the capital. Kyoto is beautiful in the autumn, did you know that, sister? And wait until the spring when the cherry blossoms are in bloom! I can show you things that will take your breath away."

Momo sighed. "I don't know, Kei. I just don't know." Suddenly, alarmingly, tears brimmed in her eyes. Kei moved to her.

"Sister, what's the matter?"

Momo pawed at her face, a curiously human gesture. "It's nothing. I just hate having to run all the time. Do you think I'll ever feel safe?"

Kei nodded. "Hey, look at me! One night ago I was tied up in some tengu's cave, about to be served for supper. Now I'm back on the road again with my dear friend. You'll never know how things will turn out, Momo."

Momo shook her head. "How can you be so enthusiastic all the time?"

"Hey, you need to enjoy life a little more, that's all! Think of it, we've survived this far. We can hide and change our forms at will. The gods have blessed us with these abilities, sister, don't think that they haven't! A few plotting humans and tengu won't get in the way of that."

Momo sighed. "I hope someday I can feel like you do." Kei hugged her fiercely.

They continued on, finally reaching the base of the mountain just after the peak of the day. Kei panted heavily in the heat. "I need some water. Are you sure you don't want to stop at the temple and rest?"

Momo shook her head. "We can't. I'm sorry Kei, but please let's not go there. I don't think…" She trailed off. "Let's go to the river. We can eat and rest there." They gave the temple a wide berth, Momo shooting it furtive glances as they skirted by. Kei could only guess at what had transpired there. When they reached the river, she happily ducked her head in and drank deep. The water was fresh and revitalizing, but then a tangy mossy taste entered her mouth. Kei sputtered and spat it out. Momo looked over. "What is it?"

"Nothing. Just slimy. I think kappa were swimming in the river here."

"Kappa?" Momo cocked her head. "What are they doing here?"

"I don't know. Most of the kappa live in Kyoto right now and they pollute the water with their muck. Ugly duck creatures." Kei said. She wiped her mouth. "Aren't you hungry, sister?"

Momo shook her head. The kitsune recalled the bodies floating down the river and the direction that they were heading.

She looked to Kei. "Is this the same river as the one by Kusama Village?"

Kei shrugged. "I guess so. Why?"

Momo had no answer, but a terrible foreboding entered her. She thought of Hiroshi and of their last night together. How she had wanted him then! At least for a time, she had felt needed by somebody and his sweet kisses had filled her with comfort. She stared at the glassy surface of the river. She realized then that she needed to see him one last time. She needed to know that he was safe, and she needed to say goodbye. The kitsune shifted back into her human form and walked over to the neko.

"Kei, let's go. We need to take a detour." Picking up the protesting cat, Momo began to walk in the direction of the river's flow.

*

Kiyoshi Hidetora rode fiercely through the gates of Kusama Village, nearly toppling the sentry as he raced by. Hiroshi struggled to keep up with his grandfather, his heart racing at the new turn of events. His grandfather had picked him up at the temple the morning after Momo had left and had wasted no time issuing him a beating. They had shouted and cursed each other and Hidetora had nearly left him behind in disgust, but their differences were set aside when a wounded soldier stumbled onto the temple grounds. The man had a severe gash on his side and as he toppled onto the priest's tended garden he spoke one final word.

"Kappa."

It suddenly made sense to Hiroshi. The bodies in the river. His cousin's warnings. Even the tengu were probably connected with this. He had wanted to go find Momo but in all honesty, he had no idea where she had gone. So he chose to follow his grandfather and help warn the village.

The townspeople swiftly reacted, barring the gates and fortifying the lone watchtower with archers. The soldiers began sharpening their weapons while the women and children collected their belongings. Rumors flooded the village, and whispers of the impending othermen sent a panicked chill through all the people. Hiroshi despondently looked for Momo in the village but there was no sign of her. He could only pray to the gods that she was safe somewhere, and well protected.

For now he had to see to the defense of his village. Hidetora had tossed him a short sword, not finely honed like the traditional samurai katana but a deadly blade nonetheless. Hiroshi immediately saw to sharpening it. He was scared but also felt wildly exhilarated. It would seem that the war he was going to ride off to had found itself right at the village gates! Hiroshi had no intentions of letting his grandfather down.

Then he saw his mother, crying and packing her things. He saw Eizo and the other young boys huddled in the inn, the only building made out of stone. It was at that moment that Hiroshi realized how very real the battle was going to be. War had come to him, true, but it had also found everyone else at Kusama Village. Suddenly, the prospect of fighting on his land did not seem so appealing after all.

VI. First Casualties

They walked with the crunch of leaves as their only conversation. Aiken tried to slow her mate down but Banken hurried with his usual stubborn pace. The wounds from the Yan ninja did not seem to bother him any more than a flea's bite, but Aiken knew how deadly the assassin was. She wondered who that human was and why she so vigorously pursued them. There were many mysteries right now that were beyond her, but Aiken was determined to see herself and her mate through all of them.

They arrived at the outskirts of Kusama Village. An old fisherman's shack lay abandoned, his tools scattered about and his boat bobbing gently in the river. It was almost a serene image that belied the danger ahead. Banken slammed his fist into his palm as he stopped by the waters and blew out air from his nostrils in a heavy whistle.

"There is no sign of him," he growled. "Where could he have gone? Do you see any trace of the kappa?"

"No, my heart. They must have taken him across the water."

"Tengu can't swim!" Banken roared. "Come, we'll backtrack and find the trail again."

"Banken, you're hurt," Aiken said, but Banken was already past her, heading back in the direction they had come. "This is foolish!"

Banken paused and stared straight ahead. His long nose trembled with tension and cords stood out of his red neck. "I swear to you," he said through gritted teeth, "if they have killed my brother, then every single one of them will die!"

"There's no need for that." Saima's high fluted voice cut through the air. He stepped out of the trees, casually extending his palms open in a gesture of peace. Other than a few scratches on one arm, the tengu looked no worse for wear. Aiken's stomach roiled.

Banken shouted in jubilation and slapped his brother on his back. "Where were you?" he asked. "Brother, we had thought you were taken by the kappa."

"Not taken." Saima had a smug expression on his face that Aiken didn't like at all. Looking him over, she saw a scythe fastened in a new turtle shell belt he had somehow obtained. "You might have been taken, dear brother of mine, but I wasn't. In fact, I convinced those fine river folk to help us."

Banken extended his spear and shifted it into his left hand.

"Where are they?" he rumbled. "I'll make them bleed for this! What are kappa doing out here anyway?" Saima let out an exaggerated sigh and rolled his eyes.

"You are as thick-witted as ever, Banken. Didn't you just hear me? The kappa are our allies now. They captured me, true, but after I spoke to them they quickly saw how useful I could be. There are two of them here right now, actually. I told them to hold back because I know of your tendency to charge at moving things."

"And what did you promise them, Saima?" Aiken spoke quietly. Saima's eyes flickered to her and he smirked.

"Well, I had to give them *something*, didn't I? Anyway, the truth is, dear sister, the kappa have always been our allies. At least, we all serve those humans in Kyoto, isn't that what you had said to me once, Aiken? Well, those humans are looking to start a war and the kappa are their loyal servants. I just happened to know a place where they can wet their bills." The dark tengu flashed them a reptilian smile. "They're approaching Kusama Village as we speak."

*

"Over there!" roared the sergeant, a burly man who had not bothered to wipe the grains of rice from his beard. "Soldiers, steady…steady. Fire!" The men responded and six arrows whistled down toward the kappa milling below. Five missed and the sixth clattered noisily off one of their shells. The brutish creatures laughed and made rude gestures as the sergeant's face turned purple.

"I don't like it," Hiroshi heard one of the spearmen whisper as the sergeant ordered the archers to reload. "What do those creatures want with us?" The defenders were crouched behind a makeshift palisade constructed of bamboo and wood. The soldiers had built it beyond the village gates in order to protect the few homes that lay scattered in the wilderness. Though it seemed crude and weak to Hiroshi, the five kappa seemed reluctant to advance.

"Who cares?" spat another man. "They killed old man Aki and his poor daughter. If they stay there, I say we charge."

The first casualties, Hiroshi thought with a shiver. He had barely known Aki, who was an infamous recluse known to beat his daughter, a simpleton. However, he would never again hear the latest gossip in the inn, never wave to the daughter as she went to market on her occasional outings. He found himself growing increasingly fearful. "Shouldn't we go back into the village?"

"Be silent!" snapped the sergeant. "We're advancing, but only when they retreat. I don't see them retreating now, do you?" As more arrows whistled out towards the indifferent kappa, Hiroshi had to wonder why they weren't.

*

While Daru and the others kept the humans distracted, Kaaro's men knifed through the river with casual ease. The kappa lord smirked at his good fortune. They might have completely ignored this village if that tengu hadn't informed them of how defenseless it was, how utterly soft these villagers were. *Strike at the peasants,* Yugotaru had ordered Kaaro back in Kyoto, and here there were plenty to fulfill that command. Slay the peasants, burn their crops, and starve the greater cities. With his people dying, the lord of these lands would be forced to mobilize his men and then Nobunaga's armies would march in and finish the job.

Kaaro signaled them to halt as they drifted near the edge of the village. Fifteen shells rose slowly to the surface like misshapen lily pads, and then their beady eyes peaked over the murky water. Kaaro's guess that these humans did not know kappa tactics had proven to be correct. The riverbank was completely unguarded, leaving this side of the village vulnerable as a ripe underbelly. The kappa swam ashore and paused for a moment. They appeared like green emeralds as the sparkling sun caught the water cascading down their backs. Then the illusion broke as they awkwardly lumbered forward, crude but deadly warriors. A lone fisherman repairing a net barely had time to gape before a scythe split his neck wide open. The killing had begun.

*

The soldiers heard the screams from the rear, down by the river. Hiroshi grabbed his sword and ran through the village toward them. He found his grandfather with a line of other soldiers, spears ready and pointed towards the water. The old man was dressed in finely polished black armor that Hiroshi had never seen before. He raised a hand to the boy.

"They're coming," he said.

Smoke descended over them, heavy and gray. It burned Hiroshi's lungs and he bent over, choking. Orange licks of flame danced across the distant straw huts while the inhabitants fled toward the line of men. Two women ran shrieking past, one so close to Hiroshi he could smell her hot, panicked breath, reeking of sour fish. The woman was clutching a small child who had blood dripping down his face and his mouth was wide open in a surprised gasp.

"Close that up," Hidetora snapped. "Come here boy, take the place next to me." When Hiroshi didn't move right away, Hidetora grabbed his arm and settled him on the line. "I'll make sure you're fine," the old man whispered in a low voice. More villagers ran by, many wounded and crying. The sky darkened as the clouds of smoke obscured the sun and the screams in the distance intensified, a high piercing sound that stung Hiroshi's ears. He moved as if in a dream, helping people past the line, grabbing at hands and limbs. Then the stream of people abruptly stopped.

For a minute there was nothing. Then, like apparitions, large bulky shapes materialized from the smoke. The kappa were a fearsome sight, with giant green and mottled shells. Their faces looked dimwitted behind the duckbills, but the eyes were intelligent and piercing. The othermen stopped before the line of soldiers and regarded them with contempt. Each had a long scythe in one hand, poised and ready to strike. One kappa with a blue sash wrapped around its waist stepped forward and issued orders in a bleating, garbled tongue. Hiroshi could feel his knees tremble and his bladder about to let go. The rivermen charged.

What happened next was an indistinguishable blur. Kappa blundered forward and crashed into the soldiers, much heavier than anyone expected. Hiroshi saw one man fall underneath a kappa and crack beneath the heavy body. His grandfather shoved him back and stood protectively in front. The old man thrust his spear with remarkable accuracy, piercing the stomach of a menacing kappa. The creature grunted and slowed but still charged forward. It was only when Hidetora put his weight forward and plunged the spear further in that the monster froze. Hiroshi saw a look of pain on its face as it spun its body away, snapping the haft in half. Remarkably, it still had enough strength to stand.

Other kappa rushed ahead to replace it. Many went right past Hiroshi, completely ignoring the boy. They had torches, which they threw onto the houses. The simple thatched roofs caught easily, going up in brilliant blazes. "Go!" he heard his grandfather yell. "Find your mother and run to the inn! I'll be right behind you, boy!" Hiroshi broke ranks and ran. One kappa turned to face him but the othermen were ungainly on two feet. Hiroshi nimbly skirted around the creature, dropping his sword from nerveless fingers. The fires licked at his heels as the village around him burned.

*

"Look," Saima said. "They've started." Smoke drifted in the distance, a stain in the otherwise unblemished blue sky.

"Saima, how could you?" Banken growled. "Those humans were innocent!"

"Innocent? They nearly killed me, dear brother! Or have you forgotten what I went through to retrieve your little neko?"

Aiken hissed and threw her axe down. "You disgust me," she said. Her frustration from the last few days overflowed and she focused her gaze onto both of the males. "You both do!" Banken looked at her in surprise. "Yes, you," Aiken snapped.

"This was all your brother's doing, true, but you went along with it. Like a fool, I trusted your judgment and followed. I'm ashamed to be a part of this...this evil."

"Aiken," Banken said, stepping forward. "My heart…"

"No, don't start!" Aiken snapped. "How many more innocent lives are going to die today? How much death and bloodshed, all for this mad hunt of ours? It's over, Banken. We've lost."

Saima sighed in mock exasperation. "Aiken, really. This sort of talk won't get us anywhere. We haven't failed yet. Or maybe we have, but just remember that Lady Jinzo doesn't tolerate failure. This I know too well."

Aiken laughed, a bitter laugh. "For once you're right, Saima. This mission is as mad as you are. We'd be fortunate if Lady Jinzo allowed us the peace of exile."

Banken tried to hug her. "No, no, it won't be like that. Lady Jinzo told us to follow Sharada, don't you remember? She won't punish us."

Aiken shoved him away. "Enough! I've had enough of both of you. I'm going." She turned.

"My heart…" Banken protested. His voice was wounded, like a small animal's cry.

"Don't follow me, Banken," Aiken warned. She bounded into the air. Banken started after her but Saima grabbed his shoulder and shook his head.

"Let her go. She'll come back to you eventually." Banken angrily shrugged his brother off.

"She's right, brother. You've gone too far with this!" Before

Saima could respond, another voice interrupted them.

"You!" Two kappa had arrived, climbing up the riverbank. Banken glowered at the small turtle creatures, but Saima stepped in front of him. "Honorable rivermen," he said with a flourish. "This is my brother, Banken."

The kappa regarded Banken with indifference, then looked back at Saima. One of them said, "We must join the battle. Are you coming with us?"

Banken shook his head. "Go fight the humans or whatever you want to do, brother. I'm going after my mate." Banken jumped into the air, his wings flapping heavily, and disappeared into the forest. The two kappa watched Banken leave and then leveled their spears at Saima. "*You* are still our prisoner, tengu. Don't forget."

Saima smirked. "Everyone is in such a rush these days. Fine, let's go. I wouldn't want to disappoint Lord Kaaro." He followed them towards the village.

*

The human deaths were piling up. Once in battle, tactics meant little to the kappa, who relied on their brute strength and ferocity to carry them forward. Kaaro grabbed a torch from one of his men and flung it onto another hut, sending it ablaze. The others charged forward, hacking and slashing with wild abandon, discerning neither age nor sex in their slaughter.

Some resistance was met. Kaaro spied one of his kind slumped over with three arrows sticking out of his chest. Another kappa caught one right in the eye before the archers were run down. It hardly mattered. Lord Kaaro waited by the entrance of a burning hut, his scythe out and ready. A woman ran out and he let her past to be killed by the others. When the second, an older lady, tottered out hacking and wheezing, he didn't even bother with his blade. He wrapped the feeble creature in his arms and squeezed once. The crack of her bones was delightful.

*

When Momo saw the smoke wafting in the horizon, she knew her worst fears had been confirmed. She stopped abruptly by the riverbank, her body erect and taut. "Momo?" Kei asked in a concerned voice. Blood dripped down from Momo's palms as she dug her nails into them. "Momo!"

It was all coming back to her. The screams. The blood. The ninja cutting Kimiko down. Momo recalled the taste of her blood as she ripped her throat out, the exhilaration of that sensation. Her mind whirled and raced and her vision rocked as if an earthquake had struck. Kei's voice became a distant hum in the background, drowned by a heavy buzzing sound. Without even thinking about it, she slid back into her kitsune form.

She growled inarticulately as she thought of Hiroshi, of his gentle smile, of the eagerness in his body as they had kissed. She remembered his sweet lips and the firm caress of his hands. These memories flowed in her, warm and heavy, and then were abruptly replaced by images of Hiroshi lying dead, his blood filling the river. Suddenly, Momo's eyes took on a yellow glow as her mind descended into a red rage. Something like a thin burning poker burrowed inside of her brain and the dull echoes of a maniacal laughter filled her mind.

Hiroshi! she screamed over the alien laughter, and then she felt a force inside her *push*. It shoved into her mind, trying to dig deeper, to infect her with the laughter. *Not in, no. Out, at them.* The force responded, almost reluctantly, and lashed outwards in a sharp twist. The energy thrummed and skipped across the river like a stone, soft ripples dancing in its wake. Momo felt a thrill course through her. It was time to make those who had hurt her for so long pay, pay for everything. Kei's voice cried out in terror but Momo had no time for her. She turned toward the village and lurched forward, slaver dripping down her face as her eyes glowed brightly in the afternoon sun.

VII. Kusama's Last Stand

Madness throbbed through Momo's body. Deep inside a small voice, the part of her that still retained some conscious thought, wept. It wept for the loss of her father, and of the simple life he had promised that would never be. It wept for Taku, the loyal brother who would never understand why she'd had to leave. It wept for Usagi and Kimiko, victims of an ever-cruel world, and it wept for Hiroshi. But most of all, that voice wept for herself. It wept because the dream that Momo could live as a human, as a nice young girl who could idle her days away farming and fishing, was forever gone.

But that voice was resigned and weak, completely ignored by the other side. That side burned with a dark animalistic hunger that quickly swallowed her feeble thoughts like darkness engulfing a suffocating candle. It reveled in its sudden freedom, a caged animal experiencing the wide world for the very first time. Her senses thrummed, heightened with new life, and she inhaled the smell of wet grass against the ground, the tang of mineral that lurked near the edges of the freshwater river, the hot blood of rodents and birds that was pumping rapidly in their arteries. Most of all, she felt utter desire, a desire to taste heat, to watch the blood spray rich and red from her enemies. Foam bubbled across her quivering lips and her eyes burned with a familiar yellow light that edged forth, until her pupils were pinpricks of black against two brilliant suns.

A burst of fresh wind shot through her nose and she snuffed it in eagerly, taking in the smells of man-sweat and fear. In the distance she also picked up a new smell, one reeking of swamps and bogs, of mud and fish. Those smells belonged to the kappa, and she was eager to meet them. The kitsune stalked onwards.

*

"I'm sorry, Banken. I can't come with you." He had caught up to her near Maruyama Temple, where she had come to pray for the gods' forgiveness. Only they could judge her now, and she knew she would have to spend years in penance before she could feel even remotely clean again.

"Aiken, my heart," Banken said slowly. "I understand why you left. Saima was a mistake, I see that now. I'm ready to give up the hunt and return. Lady Jinzo will understand our failure."

"Do *you* understand, Banken?" Aiken said. She looked carefully at him. "Do you understand what we've done?"

Banken sighed. "We have made mistakes. But we were following orders, weren't we? I don't—"

"I remember when I first saw you," she said quietly. "It was at the eve of the third Ji-ten celebration. You were the best leaper of the entire tribe." She smiled gently. "I watched you soar up above the clouds until you were a mere speck. The others couldn't jump half as high as you did that day. You were like an eagle."

"Aiken?" Banken asked, "Why are you speaking of this now?"

She took his head in her hands and gently kissed the tip of his nose. "Just a fond memory, Banken." She let him go with a smile.

"Where are you going?" Banken's voice quavered as he spoke.

Aiken stepped back. "I'm not sure. But know that I'll always be with you, Banken. Remember that." Her thick black wings beat mightily and with a leap she took to the skies, a rapidly shrinking red dot in a vast expanse of blue.

*

Hiroshi staggered into the inn and shut the door. The children were huddled in a circle in the center of the common room, covering their mouths with wet rags. The innkeeper waved Hiroshi over and motioned him to get down. Though they were safe from the fires, smoke poured underneath the door and through the windows. The air thickened and Hiroshi doubled over coughing.

"Are we dying?" Eizo squeaked. Hiroshi made his way over to him and put his arms around the small boy.

"No way," he said. He tried to grin but felt his courage fail as the door swung open. Two large kappa stormed inside, blood dripping from their scythes. Expressionless, the creatures stalked towards the group of children.

"Stop this!" the innkeeper cried. She thrust herself in front of one of the kappa, brandishing a broom. The creature plunged his blade into her side and sent her reeling with a kick. The old woman screeched until the other kappa silenced her with one quick dip of his weapon. The children wailed as the two kappa continued to advance. Hiroshi stood on weak legs and fumbled for his sword. When he realized he had lost it, he steeled himself to face his death bravely.

A crack resounded through the air. One kappa paused and looked upwards, just in time to catch the timbers falling onto its face. The roof had burned completely through, and hot embers drifted into the inn. The injured kappa howled and clutched its face while its companion choked on the fire. Hiroshi could see dry cracks forming on both of their underbellies. The heat was hurting the rivermen even more than the villagers!

The wounded kappa had fallen to its side now, writhing underneath the burning wood. Hiroshi grabbed its fallen scythe and waved it in the air. "Get out!" he screamed to the children. "This place is falling!" As the children streamed by, Hiroshi advanced on the other kappa. The creature was still standing, but its reflexes were slowed by pain. It was all too easy to plunge the scythe deep into its belly. The kappa grunted and opened its eyes, hatred pouring out at Hiroshi. It tried to extract the hilt but it was too deeply buried. Hiroshi ran past him without looking back.

Outside, the air was almost black with ash. The fires were dying out as everything that could be consumed was, but the smoke remained, as thick as fog. Coughing and with eyes tearing, the boy ran for his house. He blundered past both kappa and humans, everyone smothered in soot. Blinking, he could see the faint outline of his home still miraculously intact. Just as he started towards it, another kappa reared up in front of him. It was the one he had seen before, wearing a blue sash. Hiroshi backpedaled, but too late; he crashed face-first into the creature's shoulder. His head rebounded and he gazed in terror at the monster. With a guttural laugh, the kappa brought its hand down and then Hiroshi knew nothing more.

*

Kaaro regarded the fallen boy only momentarily before turning away. His eyes would not stop watering and now they started to ache under the blistering heat. Furthermore, his soft skin was growing brittle and hard. There was no doubt about it; the fire was weakening him. He needed a drink badly. Better yet the river, a cool place where his sensitive skin could suck up the moisture. The fires they had set were burning too hot, and now the kappa were as trapped as these humans. It was time to retreat.

Hacking and spitting ash from his throat, Kaaro stumbled for the river. Suddenly, something sharp and painful skidded across the back of his neck. Only the horny flesh that joined against his shell saved him from being skewered through the throat. He reeled around and spotted an old man dressed in samurai armor, bearing a long spear. The man had a thick white mustache that hid his mouth.

Kaaro readied for the attack. The human circled slowly around him, every muscle flexed and poised. The man feinted a jab with his spear, and then with amazing dexterity spun the weapon over his head, too fast to follow. Kaaro felt the weapon slam into his shoulder and backpedaled before the blade could find a soft spot. The old man hung back.

Kaaro charged forward, but the human countered with a thrust to his throat. The kappa snarled through his bill and crouched low, eyes firmly on his opponent. He tried to advance again but was only rewarded with another jab, this time into his stomach. It wasn't deep, but he felt blood trickle down, hot and wet. The wetness reminded Kaaro of how badly he needed the river. *Where are the others?* He could not last much longer, not in this condition. As if sensing his hesitation the old man suddenly spoke in a soft, stern voice.

"River demon, you will not take this village. Your foul brothers are fleeing, blinded as they are by their own fires. You, however, will die here."

Kaaro roared at the man's impertinence. Spinning around quickly so that his shell faced the human, he charged backward. Kappa were ungainly on two feet and even worse when walking backward, but Kaaro only had to move a few paces before feeling the spear crash against his sturdy turtle shell. The weapon screeched like a grinding stone before snapping in half.

With a howl of triumph, Kaaro spun forwards, his scythe raised and ready. The human was not there. Kaaro started to turn again and then felt a crashing blow against his head. He stood there momentarily as if shocked, and then quietly toppled sideways to the ground.

*

Hidetora dropped the blunt half of his broken spear and stepped over the body of the kappa. His grandson lay there like a broken toy. Oblivious of the fires, of the kappa, and of everything else, the old man grabbed the boy and pressed him against his chest.

*

The scent of blood and fire were all too familiar to Momo, but what she sought was something else. Smoke draped over the village like a heavy blanket, and she had a brief image of the dying circus troupe before the laughter drowned out her thoughts again.

Humans and kappa alike ran by her, barely giving her a glance as they struggled with each other. Many humans were dead, but others still stood and they outnumbered the kappa. She saw two humans take down one riverman with repeated stabs of their swords. Yet another kappa teetered around aimlessly with several arrows deeply embedded in its chest.

None of it mattered. She reached the inn and sniffed deeply. Through the blood and death she caught the thin tendril of his life, trailing forward from the inn. She followed that trail, hanging onto it tenuously. Hiroshi was near. She had to find him.

It was too late. The boy's limp body was in the arms of his grandfather. Momo saw that old man was stroking his face, wiping the ash from his cheeks. The pinpoints of her pupils completely disappeared under the wash of yellow light as her tailed vibrated like a stiff reed against the wind. She welcomed the madness, embraced it fully so that it would drown the sorrow that threatened to flood through her. The power throttled her mind and her eyes turned from yellow to white hot. Her lips peeled back, revealing a row of sharp, dark fangs.

Dimly, she was aware of a large kappa rising to its feet. Blood poured from its ears but it was fixated on the grandfather and Hiroshi. Fumbling for its weapon, the creature lurched toward the old man. Momo shook with rage. *Die.*

The creature stood stock-still, every inch of its body at attention. Then its head popped free of its body in a gust of rich redness. The blue sash wrapped around its body drifted free and floated gently onto the ground, beside legs that scrabbled aimlessly on the ground. Blood matted the earth everywhere.

Not enough. It was not enough. The power rang through her triumphantly, but there was no satisfaction from the creature's death. It only reminded her that more, much more was needed. The sky would rain blood before she was satiated.

The old man had seen her. Should she snuff his pathetic life, this old man who had thrown her out of this village and let Hiroshi die? Part of her screamed in protest but most of her simply didn't care. Human or kappa, all would perish in her wake.

A second pair of eyes joined the first. Hiroshi feebly lifted his head from his grandfather's lap and stared fearfully at Momo. "Oh gods," he said in a tiny, small voice. Immediately the world around her came crashing down. She shrank before his face, cowering helplessly as the tears came.

"Hiroshi!" she screamed over the laughter. Both humans startled at the voice.

"What is that?" the grandfather said, right over Hiroshi's "Momo?" It was too late. It was far too late. She had let loose something horrible and she could not contain it.

"Momo?" Hiroshi said again. "Is that you?" His familiar voice overcame the laughter, which abruptly tampered down to a low buzz. It hungered to come up again but the stream of emotions that his voice brought back overwhelmed it. Momo felt her eyes lose their yellow glow and her tail settle down. Exhausted, she fell panting to the ground.

Hiroshi was standing now, on his own two feet. He seemed unharmed but scared. They were both afraid, and Momo realized how terrifying she must appear. Her head pounded and her body trembled with a strange, enervating force but she struggled to her feet.

"Hiroshi…I'm…I'm so sorry." She forced her body to shift and momentarily stood before him in her human form. "Please, forgive me." The boy stared at her as only he could, with no more words. Momo turned away and hid her face. The last reserves of her energy were consumed as she slipped back into her fox form. The laughter had died down but what replaced it was an immense emptiness, an emptiness she could never fill. Darkness engulfed her senses and this time, Momo welcomed it. She stepped into silent oblivion.

*

The two of them watched the still form of the fox. Hiroshi blinked his eyes. "Is…is she dead?" Still smarting from the bruise on his head, Hiroshi gingerly stepped forward.

A hand fell on his shoulder. His grandfather held him back, shaking his head. "Look," he said.

A small white cat stood off to one side. It would have appeared ordinary, except for its curious green eyes. The creature watched them warily, until Hidetora motioned it forward with a brief wave of his hand. The cat walked to the fallen form of the fox. Hiroshi gasped as the cat shifted into the shape of a young girl, one he had never seen before.

"You are the one from the inn," his grandfather said. The girl stared impudently at him before nodding. "I thought so," Hidetora added.

"Who are you?" Hiroshi said. The girl shrugged silently and offered a mischievous grin before picking up the fox. "Wait! Where are you taking her?" The girl started to walk away but then paused. She coyly looked over her shoulder.

"To a better place, Hiroshi-chan. She belongs with us, now." Hiroshi shivered at the sound of his own name. The girl turned fully around and bowed low. "Thank you for everything," she said in a formal voice. With that, then she stepped into the forest. Her small frame soon vanished behind the thick copse of trees.

"Can you walk?" Hidetora said after a minute. Hiroshi nodded. "Then let's go. I think the battle is over." True to his grandfather's words, a thick breeze carried the smoke by them. There were still shouts and cries from the village, but the screams had ended and were replaced by cries for water and aid.

Hand in hand, the boy and his grandfather went to find other survivors.

*

Aiken watched the village from a distance. The kappa's attack had been swift and brutal, but the humans had vastly outnumbered the rivermen. After their initial surprise attack, the kappa were driven back by their own fires. Several were cornered by the inn and slaughtered, and only a few survivors had made their way to the river. Whatever madness Saima had conjured, it had passed.

So much violence, she thought wearily. *And it will only cause more.* She felt old beyond her years. The tengu peered south, where Banken would be waiting for her by the temple. She looked east, toward Kyoto and Akasaka, their ancestral home. She then turned to the north, toward the solitary mountain range capped by snow peaks, a place of isolation and rest. Where would she go?

   Aiken thought for a minute and then nodded, her decision made. She was flapping her wings when something to the west caught the corner of her eye. She started to turn her head and then her world was engulfed in green fire.

VIII. Blood Price

They found the surviving kappa in a shallow pool that broke off from the main river. There were eight in all, and they milled about, confused and wounded. One was dying noisily, emitting pitiful cries that sounded like a large bird being strangled. The others ignored it and mucked about in the water for fish and insects.

Saima approached them as Banken hung back cautiously. The younger tengu had found his brother shortly after Aiken had flew off, and had reluctantly joined him again.

"Mountain bird," it croaked. It was Daru, the one who had first captured Saima. "You have returned!"

Saima ignored the greeting and walked into their company. Up close, the kappa were a sorry sight. Their skins had lost their healthy, rubbery sheens and were dry and cracked. The dying kappa had hideous weeping burns that crept up its arm towards the shoulder and thick black fluid bubbled forth. The once implacable creatures now shied away as Saima stepped amongst them, averting eye contact as much as possible. *This is certainly interesting,* Saima thought. *Maybe…*

"You," sneered one of them, apparently regaining its courage. "You led us to that village. You've killed Lord Kaaro. Traitorous creature, you serve the humans!"

"I serve no human," Saima said quietly. "I work for the good of our kind."

"What kind?" spat the kappa. It was not injured and it lumbered to its feet, scythe in hand. "You serve tengu, and the tengu are traitorous dogs!"

Saima gazed over the others. Daru and the others watched on silently at this challenge. He spoke. "For ages now, it has always been so. Tengu serve tengu, kappa serve kappa, and humans dominate over all." His voice rose with each word. In the distance he heard Banken calling his name, but ignored it. "What say you all if I say tengu and kappa work together, to end the oppression of our kind against the foul humans?"

"Bah!" the resistant kappa spat. "Kappa do not serve the bird men. Kappa serve Kaaro, and the bird men brought Kaaro's death. You are the one that's foul, tengu!"

Saima looked at the others again. They had not joined in. It was time to risk it. "Serve me," he whispered slowly to them, pointedly ignoring the challenge, "and you will find glory in battle and for all kappa. Work with me and I will return greatness to your kind. Or do not, and die for it like the worthless fish you now are."

It was the ultimate insult among kappa and it worked as planned. The angry one roared and blindly charged Saima. The others started to get up but the tengu did not allow them the chance. His whip popped once in the air and the curved razor edge at the end found its mark on the kappa's meaty neck. A thin spray of blood jetted into the pool, misting it red as the kappa fumbled with the wound. It eventually shuddered and fell into the water, and then sank slowly to the shallow bottom under the heavy weight of its shell.

"Again, I make the same offer," Saima said when it was over. This time Daru kneeled.

"Saima," he said. "We will serve you. Take us from this misery and give us the freedom that you promise."

"*Lord* Saima," the tengu informed the kappa, unable to hide the glee from his voice. "And I will give you all that you have ever dreamt of."

*

The fire burned low over the remains of the gutted house. Hiroshi recognized the home of one of the village boys whom he used to play with. Now he was dead, like his brother and father, more lives lost in the senseless attack. Over the embers the boy's mother sobbed wildly, clutching a little silver crane for reasons that Hiroshi didn't know. The loss of her two sons and husband on the same day had stolen the woman's wits and now she only wailed like some hysterical child. Hiroshi turned away from the horrific sight.

From the inn he could hear the soldiers celebrating, drinking their fill of warm rice wine. With old Yamma dead, the soldiers had taken to her cellars liberally. Another old woman, one of Yamma's friends, complained to the villagers, but they dully ignored her as they shuffled around the burned remains with shocked expressions on their face. Hiroshi saw one man sitting in the middle of the ground, blankly staring ahead while others stepped around him. A little girl, a relative he assumed, tried to get his attention by tugging his sleeve, but the man ignored her. He looked like a withered tree, planted on the dusty road, waiting to die.

Yet half the village still stood, untouched by the fires. Hiroshi's own house was intact, his family alive. His mother had been in the fields when the kappa came and she wisely remained there, safe from the fires in the wet paddies. Hiroshi found himself thanking Lord Sano repeatedly throughout the day.

His thoughts wandered to Momo. He remembered little of the battle after that kappa had hit him over the head, but when he had opened his eyes it was like they were facing a demon from hell. A giant red wolf stared them down with fierce white eyes and then impossibly, Momo's small voice emanated from the creature. Hiroshi called her name, still in a fog, and the demon shrank into a small brown fox. A kitsune. He shivered when he remembered the night they had shared together. It would be his secret forever, to be taken to his grave.

He found Eizo by the river, watching with wide eyes as villagers dug graves for the fallen. There were so many. Aki the hermit and his daughter, Chieko, Reiko the weaver, and her husband Kenji. "Hiroshi-san," Eizo whispered when he saw him. His face was grimy with ash but he seemed wonderfully healthy compared to those around him. "I'm so sorry about your loss."

"What loss is that, Eizo?"

Eizo looked at him in surprise. "The young girl you were with. Your grandfather has been telling everyone that she died in the fight. The monsters threw her body into the river."

"He did, did he?" Hiroshi knew it would be for the best. The villagers needed no more tales about strange creatures in their village. Everyone was on edge as it was. Resigned to this fact, Hiroshi simply nodded and patted the boy affectionately. "The soldiers are saying we won a great battle today," Eizo continued on. "But it really doesn't feel like that, does it?"

"No," Hiroshi agreed. His gazed wandered across the river. Even though the battle was yesterday, the river was already clean of any sign of bloodshed. He sighed with a sad smile and turned back to the boy. "Hey Eizo, have you ever heard of the Green Lady?" The boy shook his head, eyes still fixated on the graves.

"She watched over us, you know. We're lucky to live by the river, where she is known to dwell. Because the Green Lady lives in halfway places, where the land meets the water, between night and day and at the edge of seasons."

Eizo shrugged. "I've never seen her, Hiroshi-san."

Hiroshi smiled at the boy. "I have," he said. "Maybe someday you will too." He then bowed before the river, deep and low. "Goodbye," he whispered.

"Who are you talking to?" Eizo asked.

Hiroshi just laughed. It was a small laugh, but it sounded good to his ears. "Nothing, Eizo-chan. Come, let's go find my grandfather. We've a great deal of work ahead of us."

*

Her body was still warm when he found her. Banken snorted through his nose, his head swimming. The mighty tengu shook his head to clear his thoughts. *It has to be an illusion.* Spots ran dizzily in his field of vision as he ran his fingers over Aiken's body once more. Too still, she was too still and the familiar feel of her skin felt frighteningly alien now. His heart thundered madly and he snorted air again, trying to make sense of it all.

"Aiken," he said gently, as if to wake her from a sleep. "Aiken, my love, get up." It was then that his wandering fingers traced the deep incision in her chest, right over where her heart lay and he knew that she was gone. He jerked his head back and let loose an agonized howl, sending birds flapping from their nests above the trees. Thick tears streamed down his face and he screamed again, shaking his head.

Banken swayed to his feet, grasping wildly for his spear, blinded by his own tears and lost in grief, as Saima came across him. The smaller tengu looked down at the prostrate body of Aiken, and an expression of surprise crossed over his face. "Gods," he murmured. He went over to Banken and tried to rest a hand on his shoulder. "Banken, I am so sor—"

With whiplike speed, the larger tengu spun around and wrapped one hand against Saima's throat. With a strength unnatural even for tengu, he lifted his brother one-handed into the air. His eyes shone with pure fury. His sharp teeth were curled down in a cruel snarl. Saima felt terror lance through him.

"You…you…" Banken rumbled, feeding his grief. "It was…you…"

"No!" Saima managed to gasp. "Brother, I would never…"

Banken's eyes narrowed and his fist tightened. Saima felt his windpipe start to cave in, and his lungs burned from lack of oxygen. Both of his arms were wrapped around his brother's corded bicep but he couldn't break free. Darkness blurred his vision.

And just like that, Banken let him drop. As Saima bent over, retching for air, Banken curled his hands into fists and drove them against his own face, sobbing loudly. He sank down to his knees where his lover's body lay just an arm's length away.

Behind them Saima could hear the kappa catching up, left behind when Banken took off in disgust after they had pledged themselves to Saima. He could not show weakness now, so he forced himself to stop coughing and stood up straight. With reluctance he went over and inspected Aiken's body. There were few signs of struggle; other then a single sword thrust and a curious burn around the tengu's eyes, she might have been merely asleep, her wings folded neatly behind her. Her dark red body lay gleaming in the evening light and for a second Saima saw what his brother must had seen in her.

"Aiken," he said slowly, relishing the way the word rolled off his tongue with liberating finality. "It could have happened another way." The kappa had arrived but stayed in the distance, obviously wary of the larger tengu's grief.

"S-Saima," Banken blubbered. "I-I don't know what to d-d—"

"Shh," Saima said, mindful of their audience. He knelt down and ran his hand down his brother's back. "We cannot do anything more right now. Don't show such weakness in front of our new allies."

"It's-it's Aiken," Banken sobbed on. "I think she's d-dead."

He snuffled noisily. Saima, suddenly annoyed, tried a trick that their father had often used: he slapped Banken fully across the face. Fortunately for both of them, it worked. Banken's head jerked back in pain and his eyes widened in shock, but Saima had his full attention now.

"Listen brother," he whispered rapidly. "I am sorry for your loss, truly I am. But now I beg you to reconsider my offer. Join me and join my cause. Together we will bring peace to our people, and I promise you this as well: we will find who did this! Aiken will be avenged!"

He rose then, and put his hand out for Banken. His younger brother stared at it, uncomprehending at first, and then hesitatingly joined hands. The two brothers bowed their heads together in a show of affection, outwardly sharing a mutual grief for their lost companion. Inwardly, Saima grinned widely in triumph.

*

"She won't wake up," Kei said in a small voice. "It's been two days, and she won't wake up."

"It's like you first found her, isn't it?" Penken asked. They were nestled in a small cave at the base of Maruyama Mountain, away from prying human eyes. The tanuki tended to a small fire and cursed as it sputtered out.

"She spoke to that boy, Penken, I saw her! She changed to a human and spoke. Then she collapsed. I thought she just needed rest, but it seems…" Kei fussed over Momo's prone body. The kitsune slumbered peacefully enough, but both Penken and Kei knew that no amount of prodding would wake her up.

Penken sighed as he bit into his raw fish. It was all so troublesome. Ever since that woman had interrupted his reverie of self-destruction in Okayama, he had been tormented by the demons of his past. Her words were echoes of a distant life and for a moment Penken was overwhelmed of images in a foreign land, fighting the terrible creatures that roamed there. And it would seem that he had arrived here just in time. The tanuki had found Kei weeping by the riverbank while the human village was under attack. After being reunited, they set off to find Momo, who thankfully had just stopped her rampage in the village.

"What is she?" Kei asked, for perhaps the tenth time. "Why did she do that?"

Penken shook his head. "I'm not sure, Kei-chan." He would have to leave it at that, for now.

"I think we need to take her to Kyoto," Kei said with finality. "We can find the best doctors there, you know?"

"Kei…" The fat tanuki rested his hand on her head and

patted it gently. "I've told you, I think Kyoto is the last place Momo should be right now."

The neko sighed and rolled her eyes, exasperated. "Fine, then. But we can't stay here forever, and Momo isn't waking up. Where'll we go?"

Penken considered the kitsune carefully. Kei was right – for whatever reason, the kitsune remained insensate, unable or unwilling to awaken. It was time to break camp. "We leave tomorrow at dawn," he finally said.

"But where?" Kei's voice was an insistent whine and Penken again regretted that the neko was there. She was innocent and should be uninvolved, for great danger lurked just around the bend. He fixed a stare at the neko and spoke in a serious voice that sent a chill down Kei's spine.

"We're heading south, through the Hoji planes. Do you know what lies there?" Kei shook her head. "The yokai, spirits of the dead, still roam those lands at night. But we must pass through there to reach my old friend, someone who may help Momo, someone who may provide some answers." *And maybe,* Penken silently prayed, *save us all from certain death.*

Epilogue

The wind blew frantically over a desolate mountain pass, devoid of life. Few dared take this trail down to the main road, but those who did often saved days of travel. The monk who struggled up the windy hill hardly seemed like a wealthy merchant, so at first the three bandits thought to let him by. Then the monk stopped near their hiding place and set down his walking stick, a large brass Buddhist staff that jangled with three rings attached on top. A basket hat was tied around the man's head, obscuring his face but not the lean, whipcord figure underneath the baggy white and brown robes.

The monk did not seem to notice them but instead sat down to meditate. It wasn't long until the bandits grew restless and began nudging each other. The leader nodded assent and they stepped out into the pass. They encircled the man and hungrily eyed his satchel. Perhaps such an easy target would yield a few beggar coins or at least some fresh food.

"Good afternoon, traveler," said one, the most eloquent of the three. "What brings you to these dead lands?" Another snickered in a high weasel voice. The monk only responded with a low chant, one in a language none of them could understand. Annoyed, the man shoved the monk. "Hey! I'm talking to you. What's your problem, beggar?"

The other two bandits saw the monk was making rapid hand gestures, too fast for them to make out, but before they could comment on that he was on his feet. One hand shot out and a knife that wasn't there a second ago impaled the talking bandit's eye. The other two were well trained for battle and reacted swiftly, drawing their swords and slashing at the robes. The cloth fell away, leaving no body.

"What?" one of them had time to ask before the monk reappeared behind him and slit his throat. The surviving bandit screamed at the sight of his dying comrade and fled. With a flick of his wrist, the monk threw another knife and it sang through the air, burying itself deep in the bandit's back. He sank to the ground, begging for his life, even as the mysterious traveler stepped over to him and finished him with a final twist of the hilt. Satisfied that all three were slain, the monk then returned to his original position and resumed his meditation.

*

High above, two figures clad in green stood on the rocky top overlooking the canyon. Both were bald, their pale yellow skin glinting like scales in the bright sun. The younger of the two nodded with satisfaction and bowed to the elder.

"Did you not see? Such grace, with the swift strike of a viper. I say he is ready."

The other considered for a moment. His eyes were slitted, and as they narrowed in thought, they appeared to close almost completely. His face was a horror to look at, mutilated in nose and tongue, yet he did not seem to mind the deformities. Instead he merely grinned, revealing two sharp teeth over wet pink gums, and hissed in affirmation. The younger one beamed in his master's approval.

Below, the monk also heard the hiss and so he stood. He untied the string under his chin and let the basket fall to be carried away by the gusts. Two seared chunks of flesh marked where his eyes once were, and they stared sightlessly up at the sun as the man laughed over the rising wind.

END OF PART 1

Printed by BoD in Norderstedt, Germany